WILLIAM SA

Foxe and the

Moon-Shadowed Murders

AN ASHMOLE FOXE GEORGIAN MYSTERY

RIDGE & BOURNE

Published by Ridge & Bourne 2020
Copyright © William Savage 2020

1

On a day in early July, Ashmole Foxe was sitting in the room he called his library admiring his new desk. Usually after eating his breakfast, he went for a walk around the marketplace, then called at his favourite coffeehouse. Today, however, he'd felt drawn back to spend at least a few minutes admiring his purchase. The desk was constructed from the finest Jamaican mahogany and had cost him a great deal of money. As he looked at it, he did not begrudge a single penny. The top rested on pedestals either side which contained cupboards. The edges and the door panels were worked into an intricate pattern of concave and convex strips. The wood was so richly coloured, it appeared nearer to maroon than brown in shade, and the whole was faultlessly polished. Best of all, the top was covered with a fine kid leather which felt wonderful under his fingers as he lightly slid his hands to and fro across it.

This pleasant reverie was interrupted by his apprentice, Charlie Dillon, knocking on the library door and calling out that he had important news.

'The Alderman's servant met me outside, master. In a real muck sweat he was. Said he'd been pulled from his duties and sent with a message for you and the instruction to run all the way. Seems there's been a right panic going on.'

'Come inside, lad' Foxe called out angrily. 'Don't stand there shouting through a closed door. Now, tell me what the Alderman wants and try to do it calmly and in proper order.'

"Tisn't the Alderman as wants anything,' Charlie said, lapsing into the speech of the streets in his excitement. "Tis the mayor, as I heard, and him all in a tizzy because of the bishop.'

Foxe turned in his chair and glared at Charlie in irritation.

'The mayor, the bishop ... I can make no sense of what you're telling me, boy. For the last time, give me the Alderman's message in a sensible way. What does Alderman Halloran want?'

'He wants you to go to see him right away, master. There's been a murder in the cathedral and the bishop wants you to find out who done ... did ... it?'

'A murder in the cathedral itself?' Foxe asked. 'Is that what you're telling me.'

'Not exactly in the church,' Charlie replied. 'More like in a part of the Cathedral Close. Some young parson has been done to death, and him a kind of pet of the bishop's too.'

'I can see I'll understand none of this until I can speak with the Alderman myself,' Foxe said in exasperation. 'Tell Alfred to bring me my coat and hat. Its a nice day, so I'll walk there. Now, back to your duties in the shop, Charlie — and do try not to get so excited next time someone brings me an important message.'

'It's really quite simple,' Alderman Halloran said to Foxe, when the two of them were settled in the Alderman's library in his house in Colegate. 'The body of a young clergyman was found this morning, lying on the pathway outside his own house. It was quickly reported to the dean, who told the bishop. The victim was the present Warden of St. Stephen's Hospital.'

'Not the Great Hospital?' Foxe said. He knew where that was. This other place meant nothing to him.

'No. Different place entirely, rather tucked away on the other side of the Close. I'm not surprised you haven't heard of it. It's an old building. Dates from mediaeval times, I would estimate. The inmates are all old male servants or similar people who previously worked for members of the cathedral clergy: the dean, the canons in residence, perhaps even the bishop. Butlers, grooms, those sort of people. They're too old or frail to work any longer and all alone in the world, with no one to look after them in their old age. As an act of charity, the church feeds and houses them and provides each one with a small pension for spending money. There they stay until they die. They're looked after by a warden, usually a newly ordained priest waiting to be presented to a suitable parish living. The position of warden gives the priest a home and a modest income. The duties are few, other than to keep the old men in order, manage the hospital's money, and make sure they all go to services in the cathedral wearing their distinctive blue and gold jackets and red stockings.'

'It doesn't sound much of a job for a young man eager to serve God and his fellow men,' Foxe said.

'On the contrary, Foxe. It's a prestigious appointment, since it lies in the personal gift of the bishop. Successive bishops have used the position of Warden of St. Stephen's Hospital as a stepping-stone for favoured young men on their way to becoming rector or vicar of a rich and important parish. Such parishes are rather few in number, so it's not unusual for there to be none vacant at the point an up-and-coming young man is ordained. Giving someone charge of St. Stephen's tells the world that he is not to be sent to serve in just any available place. He is to be kept close at hand, under the bishop's eye, until a suitable living falls vacant which will match his outstanding abilities or his status.'

'I see,' Foxe said slowly. 'That's what Charlie meant when he said the murdered man was the bishop's pet.'

'A most inelegant way of putting it, but essentially correct. Henry Pryce-Perkins, the young parson who's been murdered, was the third son of the Earl of Westleton and thus something of a protégé of our current bishop. Hearing he'd been murdered, the bishop, as it was reported to me by the mayor, was greatly upset. Naturally, he's determined to bring the murderer to justice as swiftly as possible. Knowing of your record in such matters, he sent an urgent message to the mayor asking for your help. The mayor then reacted as if the Archangel Gabriel himself had descended on him. He gave himself over entirely to panicking and fussing and passed me the practical matter of contacting you and explaining what has happened. You are to present yourself at the Bishop's Palace this afternoon, where the bishop's secretary will give you all the details.'

'I'm not to see the bishop?'

'Alas, no. Having disposed of the matter to others, the Lord Bishop of Norwich departed for London, where he is to be engaged on business in the House of Lords and the Court for the next two months as least.'

Foxe frowned as a thought came to him.

'Surely the Cathedral Close lies outside the City's jurisdiction? That's what I've always understood. Why is the mayor involved at all?'

'You are quite correct, Foxe. Just as the City of Norwich is a separate entity within the county of Norfolk, governing itself under the king, so the environs of the cathedral are separate from both city and county. Several of the canons act as magistrates and the dean holds much the same position as our mayor. It dispenses its own justice, so, if you find the killer, he will be tried first in the cathedral's court before being sent to the assize.'

'Why contact the mayor then?'

'Because the Lord Bishop of Norwich doesn't involve himself in such sordid matters as finding you and persuading you to take on the investigation. He probably wouldn't even know where to send his servant to bear you his summons.'

'The dean would,' Foxe objected. 'I've sold him several books over the years. From time to time he now sends me lists of books which interest him in case I hear of any available copies.'

'Maybe, Foxe, but that is not the way of such ecclesiastical dignitaries, any more than the Duke of Norfolk would think of banging on your door in person to ask you a favour. I imagine the bishop spoke with the dean, who reminded him of your suitability for the job, and commented that you often undertook investigations at the request of the mayor. A message was thus sent to the mayor requesting, in suitably polite terms, that he oblige his lordship the bishop, by setting you at once on the trail. The mayor delegates such matters to me, and so here you are.'

'I am not to present myself for duty until this afternoon, you said?'

'That is correct. Later this afternoon. The bishop's secretary is accompanying the bishop as far as Thetford, where there are some church matters to be dealt with. He needs time to return to Norwich to meet you. I suggest you go about an hour or so before dinner. Say at around four o'clock. No sense in having to go there twice.'

'Just one more question,' Foxe said. 'Charlie told me the servant sent to summon me had been told it was a most urgent matter and he was to run all the way. Now I am to cool my heels until four o'clock this afternoon before getting any of the details?'

'It is urgent,' Halloran replied. 'I need to be able to send a note to the mayor as soon as possible, letting him know I have passed on his request to you. If I delay, he'll bombard me with more messages until I do. I want to spend a quiet morning with my books and don't want him badgering me every five minutes. By the way, Foxe. How are you getting on with finding me a suitable old copy of *Froissart's Chronicles* to add to my collection?'

As he walked home, Foxe mulled over this new mystery in his mind. Who would wish to kill a young clergyman, especially one who was a member of the nobility? It wasn't unusual for peers of the realm to despatch third or fourth sons into the church as a suitable way of gaining an income for life in a respectable way. Who was the Earl of Westleton anyway? Foxe thought he knew of all the members of the nobility who lived close to Norwich, but he'd never heard of this one. Ah well, the bishop's secretary ought to be able to enlighten him. He'd have to be patient until later in the day.

The bishop's secretary turned out to be a cheerful, round-faced man in early middle age. Had it not been for his conservative clothes and neat periwig, he could well have been a prosperous tenant farmer or a successful tradesman of some kind. He rushed forward the moment Foxe was shown into the room to proffer an outstretched hand and hearty 'Good day to you, Mr Foxe,' in greeting. Then he pumped poor Foxe's hand up and down several times with enormous vigour before ushering him to a chair by the fireplace.

Foxe had never been inside the bishop's palace before and so had been at a loss over what to expect. It turned out to be a commodious and elegant dwelling of fairly modern design. The walls of the hallway were finished with fine plasterwork and adorned with some remarkably good paintings. The butler had told him that the room where he was to meet the bishop's secretary was the study. To Foxe's mind, no finer study was likely to exist in the home of any Norfolk gentleman. Not only were its walls were panelled in oak in the style known as linenfold, there were tall bookshelves either side of the massive carved fireplace. The furniture too was of a most superior kind, with richly patterned walnut and deeply coloured mahogany the most prevalent of the woods on display. Foxe's eyes were also drawn to the Chinese porcelain vases on the mantel, the huge long-case clock in one corner and the long windows looking out onto a view towards the river and the Bishop's Bridge beyond.

The man standing in this magnificent room, waiting to greet him, matched t,his opulent environment perfectly. His rotund figure and florid complexion revealed something of the magnificence of the bishop's table and the abundance of his wine cellar. The bishop himself might be something more akin to a holy ascetic. Foxe didn't know. This fellow was the perfect resurrection of a fat and jolly mediaeval friar, even Friar Tuck himself.

'Oliver Lakenhurst,' the man said, 'secretary to his Lordship the Bishop of Norwich, the dear old fellow.'

Those last few words, and the beaming smile with which they were delivered, both relaxed the atmosphere and came close to reducing a great dignitary of the Established Church somewhat to the status of a favourite uncle.

'Delighted to make your acquaintance, Mr Foxe,' the secretary added, scarcely pausing for breath. 'So sorry to have dragged you over here, but Pryce-Perkins's death has somewhat upset his Lordship. He was most insistent that I should speak with you as soon as possible. Set you on the trail of the murderer, as it might be, before the scent grows cold.'

'Ashmole Foxe, Mr Lakenhurst,' Foxe said weakly. 'Your servant, Sir.'

'Quite the other way around, I assure you,' Lakenhurst replied, 'and it's just Lakenhurst. I'm one of the bishop's servants, you understand. Nor a cleric of any kind and certainly not with the status of a gentleman, like yourself.'

While saying this, the secretary had stepped to one side and tugged firmly on the bell to summon another servant, presumably of a more lowly status than himself.

'Would you care to take some refreshment before we begin. Mr Foxe? A glass of the bishop's fine ale, perhaps? Punch? I think I'll have the ale myself. It comes from a brewery just on the other side of the Wensum, and the brewer there truly knows his trade. Ah, Simkins. A jug of the good ale and two glasses. A large jug, you understand.'

Still reeling from the overwhelming nature of this welcome, Foxe merely nodded his acceptance. When the ale arrived, it proved to be everything it was claimed to be. Foxe therefore made a mental note to ask the name of the brewer before he left. If he managed to get a few words in edgeways, that was. Now, still quite unclear of the direction to take, he made small talk instead.

'You accompanied his lordship as far as Thetford, I understand.'

His innocent remark produced a sudden silence and a look of astonishment on Lakenhurst's face.

'Thetford? Thetford? Whatever gave you such an unlikely notion, sir? If I had gone with the bishop to Thetford, I should hardly be here talking with you. It must be twenty miles and more from here. I could not have gone there and back in the time between the bishop's departure at ten and now. Who told you such a thing?'

'Alderman Halloran. He said that was what he had been told by the mayor.'

'I do hope that doesn't indicate the mayor's general grasp of geography. I should have been with the bishop, of course. Heaven knows what muddles he'll get himself into without me. He may be a fine churchman and a great speaker in the House of Lords, but he's quite unable to deal with anything practical. If I didn't organise his days and handle his correspondence, he'd miss most of his appointments and reduce the administration of this huge diocese to chaos in a week. Even though I write out a detailed timetable and list of engagements for him every morning, he's still always asking me what he's supposed to be doing next. That was what I was doing this morning when the news came. That and making sure all his luggage was properly stowed on the carriage. You know, he'd only managed to leave his bishop' crozier in a corner of the dining room! Heaven knows why he thought he needed it there! To bless the loaf and the fish course, perhaps?'

'So you didn't travel with him at all?'

'Only as far as the boundary of the city. On my return, I called on the rector of St. Peter Mancroft, for who I had a message from the bishop. He is a most hospitable man and invited me to join him in a midday meal. I was certain he would, which was why I suggested to the bishop that he should ask you call on me at this hour. Thetford? I still can't even imagine where the mayor got that notion from. But then, I believe he has something of a reputation for getting himself muddled. Thetford!'

Foxe now felt desperate to return to some kind of stability and order by putting a stop to this torrent of mostly irrelevant information.

'What time was it you actually heard of the murder?' he asked. 'Perhaps you could tell me exactly ...'

'It was a quarter before nine,' Lakenhurst began. 'I remember that exactly, because the bishop had taken his breakfast early, at eight o'clock, and was just finishing his coffee. He always has coffee with breakfast, as I do myself. We often breakfast together, so that I can remind him of his appointments and he can give me instructions on various matters. Not just hot rolls and jam either, though the bishop tends to eat sparingly. The cook usually provides eggs and ham and sometimes some fish —.'

'The bishop left after that?'

'Oh no,' Lakenhurst replied. 'As a priest, he's obliged to say the Morning and Evening Offices, if only to himself, you understand. I'd been making sure the chapel here was ready for all the servants to assemble there at nine for him to say his Office with them before he left for London. He's staying tonight with the rector of St. Mark's in Newmarket, you know. Should be there by now.'

'The news was brought to you first?'

'Of course. Simkins, the footman who brought us this excellent ale, came to tell me of it. One of the old men from St. Stephen's Hospital had called to say that P-P's body — I hope you don't mind me calling him P-P? The Rev Henry Pryce-Perkins is such a mouthful — had been found on the pathway at a little distance from the front door of his house; I'm not sure exactly how far away it was. The warden's house is part of the Hospital itself, you see. The old men live in a long row of neat little houses with small gardens front and rear. The warden has a separate, larger house at one end of the row. The building at the other end holds the kitchen, the communal hall and dining room and an area for washing. The inmates are required to gather in the hall for prayers every morning and evening, led by the warden. That's why it's always a clergyman —'

Foxe interrupted this time. He feared that, if he didn't, he'd be given the complete history of St. Stephen's Hospital and the biographies of all the inmates.

'So what did you do when the news reached you?' he asked.

'Spoke to the bishop, of course. Nothing else to be done here. The affairs of the Cathedral Close are strictly the concern of the Dean and Chapter. It was up to them to notify the coroner and that kind of thing. I must say the bishop was quite upset at the news, poor old fellow. P-P was supposed to be under his special care and protection. Not that anyone would imagine he needed to be safeguarded from being murdered in his own front garden.'

'And the bishop asked for me to be involved? Not the dean?'

'Have you ever met the dean?'

'Yes, I have.' Foxe thought it wise not to elaborate. Lakenhurst was doing enough of that by himself.

'The areas of responsibility will not be very clear to a laymen, I'm afraid. The cathedral itself and the Close are under the control of the dean. The dean is a most efficient administrator, who will do all the law requires. Some of the canons — privately, of course — complain that he's almost obsessed with keeping order and decorum in the Close and the cathedral. Being killed in his Close would be bound to strike him as an insult to the proper atmosphere which should surround such an important church. I'm sure he'd communicate with the proper authorities as quickly as possible. The Hospital, for some strange reason, directly and exclusively lies within the purview of the bishop. It's not clear whether the spot where poor Pryce-Perkins's body was found is within the precincts of the Hospital — and thus the bishop's responsibility — or part of the Close, and thus a matter for the dean. It also arose in the thirteenth century, when Bishop —'

Foxe was in no mood for a lesson in the intricacies of ecclesiastical politics and areas of jurisdiction. 'Do you know when the inquest is to be held?' he asked firmly.

Lakenhurst looked puzzled, then his brain registered the question and he provided an answer. 'I gather from speaking with the dean's butler that the coroner will hold an inquest in the Chapter House at eleven in the morning tomorrow. I suspect, after that, the whole disgraceful affair will be consigned to history. It was probably some vagrant who killed him, wasn't it? If it was, he'll never be caught."

' At this stage, I don't know who the murderer was. That's what the bishop has asked me to try to discover. He obviously doesn't know either. If he did, he wouldn't bother to set up an investigation. What I'm most unclear about is why his lordship should ask me? Why not rely on his own resources, whatever those may be?'

'It seems he's been following your exploits for some time,' Lakenhurst replied. 'He holds you in the highest regard. That amazed me, to tell the truth, since he's not normally concerned with events in the city. Anyway, I was to send for you and ask you to undertake an investigation to unearth the murderer. I wasn't quite sure where to find you, so I contacted the mayor and he said he'd handle it. That's partly why I'm still here and not with the bishop where I belong. He said I should tell you all I could, then hurry to find some needy curate who can be persuaded to serve as warden until a proper replacement for P-P can be found.'

Foxe now found he had a hundred questions, but felt he needed a lengthy rest from being with Lakenhurst before asking too many of them. He would attend the inquest next day, where some at least should find answers. He therefore contented himself with a single query.

'How long will you be remaining here? I may need to speak with you again.'

'For as long as you need me to stay,' came the reply. 'The bishop said I should assure you of his complete support in this matter and put myself at your entire disposal for as long as may be needed. He told me he could cope perfectly well on his own in the meantime. Not that I believed him, of course. He'll probably forget some audience with the king or arrive at St. Paul's for a formal service and leave his mitre behind at Lambeth Palace. That's where he's staying, you see. With the Archbishop. They're old friends from their days at the same Oxford college. He almost always stays there when he's in London. Handy for the Palace of Whitehall too. Just across the river, you see. His Lordship would probably get lost if he had to go much further without an escort.'

Foxe, feeling increasingly desperate, tried to stand up to take his leave.

'Wait!' Lakenhurst said at once. 'I haven't told you what I did next.'

'Which was?'

'As soon as I'd seen the bishop on his way, I took his chaise and went to the Earl of Westleton's house near Horsham. The Dean's message had got there before me, of course, so I must have passed the earl on the way as he hurried into Norwich. The countess was at home, so I conveyed the bishop's condolences as I'd been told to do. She was very cold in her response, I must say. Made some remark that if the bishop had watched over her son as he'd been asked to do, this would never have happened. When I said I'd been asked to request your help to make an investigation, she was dismissive of the whole idea.

'"What did you say the fellow is?" she said to me. "A bookseller? What can a mere tradesman in dubious literature know about finding the murderer of my son? My husband will ensure the finest minds amongst the magistracy will be set that task, not some paltry shopkeeper of no account. I'm surprised the bishop would entertain such a notion. We are aristocrats, Lakenhurst. Not common people. It's an insult."'

'Don't you take it to heart, Mr Foxe,' Lakenhurst continued. 'The woman likes to play the grande dame, but everyone knows there's not a groom, or a footman on their estate who hasn't been called upon to service his mistress on at least one occasion. And that's to say nothing of other members of the nobility, music teachers, her daughters' dancing masters and almost anyone who looks personable and wears breeches. The woman has the morals of an alley cat and the sexual urges of a Messalina. Quite disgusting, I call it.'

'Her response doesn't surprise me,' Foxe said. 'I've had worse said of me many times by far less exalted people. I'll not bother you further at this time, Lakenhurst. I have many things to set in motion.'

'But I haven't told you anything about P-P,' the secretary wailed. 'The Reverend the Honourable Henry Pryce-Perkins.' He looked completely downcast at the idea that the meeting should be brought to an end so soon.

'His elder brother is in the navy, you know. A captain already and doing frightfully well, by all accounts. The heir looks after the estate mostly, so everyone says —'

'I assure you I'll be back,' Foxe said. That that seemed to raise Lakenhurst's spirits a little. 'Probably in a day or so. After that, you may very well be able to rejoin the bishop in London.'

Now Lakenhurst was all smiles and excitement.

'Really?' he said. 'That would be splendid! The poor old bishop can scarcely manage without me for a few hours, you know, let alone several days. Are you sure I'll not be needed here? I mean, you know your own business, I'm sure, so you wouldn't say it if you didn't mean it. You do mean it, don't you?'

'I do. Once my investigation gets fully underway, I'll be dealing with information you would have no way of knowing about. I'll be back to hear what you can tell me of the victim, I assure you. But there are things I need to get underway at once.'

'Before the scent goes cold, eh? Just as the bishop told me. Clever man, our bishop, even if he's unable to look after his affairs without me. I'll see you again soon then. Make sure we have good supplies of ale in the house, eh?'

In truth, though the large jug of ale was now empty, Foxe had barely finished a single glass. He rose firmly, shook hands again, retrieved his coat and hat from the ever-present Simkins, and hurried away before Oliver Lakenhurst could begin again.

###

Foxe reached home feeling exhausted from deal with the constant flow of words from the bishop's secretary. How his lordship coped with him, he couldn't imagine. Perhaps the bishop was going deaf!

Now he needed time to try to recall what he had been told and get it into some sensible order. Only then would he be able to determine what he should do next — other than attend the inquest, of course. He therefore retreated to his library, paused a few moments to indulge in further admiration of his new desk, and set himself to thinking.

It was only much later, when he was in bed composing himself to sleep, that it struck Foxe that he hadn't visited his semi-permanent mistress, Lady Cockerton, for several days; and that they hadn't made love together for a week or even longer. He also realised, almost at the same moment, that he didn't miss her.

'Damnation!' he said to himself. 'I don't need complications like that with Halloran breathing down my neck and the mayor and the bishop eager for progress. I'll have to explain somehow and try to make my peace with Arabella when I can. I'll have no time tomorrow, that's for certain. Perhaps I'll buy her something nice to help smooth any ruffled feelings.'

And with that comforting thought, he feel asleep.

Next morning, Foxe rose early and spend half-an-hour in his library with pen and paper, composing a suitable letter to Lady Cockerton. In it, he explained that this request from the bishop had arisen entirely unexpectedly and was bound to occupy much of his time for the next few days at least. He contrived what he thought were suitable phrases of sorry and regret at being forced to occupy himself elsewhere than with her; added statements of how much he missed her — even if he now knew these were mostly fabrications — all couched in suitably affectionate terms; and concluded by assuring her that he would make it all up to her, as soon as that should be possible.

That done, he took breakfast, but cut it short to hurry into his bookshop to ask Mrs Crombie to collect all the gossip she could about the dead man and his family history. By then, there was no time for his usual walk around the marketplace, already busy with traders of every kind. The best he could do was call for his carriage and have himself taken to his favourite coffee-house, where he hoped to find his friend, Capt Brock. He'd sent him a message via Charlie first, asking that they meet early enough to talk before Foxe went to attend the inquest on Pryce-Perkins. If he kept his carriage waiting, it would just give himself sufficient time to reach the inquest as it was starting.

He was in luck. Brock was there already.

Foxe waved a hand at the proprietor to indicate he wanted his usual order and sat down across the table from his friend.

'What do you know of a Capt Pryce-Perkins, Brock?' he asked. 'I gather he's a naval man as you were.'

'Getting involved in finding his brother's killer, are you? Brock replied. 'Thought you would. I'm surprised you haven't read a good deal about the brother in your newspaper. In the war with the French that's just ending, he distinguished himself multiple times as a frigate captain. Right kind of ship for him, if you ask me. All dash and excitement. Pryce-Perkins will undoubtedly become an admiral in due time. If, that is, he doesn't get himself killed first.'

'That kind of fellow, is he?'

'Brave to the point of foolhardiness, I understand. Also reckless and prone to endanger his ship in his eagerness to come to grips with the enemy. But he's a good seaman and it's said his men love him. Show Pryce-Perkins the enemy and he sails straight for them, all guns primed and at the ready. I gather the Frenchies are terrified of him. On the other hand, I imagine the wiseacres in the Admiralty are shaking their heads and muttering about him needing to calm down and display a more mature judgement and a better grasp of naval tactics.'

'What about the rest of his family?'

'There I can't be much help. I'll ask my wife. She's bound to know a great deal more than I do. All I know is that the earl is a pompous fool, the countess has the morals of a common prostitute, and the eldest brother spends all his time roaming about their estates killing things. He also prefers the tenant farmers for company than young men of his own circle.'

'Not the normal behaviour of the heir to an earldom.'

'Not at all. The countess has all the ambition. She wanted her eldest son to be a leading light at court and the next one to rise to be one of the Lords of the Admiralty. The youngest — the one who's just been murdered — was destined in her mind to become a prince of the church.

She may get what she wants with the second son, but the other two looked set to disappoint her, even before the youngest one's death. As I said, the heir is a farmer at heart — good one too, as I hear it — and the young parson was better fitted to be a scholar and a recluse than anything else. My wife will know more, I'll ask her.'

'Thank you, Brock. Please give Lady Julia my very warmest regards, won't you? Tell her I'll be grateful for any information she can give me.'

Lady Julia's family included the Earl of Pentelow and a good many other members of the nobility and upper gentry. She would have sources of information Foxe would never hope to draw upon on his own, even with the bishop to back him. He had thought of visiting Pryce-Perkin's parents himself, but all he had heard of them had convinced him he would never be allowed entry. That was their loss, not his. He would manage without them and show them what a mere bookseller and tradesman could accomplish without their help.

Now he hastily downed the rest of his coffee and had himself driven along Cockey Lane towards the cathedral, just managing to arrive in time be be present when the inquest commenced. As he slipped into the room and took a place towards the back, the coroner was taking his seat behind the table set for him. From where he was, Foxe could remain partly hidden, while still having an excellent view of those attending the court. He could also see the witnesses, as they came up and took their seat on the coroner's right to give their evidence. Only the faces of the jury were hidden from him.

Foxe decided at once that the man sitting rigidly upright at the end of the front row, must be the Earl of Westleton. It was partly because the seats either side of him had been left empty; partly because the clothes he was wearing had probably cost more than the annual incomes of everyone else in the room taken together, excepting only himself; and partly because, when he turned his head to look around the room at one point, Foxe could see a look of utter contempt on his face.

The coroner nervously opened proceedings under the earl's basilisk glare, calling first for whoever was to give evidence of identification of the deceased.

That proved to be a man of late middle age, gravely serious in his delivery. He gave his name as Thomas Swanton, butler to the Earl of Westleton. When he had stated clearly that the dead man was 'The Reverend the Honourable Henry Pryce-Perkins', the earl's youngest son, the coroner rashly turned to the earl himself and asked if he could confirm this. The only response he got was a sneering expression and a small inclination of the head to indicate assent.

Wisely, the coroner hurried on, calling the next witness to describe the manner of finding the body.

An elderly man stepped up to the witness's chair and, having taken the oath, gave his name as Benjamin Gunton and his profession as pensioner and deputy warden of St. Stephen's Hospital. It was obvious neither the court atmosphere nor the earl's baleful presence affected him in any way, for he gave his evidence in a firm, clear voice throughout.

'It was like this, Your Honour,' he began. 'We was all assembled as usual in our hall, waiting to get through morning prayers before having our breakfast. Time passed and the warden failed to appear. That was odd in itself, 'cos he was always punctual in carrying out his duties. Some of my fellow pensioners began muttering and shifting about, being hungry as we all were. I decided to go and look for the warden and remind him of the time. Two or three others joined me.

We found his corpus, as you might call it, on the ground about ten yards away from the door of his house. Lying face down, it were, and blood all over the back of his head. 'Twere obvious that the poor fellow were dead, so we fetched us a blanket and covered him over, decent like, then went back and had our breakfast.'

'You all ate breakfast before doing anything more?' the coroner said in astonishment.

'O'course we did. We was all hungry, like I said, and the warden weren't going anywhere, were 'e?'

The coroner was reduced to an incredulous silence.

'After we'd ate, I sent Francis Negus to tell the dean and I went to take the news to the bishop's secretary, Mr Lakenhurst. I suppose I was a bit longer at the palace than I expected, because Mr Lakenhurst invited me to share a glass of ale with him to refresh me after my walk across the Close. By the time I got back, you was standing by the body with various other men about you.'

'And after that?'

'Your fellows took the body away and that was the end of it.'

The coroner wrote himself a hurried note.

'Do you know if the warden had any enemies or had upset anyone particularly of late?' the coroner continued.

'Not so far as I knows,' the old man said. 'Not amongst us pensioners anyhow. We was a bit annoyed when he tried to preach, but that was mostly because no one could understand more than one word in five. Aside from that, he was an inoffensive young fellow, usually with his nose in a book. Clever, you see, but not in the same world as the rest of us.'

'Did he have many visitors, to your knowledge?'

'Only a few and them fellow members of that strange group he belonged to — freemasons or something like. Certainly they was like the warden in looking as if they was seeing something the rest of us mortals couldn't. Not exactly arrogant. More as if they was always detached from anything normal. Kind of dreamy and attentive at the same time. Gor! I can't do no better than that to describe 'em.'

'Freemasons, you said.'

'I said freemasons. I don't know whether they were actual masons or something else. Secret society I'd say it were. What kind, I dunno.'

There the coroner decided to leave Gunton's evidence.

'Before I continue,' he told the court, 'I need to be clear about jurisdiction in this matter. Is there anyone present who can give evidence on this point?'

An elderly man rose to say he was a canon of the cathedral and could probably provide what the court required. He was swiftly sworn in and proceeded to explain that, while the Close was within the jurisdiction of the dean and chapter of the cathedral, St. Stephen's Hospital was what was known as a peculiar of the bishop. That meant it was wholly under his jurisdiction and control. Since, so far as he could say, the body had been found just within the boundaries of the hospital, it was not the dean's affair.

The coroner shook his head of such complexities, but thanked him nonetheless and allowed him to resume his seat. His next call was for medical evidence regarding the cause of death. That was given by a man who identified himself as Thomas Bradsome, surgeon. He stated that he had examined the body and that death had been caused, in his opinion, by a single, heavy blow to the back of the head. The blow had produced a compound fracture of the skull and heavy bleeding in the brain. Death would have followed within moments.

Asked about the item used to inflict such a blow, he explained that he had found an irregularly shaped piece of flint not far from the body. There was blood and hair on one part of the flint, and its size and weight were consistent with the nature of the wound.

'In your expert opinion,' the coroner said, 'was this the weapon that killed the warden?'

'I cannot be more definite that to say the evidence points that way,' the surgeon replied. 'There was the blood and the hair for a start. Then the size of the flint was consistent with the size of the wound. Wielded with a sufficient force, it could well have proved fatal with a single blow. All that puzzles me is the location of the wound.'

'Where was that?' the coroner asked.

'On the rear of the skull, as I would have expected of a blow struck from behind. Yet very high in that position. Almost on the top of the skull. The deceased was of slightly above average height, so only a very tall man could strike in that position.'

'A very tall man, you say? Yet even a shorter fellow would have to raise such a stone above his head to add sufficient force to the blow.'

'That's true, sir, though I would have expected the wound to be more on the back of the skull. Unless the assailant stood very close as he struck.'

'Mightn't that be a simpler explanation than some giant?' the coroner said. 'It was dark after all. Maybe the attacker crept up on him.'

'Maybe he did, sir. But all this is mere speculation.'

'And, as such, not the business of this court,' the coroner added hastily. 'My task is to establish the cause of death and circumstances in which it took place. That has now been done. Gentlemen of the Jury. You have heard the evidence. To my mind, only one verdict is possible, that of 'Wilful murder by person or persons unknown' and I direct you to find accordingly.'

The jurymen glanced at one another, a few nodded, and their foreman rose to pronounce their verdict as directed by the coroner.

It was over.

As Foxe returned home, Mrs Crombie stopped his carriage outside the door of the bookshop and requested a few moments of his time to speak with him privately. For an instant, Foxe's eyes lit up at the notion that she had already heard something important to his investigation. That was not so.

'It's not that, Mr Foxe,' she said ruefully, recognising his disappointment. 'I've sent Charlie on a lengthy errand, which will give me time to talk with you about his situation. Shall we go into the workroom? Charlie won't return for at least an hour, maybe more.'

Their discussion didn't take nearly that long. Foxe had already noticed that the apprentice was growing restless, and had begun to wonder if the bookshop gave enough scope for his lively and enquiring mind. Now Mrs Crombie confirmed this. While Charlie was perfectly competent to look after the customers in her absence and deal with all the routine of the shop, she told Foxe, his true interests lay elsewhere. What he most enjoyed was tinkering with the old printing press in the workroom. The one which Foxe's father had used thirty and more years before. Charlie had already managed to teach himself how to print simple pamphlets and notices for the shop. He'd also produced a few pieces for various nearby businesses to use to advertise their trades. To go further, he needed to train under an established master printer. He would never make more than a competent bookseller. He lacked the necessary education for a start. Nor could he follow his master into the trade in specialist antiquarian and rare books. He would never attain the ease of manner needed to move amongst the gentry. What she thought did mark the lad out was his natural facility in dealing with machinery and his love of the intricacies of typesetting and printing.

It took barely a few seconds for Foxe to agree with her judgement. He promised to speak with Charlie on the matter. If the lad agreed, Foxe felt sure he could find a master printer who would be willing to take him on.

2

As he lay in bed that night, Foxe remembered that it must only be a few days now before the Catt sisters, his first two serious loves, would be arriving in Norwich for an unknown length of time. He'd done nothing about it so far, mostly because he didn't know what might prove best. He had only Gracie's casual suggestion of resuming their former relations during their stay in the city. She might or might not have meant that seriously. He didn't know, and would have to wait to find out when they finally arrived,

Of course, this request for his services by the bishop would provide the perfect reason for him not to be able to squire them around as they so obviously expected. Even they could hardly expect him to turn down a request for help from the bishop in favour of spending all his time with them. He would explain the position and they would understand.

That decision made, Foxe found a comfortable position in the bed and composed himself to sleep. He was beginning to find that having a bed all to himself had considerable advantages.

The next morning dawned bright and fair. Foxe rose at his usual time, drank the cup of hot coffee his man, Alfred, brought for him, and decided to take a walk in his garden and enjoy the lively air before taking his breakfast. He would tell his groom to make the carriage ready for later. There were one or two visits to the city outskirts he needed to make soon to replenish his stock of rare books. He'd had several requests for titles from previous customers, together with the suggestion that they would, in fact, be interested in considering whatever he had available for sale.

Foxe had always kept his trade in antiquarian and rare books in his own hands. The business demanded a knowledge of markets and dealers it had taken him many years to amass. It was also far and away the most profitable part of his many enterprises. It was his success there which was primarily responsible for making him the rich man he was. Though he had found it difficult to establish himself at the outset — To purchase a complete library, or even one or two highly desirable volumes, from some spendthrift nobleman demanded considerable capital — over time he had gained experience in what to buy and, more important, what to pay for it. He had also developed a keen eye for the market. Buying at the right price and selling to the right buyer might yield him many hundreds of pounds in profit from mere a handful of transactions.

The Earl of Pentelow was always in need of money, and had given Foxe permission to enter his library at any time to seek out volumes to purchase. What had once been one of the finest libraries in the county was now sadly depleted. So long as the shelves were filled with books in fine leather bindings, the earl cared nothing for what the books themselves might be. Foxe would take with him a number of well-bound volumes of little other interest he had bought from a London dealer, and swap them for a few valuable items he could sell at a price to gladden the earl's heart and bring himself a substantial profit.

It was a fine late spring day and the short journey to the earl's home raised Foxe's spirits. The rich countryside through which they were passing acted like balm to his spirit. As they came out onto an open part of Mousehold Heath, he let his attention be caught first by the rapturous singing of a dozen or more skylarks high above, then by the sensuous purring of turtle doves in the birch trees which lay to one side of the road.

The view to his right over his beloved city was more than enough by itself to drive all other thoughts and worries from his mind in an instant. Norwich lay stretched out before him, many of its buildings hidden amongst trees. The many gardens within the city's boundaries, right up to the city centre itself, were one of its unique claims to fame amongst all English cities, especially those of such a vast extent. Only the massive castle keep and the lofty spire of the cathedral rose completely above this warm blanket of greenery. For the rest, all that indicated the dwellings and workplaces of more than thirty thousand souls were the roofs of the highest tenements and the towers of the more than forty parish churches which served their inhabitants.

Foxe spent several happy hours in the earl's library, renewing his acquaintance with old friends amongst the thousands of books it contained and making several new discoveries. As was his normal practice, he selected the smallest number of volumes to take away that would yield the kind of money, when sold, that the earl was likely to relish. There was no need to be greedy. The books were mostly in excellent condition and free from the ravages of bookworms and the destructive nibbling of silverfish. They could best stay where they were until a future date, when Foxe should know of suitably appreciative new owners into whose care they could be transferred.

Only on his journey home did Foxe let his mind turn from the beauty of nature to the many questions confronting him concerning the death of Rev Henry Pryce-Perkins. This stage of an investigation was always confusing and frustrating. He longed to have some definite tracks to follow, but still lacked all the detailed information that would allow them to become visible.

One matter bothered him especially that fine afternoon. Who were these shadowy figures, seemingly members of some secret or secretive society, with whom the murdered man had been spending his time? Were they truly members of a Masonic lodge? Norwich possessed several to chose from. On the other hand, it was also home to a vast array of other clubs and societies, from serious and high-minded groupings of men interested in philosophy, or the latest discoveries of science and medicine, to those devoted to the delights of the table and the bottle. There were even clubs, necessarily avoiding becoming widely known, those members dabbled in matters such as alchemy and magic. What kind of group was likely to draw the attention of an up-and-coming young clergyman, yet still chose to operate in secrecy? Did it have anything to do with his murder anyway? Foxe had not the slightest idea where to start in uncovering the identity of this group, even though it appeared at present to be the principle way Pryce-Perkins had spent his time, other than his duties as warden of St. Stephen's Hospital.

He was still turning over this problem in his mind when his carriage came to a stop outside his front door. He collected the pile of precious books together and was about to descend to the street and go inside, when he became aware of a shrill female voice calling his name repeatedly.

Looking around to discover who the owner of the voice might be, he found a girl of perhaps fourteen or fifteen years of age. She was holding onto the edge of his carriage with one hand and waving the other in the air to attract his attention. She would have been a pretty girl, for she had a fine womanly figure for her age, had she not been far too thin and somewhat grubby. Clearly one of the street children, Foxe thought, for her gaudy clothes and bold manner revealed in a moment how she earned her meagre living. Yet the stick-thin arm she was waving, and the pallor of her face under its crudely applied layer of powder and rouge, made it clear that she barely earned enough to keep her from starvation.

As he looked down at her from the carriage, Foxe could see she was accompanied by five or six other children, all as thin and skimpily dressed as she was. He opened the door of the carriage and prepared to step down to discover what this group of street children wanted. For that was undoubtedly what they were. Mostly petty thieves, pickpockets and more child prostitutes. But before he could get a single foot on the ground, the door to the bookshop flew open and Charlie Dillon came rushing out to discover what all the fuss was about.

'What you doin' here, Kate?' he said, his voice full of disapproval. 'Why are you yellin' at Mr Foxe like that? Haven't I told you a hundred times that when you wants something you comes to me? You don't go bothering the master. What will people think if they sees a young tart like you pestering him in this way?'

'That she has something urgent that needs my attention,' Foxe said calmly. He turned to the girl. 'What's your name?' he asked her.

'Kate, your honour ... sir. Kate Sulyard.'

'So this is Kate Sulyard, who's taken over as leader and guardian of the street children now that you have a respectable position and a roof over your head, is it, Charlie? Now, Miss Sulyard, calm down and tell me what has brought you here?'

To be called Miss Sulyard calmed her down better than anything else could have done. It was almost she'd had a bucketful of cold water thrown over her. For several moments, she seemed incapable of speech at all. All the hard surface produced by her dealings with men of all kinds fell away and revealed the frightened and uncertain child beneath. She had to swallow several times before any words would come.

'It's a body, Mr Foxe, sir, your honour. I knows well enough not to bother a great gentleman like you normal like. Only I thought you'd want to know soon as possible, see? I'm ever so sorry if I've acted out of place and caused you to be angry.'

'I'm not angry in the least,' Foxe said to her in a kindly tone, 'and you've done exactly the right thing. I expect you saw me here in the street when you were on your way to speak to Charlie, didn't you? That's why you got excited and rushed up to speak to me yourself.'

'You know very well to go to the back gate, not come to the bookshop door and scandalise our customers,' Charlie growled. 'I told you enough times.'

'All you other street children go about your business,' Foxe continued, ignoring his apprentice, 'whatever that is. Here's a few pennies for you to make sure you can eat tonight. You come inside with me, Miss Sulyard. Charlie too. Then we can talk like civilised people and I can put these books somewhere safe.'

Now it was Kate's turn to be scandalised. 'On, no, sir! I couldn't do that, 'Twouldn't be right, me goin' into your fine house. I'm not dressed proper and I ain't too clean either.'

'You will do perfectly well as you are, I assure you. I'm not inviting you to take tea with me, though I'm sure my cook can find something for you to eat when we have finished. Now, may I call you Kate? Miss Sulyard is rather formal, you know.'

Poets have often rhapsodised about the idea of love at first sight. The look on Kate Sulyard's face, as Foxe held the door open for her and waved Alfred aside, was such a compound of awe and helpless devotion as had not been seen in the world in many long years. She had arrived that day as a hard-bitten young tart. Now she had become Foxe's abject slave and his most fervent devotee, all in the space of five minutes.

'Do take a seat, Kate,' Foxe said when he had ushered the two young people into his library. The expression on the young streetwalker's face at this suggestion was a sight to behold. She would have been far less shocked if he'd asked her to take off all her clothes and stand on her head.

'Oh, no, sir!' she cried. 'I couldn't do that. Not on your expensive furniture and all. That wouldn't be right, that wouldn't. Not at all.'

'Very well,' Foxe said, continuing to stand himself. 'Now, tell me about this body. Where is it, for a start?'

'In that haunted house what stands in front of Mancroft Yard. You must know the one. It's hard under the tower of Peter Mancroft church.'

'I know where it is, master,' Charlie interrupted. 'The yard is behind it. You can only get in and out through a narrow gateway what stands to the left of the door to the house itself.'

Norwich was full of yards of that kind. During the mediaeval and Tudor periods, the centre of the city had boasted a good number of large houses, all wooden-fronted with infills of lath and plaster. Behind each one would be a substantial yard for stables. Most had a long garden beyond that, running the full width of the house. When Norwich's population had risen greatly in Queen Elizabeth's day, mostly due to a huge influx of protestant Huguenot refugees from France and the Low Countries. These newcomers — 'the strangers' the locals called them — were welcomed for the new skills in cloth weaving they brought. As their numbers increased, there were not enough houses for them. In a rapid burst of development, buildings were thrown up on the yards behind many of the large houses, too often by unscrupulous landlords. Tenements were crammed in, two and three stories high or more, leaving only a small central space open for a communal well and privies. The entrances to the rear of these houses, only ever large enough admit to a horse with its rider walking alongside, generally remained as they had always been. Most were set to one side of the ground floor of the original house and formed the sole entrance to whatever now lay behind. Up to fifty or sixty poor people now lived huddled together there in wretched airless, insanitary tenements, often several in a single room. The yards were the worst breeding places for disease in the whole city.

'Where in the big house?' Foxe asked.

'In what we thinks were once the dining room,' Kate replied. 'Seems some wanderin' ole tramp crept in there to find a place to sleep. When he woke up near noon today, he raised a mighty yellin' an' screechin' when he finds he's been sharin' 'is sleepin' place with a corpse.'

'He didn't see it when he went there the night before?'

'It were pitch black in there an' he ain't got no candles or nothin'. It was a miracle 'e 'and't tripped over it.'

'Is the body of a man or a women?'

'A young woman, as I were told. Right pretty too, an' all dressed in fine clothes like a real lady. No one knows who she were, but it's certain she didn't live anywhere around there. More like a gentleman's daughter they said. I 'spect she's still there, if you want to go an' take a look.'

'Did anyone send for the constable, Kate?'

'Yes, they soon done that right enough. Mind, as usual, they took their time comin'. No constable ever manages to 'urry 'imself, the lazy bastards.'

She stopped, blushing furiously in shame at having used such a word in front of a gentleman. Foxe never blinked.

'So you think the body of this poor young woman is still were it was found?' he said.

'Probable like. One of they constables would need to go to fetch the crowner's men afore it could be moved.' She used the mediaeval word for a coroner — the local representative of the Crown in all cases of unexplained death — as a few old people still did.

'Very well,' Foxe said kindly. 'You did a very sensible thing in coming to tell me right away. I'm grateful. Charlie will take you into the kitchen and see you get something to eat before you leave. Here's something for your trouble as well.'

The sight of two whole shillings Foxe placed in the palm of her hand was too much for the girl's over-stretched nerves and she burst into helpless tears.

'Now then, Kate.' Charlie said, leading her towards the door. 'Don't take on so. I'll show you the way and Flo will take care of you and see you gets a good meal. You surely remember "Quick-fingers" Flo, don't you? She works here now and has given up dipping to earn a living.'

'When you've settled Kate in the kitchen, Charlie,' Foxe said to him, 'come straight back here. I'll just put these books in a safe place and you can show me where this Mancroft Yard is. I'd like to see the body before they take it away. It might give me some clue as to who this unfortunate young woman might be. Why she met her death there is another question, isn't it? I suppose she was murdered?'

'She were, sir,' Kate managed to mumble through her tears and sobs. 'Throttled, they said, though she were laid out neat enough, with her skirts round 'er ankles as is right an' proper.'

'Stranger and stranger,' Foxe muttered to himself as he found an area of empty shelf where he could put his books from the Earl of Pentelow's library. 'Now I've got two murders to look into. Not that the alderman or the mayor will care much about some young woman killed in a place like that. Even if she was dressed like a lady. I wonder if she came from one of the better brothels around that area?'

That thought suddenly brought Gracie Catt vividly into his mind. Despite being the daughter of a wealthy merchant, she had been the madam of just such an establishment before giving it all up to follow her younger sister's acting career when it took her to London. Now she and her sister were going to arrive back in Norwich within a few days. The latter Gracie had written implied they expected to resume their previous level of intimacy with him. Foxe was far from sure that would be a good idea, and not just because he had promised Lady Cockerton to be faithful to her. The Catt sisters were unlikely to stay long and he'd suffered enough pain the first time they had left for London to pursue Kitty's acting career.

Foxe pushed the memories out of his mind, picked up his hat again, and almost collided with Charlie as he opened the door to leave.

Along the way, Foxe took the opportunity to rebuke Charlie gently for his treatment of Kate.

'Save your anger for when it really matters,' he told the lad. 'That way, it comes as a surprise and has far more effect. The girl was upset, you could see that. All she wanted was to get her message to me as quickly as she could. Seeing me arriving in the carriage must have seemed a perfect opportunity to speak with me directly. You could have waited until she'd done what she came to do, then quietly reminded her of her mistake.'

'She could easily have come to the back in the first place,' Charlie said, his tone sullen. He hated it when his master criticised him, especially when he knew the criticism was deserved.

'If she had been coming directly from St. Peter Mancroft, she needed to pass the front of the shop and house to get around to the back gate. For all you know, that might have been what she was doing, until she saw me arrive. Anyway, let us say no more about it. Tell me about Mancroft Yard and why people think the house on the street is haunted.'

This request was much more to Charlie's liking, and he swiftly regained his normal cheerfulness.

'It's not as bad as some of the yards, master,' he said. 'Those are so filthy and overcrowded you can smell them a hundred yards away. Mancroft Yard is still a wretched place to live, mind you. It's almost two yards nowadays. There's a rickety building that's been built sticking out from one side. It leaves no more than a narrow pathway to the part of the yard beyond it.'

'And the original house? I presume that stands right on the street?'

'It does. Must have been a fine enough place in it its day. Built of timber, of course, but someone replaced the lath and plaster with brick to make it sturdier and warmer inside. It's been empty a few years now, on account of the stories of it being cursed and haunted.'

'Cursed as well as haunted,' Foxe said. 'Why should that be?'

'According to the stories, the last person to live there was an old, old woman with one servant, who was near as old as she was. The mistress was an ugly old biddy and foul-mouthed if you upset her . She kept a passel of cats too. Some of the wilder boys in the area used to chase and torment them. That made the old woman real angry. She'd call down all sorts of curses on them for doing it.'

'I don't blame her. Cruelty to any creature, human or animal, shows an evil nature. Did it stop them?'

'Not at first. They just laughed at her. Then two of them, while they were running away, got badly hurt. One ran into the path of a heavy cart and had both his legs crushed. He lingered on a few days, but died of his wounds. The other tripped and fell face down in a pile of dung. He must have swallowed some, because he soon got some sickness in his stomach which nearly killed him too. People said it was the old woman's curses what did it, so she must be a witch. There was no more taunting of her cats after that.'

'I'm sure both were accidents,' Foxe said. 'No more than that.'

'That wasn't all, master,' Charlie objected. 'Carters said their horses wouldn't pass the old woman's house without rearing up and making a terrible fuss. Even the people who lived in the yard itself hurried past her door and stayed at home after dark.'

'I assume the old woman isn't still there, as you say it's empty.'

'She died. By this time, she has such a bad reputation the parson wouldn't let her be buried in the churchyard. Instead, the people in the yard put the body in a cart and took it to one of those holes which sometimes open up in a garden or a piece of waste ground.'

'A sinkhole?' Foxe said

'I don't know what they're called properly,' Charlie replied. 'Anyhow, they dropped a stone down and couldn't hear it hit the bottom, so they reckoned that must be bottomless. They threw the old woman's corpse into it, so she'd go straight to hell where she belonged.'

'What happened to her servant?'

'No one knows. She just upped and disappeared, along with most of the cats. Folks believed they was the witch's familiars and had gone back to hell .'

'You still haven't said why people think the house is both cursed and haunted,' Foxe objected.

'Though it was empty, folks say there are lights seen in it at night and something could be heard moving about. One fool who ventured inside to see what he could steal said he was met by a ghost that screamed in his face. All white it was, and moved about without making a sound. It was the demons, master. They'd got the old witch, but they still weren't satisfied. Everyone knows witches call up demons and force them to do their bidding by spells and the like. It seems some of them are still there.'

'And people believe this?'

'Right enough, master. That old tramp they said found the body must have come from somewhere outside the city. No Norwich man or woman — at least none from round about that area — would dare to take a step inside that place after dark.'

Charlie's story had lasted all the way to Mancroft Yard. Ahead, Foxe could see a small crowd of nosey people right by the house doorway, being held back by one of the constables. Rather than convince the man to stand aside for them, Foxe and Charlie slipped quietly through the small archway into the yard itself. The house must have a back door. If one constable was still away, fetching the coroner's men, it ought to be unguarded.

Instead, standing outside the door was a large man with a determined expression. It looked to Foxe that getting inside, where the body was said to be, might prove something of a problem.

He hadn't bargained on anyone barring his way. He therefore took a deep breath and prepared to try to argue his way inside.

'It's Mr Foxe, isn't it, the bookseller?' the man guarding the back door said, as soon as he saw master and apprentice. 'I'm right surprised you've come, and so quickly. I wonder who it were what tipped you off? Whoever it was, you've had a wasted journey. We can look after ourselves, so you can go away again. This ain't your kind of place at all.'

'I'm told there's been a murder inside,' Foxe said sternly. 'Stand aside, whoever you are, so I can see for myself.'

'I said there were no call for you to interfere. We've all 'eard of you and your 'abit of meddling in things that don't concern you. You're not wanted 'ere.'

Foxe stood his ground. 'Stand aside, I said,' he snapped. 'I've been threatened by many better men than you. You don't impress me with your bluster. Maybe I'll wait for the magistrate to arrive and suggest your unwillingness to allow an outsider to see the body is worth looking into. You might be involved yourself in this killing, for all I know.'

Foxe's words had the desired effect. Faced with a magistrate enquiring into his own affairs, the man backed down at once.

'Now you 'ave come,' he said grudgingly, 'I suppose I'm stuck with you. Maybe you can at least stop those damned fools of constables from pinning the blame on one of the people who live in the yard here. The moment the fools arrived, they began trying to sniff out a suitable victim. All they want is someone to take the blame. Never mind if he's as innocent as a new-born. If I have to cope with them on my own much longer, there'll be another murder done.'

'First, you have the advantage of me, ' Foxe replied. 'You know my name, but I do not know yours.'

'My name is John Holtaway,' the man growled. 'A carpenter by trade, as I imagine you can tell by my clothes. I'm by way of being a kind of leader of the people of Mancroft Yard. They turn to me when they're in trouble, which is often enough, and I help settle their disputes.'

'Very well, Holtaway.' Foxe replied. 'What can you tell me of the murder which has taken place here?'

'Little enough,' he said, 'save that it 'as nothing to do with any who lives 'ere. We're poor folk, but I'd be tellin' you a lie if I said we were all honest. There's plenty in these tenements who earns their crusts in ways no preacher or magistrate would approve. A few are artisans, like me. Others gets money where they can, 'onestly or not, and the rest are sometimes the one and sometimes t'other, depending on whether they can get work at all. What I am telling you — and tellin' you firmly — is that none of 'em would stoop to killing a fellow creature in cold blood, whatever those constables tells you.'

Holtaway was obviously trying his best to distance himself and all who lived iin Mancroft Yard from what had happened.

'And in the heat of anger?'

'If they did, it wouldn't be intended. But this ain't a matter of a fight, is it? This is a young 'ooman, killed in cold blood.'

'That I will judge for myself,' Foxe told him. 'Now take me to where the body is.'

'I suppose i'll 'ave to. It's not been moved at all. Follow me, then, and I'll show you the poor crittur.'

'You stay here,' Foxe said to Charlie. 'I want you to keep watch. Let me know if you hear or see the other constable coming back with the coroner's men. I don't want any of them to know that I'm here.'

If they did, they would tell the coroner, who would tell the magistrate. Then the mayor would soon learn of it too. The last thing Foxe wanted now was a lecture from Alderman Halloran on sticking to what mattered — the young clergyman's death — and not pushing his nose into something which was none of his concern. Anything they thought might distract him from the problem the bishop was expecting them to solve, would have them chattering and screeching at him like monkeys in a menagerie.

'It's not far,' Holtaway said. 'Just in the first room, on the left off the hallway.'

Inside, the old house looked much as it would have done when the woman everyone said was a witch lived there, save for a thick layer of dust over all the furniture. Foxe could see it had once been a fine dwelling, with a spacious entrance hall flanked by a large panelled room to either side, and a kitchen and storage areas to the rear. The furnishings it now held were undoubtedly old-fashioned, but well-made enough for all that.

'I wonder why no one's helped themselves to this furniture?' Foxe muttered, just loudly enough for Holtaway to hear him.

'Din't you know the place be cursed? I thought you knew everythin' in this city,' Holtaway replied. His surly impudence was starting to get on Foxe's nerves.

'If you don't keep a civil tongue in your head,' Foxe snapped, 'I'll tell my people to give you a good hiding to teach you manners.' Who these imaginary people were, he had no idea, but the threat seemed enough to cow Holtaway somewhat.

The room they entered also had its furniture still in place. There were even hangings on one of the walls, though they were now marked by frequent holes where the moths had been feasting. A carpet, going mouldy, still covered most of the floor. Everything here was also thick with dust and the room smelled strongly of damp and decay. It was a miserable place to die, if indeed the dead woman had died there. That remained to be seen.

For several moments, Foxe stood still, taking in all he could see and touching nothing. Finally, he steeped closer to the corpse and looked down at it, noting how the body lay stretched out neatly on its back, with her clothes seemingly undisturbed, just as Kate Sulyard had told him. Probably not a rape then, though some perverts had been known to try to hide what they'd done the moment the frenzy left them. Probably no older than twenty-five, Foxe though. Most likely a few years younger. Her face must once have been pretty, before the effects of strangulation had ruined it. Her hair was blond and neatly arranged under a lace cap which still clung to the back of her head. She was dressed in excellent clothes, typical of those of a gentlewoman, again as Kate had said. It was odd they had not been plundered by those who found her, for they would fetch a good price from the dealers in second-hand clothing in the city. But there they still were. A richly embroidered bodice over a lawn shift, with skirts of fine brocade and a flowered petticoat of typical Norwich calamancoe. All seemed to testify to a person of above average wealth.

Having seen all he could standing up, Foxe knelt down and studied the mottled, discoloured skin of the face for a few moments, then the marks about her neck. He next lifted each hand in turn and took some time to inspect the palms and fingertips. The body was stiffening in death, but was not fully stiffened. She must have been killed not that long before the tramp who was said to have found her awoke from what was doubtless more of a drunken stupor than sleep.

Having seen all he could on the upper part of the body, Foxe lifted the edge of the skirt to examine the young woman's ankles and lower legs. Her shoes were of good leather, well cut and stitched, though more like walking shoes than the pretty embroidered creations which so many young ladies wore. Those were fine indoors, but became swiftly ruined by walking a few yards in the mud and filth of the street outside. These shoes did indeed show some marks of mud and dampness still about the soles. Their wearer had probably walked to meet whoever killed her rather than ridden in a carriage.

He was just about to rise from where he had been kneeling by the body, when he saw the carpet beneath the girl's head was stained with blood. This murderer, it appeared, had wanted to make quite sure his victim was dead. He had probably hit her first, making her unconscious, then knelt beside the body, as Foxe was doing now, and strangled her to make sure.

A low whistle from Charlie outside alerted Foxe to the need to leave right away. He rose and roughly pushed Holtaway out of the room in front of him, collected Charlie and slipped back out into the street as unobtrusively as he had come. In moments, he was back on the edge of the marketplace, walking along towards his home in his normal, carefree manner.

'Well, master?' Charlie said after a few more moments, his curiosity getting the better of him.

'A pretty young woman most cruelly killed and another mystery for us,' Foxe replied. 'Whoever did this foul deed richly deserves the attentions of the hangman. I will make it my business to see that he does.'

3

Foxe had been looking forward to some peace when he reached his home and time to mull over what he had just seen. To his mind, there were a number of jarring inconsistencies in this affair, which suggested it was neither an attempt at rape, a lover's quarrel nor a botched robbery. If the constables and the magistrate persisted in trying to fix on someone in Mancroft Yard as the killer, they would, in his view, be wasting their time. This was no sudden, opportunistic attack, but a deliberate murder by someone. It might even have been planned it in advance, though for what reason he could not even guess at present. Even so, he felt sure one could be found, if he tried hard enough. Then, with luck, the reason would point him to the identity of the killer.

As Alfred opened the the door to him and took his hat and coat, the valet also added two pieces of news. There was a letter waiting for him and he had a visitor. According to the sender's name above the seal on the back of the folded sheet, the letter was from his cousin, Nicholas Foxe.

'Your visitor is Lady Cockerton's maidservant,' he told his master. 'She arrived perhaps five minutes ago and I explained that you were not at home. She insisted on waiting until you returned, so I've put her in the drawing room and provided coffee.'

Foxe was puzzled. It had never occurred to him that Lady Cockerton would send her maid, rather than send a letter or come herself in response to his message. He was far from sure what this might mean and needed a little time to think.

'Very good,' Foxe said to Alfred. 'Bring me some coffee to the library. First I'll read the letter you mentioned. After that, I'll ring and you can show the young lady in to me there.'

Once in his library, Foxe retreated behind his magnificent new desk. He had bedded Maria Worden several times before she had gone to serve Lady Cockerton, and he was very fond of her. There had even been hints dropped that a blind eye would be turned to him continuing to enjoy her favours after his promise of fidelity to her mistress. But for Foxe, a promise of faithfulness to one woman alone could only ever be absolute — however much he felt afterwards that he had given it without proper thought. Once an exception was was allowed, others would be bound to follow. He was determined to keep his promise to the letter. If anyone was going to break it, it would not be him. Since then, therefore, relations between him and Maria had been conducted with a proper attention to propriety.

He set all that aside for the moment and took up the letter from his cousin.

Nicholas Foxe was currently an articled clerk to a firm of legal attorneys in Diss. In the letter, he asked if he might shortly pay Foxe a visit. There was an important matter on which he wanted his elder cousin's advice. If possible he would like to stay for a few days, since what was at stake was his future. The partners in his present firm had indicated they would be very willing to offer him a partnership when his articles were completed later that year. However, all his present firm could offer him was a lifetime of drawing up leases for land and wills for local farmers. Might his cousin Ashmole be able to help him find more congenial and demanding employment with a legal partnership in the city? He wouldn't mind if it involved prolonging his period of articles to undertake further study and gain fresh experience. He had become used to working hard and had won golden opinions from his present employers. Indeed, they had told him they fully understood his dilemma and were willing to hold the offer of partnership open for a year, in case he later changed his mind

Foxe at once took up pen and paper to write a swift reply, indicating that Nicholas would be welcome at any time and might stay as long as he wished. His letter could be taken to the post office after he had dealt with Maria Worden.

He composed himself and rang the bell as arranged.

'Maria Worden, Sir,' Alfred said as he ushered her into the library.

Foxe stood up and Maria curtseyed gracefully. 'I have brought you a letter from my mistress, Mr Foxe,' she said at once. 'She has asked me to wait and take back your reply.'

'Why didn't your mistress come herself?' Foxe asked. 'Surely that would have been more usual. This seems very formal.'

'That I don't know,' the maid replied. 'Her instructions were to bring you her letter and await your reply.'

In many ways, Maria had changed a great deal from when he knew her first. The she was typical of the servant class, although prettier and somewhat bolder in her manner than most. Now, some ten months of living in Lady Cockerton's household had refined her speech and manners. It had also allowed her to dress in finer clothes than she had in the past and make her look more like a lady's maid that she now was. Her clothes were neat and unassuming, yet obviously the product of a superior dressmaker. Her hair was well brushed and curled and peeped out enticingly from beneath what looked like a new bonnet in the latest style.

Foxe stayed well away from temptation behind his desk, merely leaning forward to take the letter from the young woman's hand. She stood there quietly waiting while he read it.

Lady Arabella's words laid a chill on his heart and shocked him to the core.

He had assumed it would contain complaints about his absence and lack of attention to her. Maybe declarations of pain and hurt, probably mixed with reports the tears she had shed and the sleepless nights she had passed without him. There were none of those. Instead, her letter contained something akin to a large charge of gunpowder designed to dash his nerves and composure into a million burning fragments.

It began sternly. No suggestion of missing him or concern about why he had not been to see her. Not even any reference to his own letter.

'Since I find that you are neglecting to pay me the respect and attention due, I have no option but to bring the matter to your mind more forcefully. There can be no acceptable excuses. When you committed yourself to our relationship, I made the reasonable assumption that I would come first in your life. This apparently is not so. Now I expect a full apology and an undertaking to amend your behaviour for the future.'

Lady Cockerton wasn't sad or miserable at his absence. She was quite plainly furious.

What was even worse was that she next announced she was going to leave for Bath in four days time and expected to stay for at least three weeks. He must ignore all his other concerns and go along to act as her escort.

'Mrs Crombie is more than able to look after your shop. You hardly ever seem to be in it yourself anyway. It is high time you had a change from dull, old Norwich, set aside books and trade, and in particular, stooping to involving yourself in dealing with sordid crimes. It is unbecoming in a gentleman, and especially one who expects to be closely associated with me. Now is the time to stop such nonsense and give me the attention you owe me. I fully intend to enjoy what pleases me and will not allow any man to prevent it.'

After that, and for another half page, she rhapsodised about the leading actors and actresses who would be performing at the theatres in Bath; the balls, assemblies and routs to be held every evening during the season; the presence of most of the leading members of society, who would arrive from every part of the realm; and the unrivalled opportunities to see and be seen, as well as observe the very latest fashions from London and Paris.

What on earth had happened to make her behave like this? She had always been demanding, even somewhat vain, but had never before acted as if placing herself amongst the most fashionable members of society was her sole purpose in life. What had Bath to offer that Norwich did not provide already? As for the so-called attractions she had listed, they were hateful even to contemplate! He'd rather face imminent death than have to deal, day after day, with all those braying members of the *ton* and their empty-headed womenfolk.

The letter ended much as it had begun.

'If leaving in three days is too short notice, you must follow me to Bath as soon afterwards as is possible. I will write when I arrive to let you know where I am lodged and will arrange suitable accommodation for us both. Come without fail and bring your finest clothes.'

This imperious summons left Foxe hurt and confused. He wasn't going to Bath, in four days time or possibly ever. Nothing would change his mind about that. The problem which before him lay only in how he should respond to this epistolary slap in the face. He was fond of Maria and wanted to spare her from hurt, if he could. If he said exactly what he felt, she was likely to get a severe scolding when she reported his reply to her mistress.

'Did Lady Cockerton tell you what was in her letter to me?' he asked.

Maria's smile wavered as she replied. She seemed to sense something was badly wrong.

'No, Mr Foxe. She just told me to give you the letter and wait for your reply. It seems she wants to avoid the delay in letters passing to and fro. At least, that's what I assumed.'

'Please understand, Maria,' Foxe said, as kindly as he could, 'that you have no blame in this matter. It pains me to have to give you the response I must. To my mind, it was quite wrong of your mistress to entrust her letter to you to deliver. Even worse to expect you to take back my reply personally. However, that is what she has done. Please tell your mistress I will be unable to leave Norwich at any time in the foreseeable future, in view of important business which requires my presence here. That is all.'

The poor girl responded as if he had thrown a glass of cold water in her face. For a moment, it was clear she did not even believe what she had heard. Then she frowned and tried a second time to elicit a more suitable response to take back to her mistress.

'Is that it, Mr Foxe? Is that what I am to say to my mistress? You know how upset it will make her.'

'That is my answer, I'm afraid,' Foxe said. 'As I said, I am extremely sorry to burden you with it. None of this will change in any way the warm regard in which I hold you. It is your mistress whose imperious manner makes it impossible for me to give you a more conciliatory reply.'

Foxe tried hard not to see the tears in Maria's eyes as she bobbed another curtsey and turned away to leave. As the door shut behind her, Foxe sat sat back, his breath coming in irregular gasps and a cold feeling gripping his stomach. He knew clearly what he had done and he hated being forced into doing it. What on earth had come over the woman? Did she expect him to be her lap-dog? She hadn't asked whether he wanted to accompany her to Bath, nor whether it was convenient. She hadn't requested his company with suitably loving phrases. Instead, she had assumed his obedience to her wishes, whatever else he might be engaged in. It was too much to be borne. Foxe could be asked, persuaded or enticed. She should have known better than expect him to take orders from her or anyone else.

Foxe spent the rest of the evening alternately boiling with anger and cursing himself for responding so coldly to what might not have been intended to be seen that way. It was no use. The blow to his pride of Lady Cockerton's message was simply too much. No one treated him like a dog that was expected to come the moment it was called. Whatever her reason for acting in this way, it was not to be borne. Was there perhaps another man eager to take his place? If so, he was welcome to it.

If he had been asked at this point whether he definitely wished to end his relationship with Lady Cockerton, Foxe might still have denied it. He mostly wanted to remind her to treat him with respect. Nevertheless, the seeds had been sown which would cause him to abandon her altogether very soon.

Needless to say, he slept badly that night and arose full of all manner of anxieties, picked at his breakfast and decided to forego his usual walk and cups of coffee. Instead, he resolved that he would try his utmost to forget about Arabella Cockerton altogether for the moment. Hopefully, she would come to her sense. If not, well . . . It was time to turn his mind back to the mysteries he was investigating. He would give Alfred careful instructions on what he was to do that morning. Then he would walk off some of his remaining anger by going to see Alderman Halloran.

The coroner would almost certainly hold his inquest on the dead woman sometime that day. It was the usual practise to do so as rapidly as possible, thus allowing the jury members to view the body, as the law required, before decay had begun to render that task even more distasteful. A suitable medical adviser would conduct a rapid autopsy, witnesses would be summoned while events were fresh in their minds, and the business completed as expeditiously as possible.

There was no question of Foxe attending in person. Not if he wished his interest in the murder to remain unknown for the moment. It might have leaked out already, of course. He was far too well known in the city. That was why he planned to see Halloran at once; to find out if he had any inkling that Foxe was not directing his entire attention to the death of Pryce-Perkins, as the mayor and the bishop would clearly expect him to. If he needed an excuse for appearing so soon, with nothing to offer in the way of progress with that mystery, there were always the books he had obtained from the earl's library. Halloran was an avid collector of rare books and could always be distracted by hints that some especially desirable title might soon be available.

'Listen carefully,' Foxe said to Alfred, when the manservant brought him his coat and hat. 'An inquest will be held sometime today on the body of a young woman, found in Mancroft Yard. You are to attend, taking care to draw as little attention to yourself as you can. I need you to bring me a full report of what is given in evidence. I am especially interested in what the medical examiner tells the court. Listen most carefully and be prepared to tell me every detail this evening. Now do you understand what you are to do?'

'Fully, sir,' Alfred replied. 'I will return with an exact account of all the takes place.'

Setting out for Halloran's house in Colegate, Foxe found himself waylaid by Mrs Crombie as he tried to pass his own shop unnoticed. The only way to deal with her would be to step inside for a moment and satisfy at least some of her curiosity.

'Mr Foxe,' she said, as he closed the door on the street. 'Is it true that you were seen to escort an young street-walker into your home yesterday? And what is this Charlie tells me about going to a haunted house to see a dead body?'

'I am on my way in some haste to see Alderman Halloran.' Foxe told her. 'If I am delayed now, he may leave the house on some business or another before I can get there.'

'Don't worry on that score,' Mr. Foxe,' she replied immediately. 'His wife was in here yesterday and told me he is determined to spend the whole day with his book collection. Now, tell me all, for I am consumed with curiosity. As you see, business is light so early in the day. Cousin Eleanor can deal with any customers, while we go into the storeroom, where we can be private and uninterrupted. Even Charlie is busy with that old printing press.'

'The young woman I was seen with is called Kate Sulyard, Mrs. Crombie. She is one of the street children — and also their leader now, I understand, since Charlie lives with me. Yes, she is a prostitute, but only from dire necessity. Whatever she may be, she is still a human being, like you or I, and entitled to be shown respect. She came with an important message and I took her inside, where she could tell me about it privately. I don't care to have all my doings overheard by any passer-by.'

Mrs Crombie blinked. Unbeknown to Foxe, some echoes of his anger with Lady Cockerton must havel lingered in his voice.

'I did not mean to annoy you with my questions, Mr Foxe,' she said swiftly. 'Merely to tease you a little on the matter. You know I would never wish to offend you in any way.'

'I am not offended, Mrs Crombie,' Foxe said. 'Nor have you annoyed me. If I spoke with less kindness than usual, it is because I slept badly and have a great deal on my mind at the moment. Please accept my apology. There is another point. For good reasons, I do not want my interest in the murder in Mancroft Yard known for the time being. Please collect all the relevant gossip you can, but don't even suggest that I'm involved. Will you do that for me?'

'Of course I will. What about Charlie?'

'Perhaps you would be kind enough to tell him to stay silent about the murder, at least for the time being, please. He was with me last night and may be tempted to boast of being there so soon after the body was found. By the way, have I told you that my cousin, Nicholas, is coming to visit for a week or two?'

Nicholas had become a great favourite of Mrs Crombie during his last visit, so this remark served well to deflect any further questions. It also allowed Foxe to escape without explaining any more about the body in the haunted house.

5

Alderman Halloran greeted Foxe with some surprise when the butler announced him. He was busy amongst his books, exactly as Mrs Crombie had said he would be. Each had to be dusted periodically and checked for any signs of damage from bookworms or silverfish. Many library owners left this task to servants or even neglected it altogether. In that case, books of some value could be made worthless in a year or less. Foxe knew Halloran allowed no one to touch his books other than himself; not even his wife or his two nieces. If they wished to consult a book, they had to ask him to fetch it for them, then tell him when they had finished with it, so he could return it to its proper place.

The alderman loved his books as a man might love a favourite child. Even this routine task of dusting and checking them gave him considerable pleasure. It therefore often took a long time. He would often spend many minutes — sometimes hours — renewing his acquaintance with the most cherished volumes.

'What brings you here so soon?' he said to Foxe, setting down the book in his hands with great gentleness. 'Take a seat and I'll ring for coffee. Have you discovered something useful about the murdered parson fellow already?'

'Not yet,' Foxe replied easily, 'though I have organised several people to start searching for me.'

'You've talked to the bishop's secretary, I hope. Terrible windbag, I'm told. Totally loyal to the bishop and good at what he does, but even more boring to listen to than most preachers.'

'Yes,' Foxe said. 'I've seen him once and intend to go to see him a second time after I leave you.'

Halloran laughed. 'Good luck to you then. Let's hope there's something useful amongst all the digressions and verbiage.'

Foxe felt himself beginning to relax. The alderman clearly knew nothing of his involvement in the other murder. If he had done, Foxe's reception would have been very different. Like most men, Halloran's sense of priorities was determined more by the status of the person who raised some problem than any regard for its inherent importance. He, the mayor and the bishop would not be at all pleased to realise that for Foxe, murder was murder, regardless of the status and connections of the victim.

'Did you try to speak with the Earl?' Halloran asked idly. 'Damned prickly fellow, I gather. Wouldn't even agree to see the mayor, when he wanted to go and offer his condolences.'

'I didn't try,' Foxe replied easily. 'Besides, I have grave doubts that he would know anything about his youngest son's activities outside the family home. Most parents don't. Their grown-up offspring also much prefer it that way. What I came to tell you is that I have a notion that before long I will be able to lay my hands on a copy of Euclid, complete with diagrams. Printed in 1493 in Venice, I've been told, and in near fine condition.

In fact, that same book was presently sitting in Foxe's own library. It was one of those he had selected from the Earl of Pentelow's library on his last visit. However, creating excitement and anticipation in the mind of the intended purchaser was a great help in making sure of a profitable sale.

Halloran stopped dead in what he was doing, took several deep breaths, and stared at Foxe with wild eyes.

'14 ... 93, you said? Venice ... fine condition ... with diagrams?' He was now barely capable of coherent speech 'How much?'

'Not sure yet,' Foxe replied in his most casual manner. 'It depends what I might need to pay the seller. It will probably cost a purchaser a great deal, naturally. A very rare volume. I don't need to tell you that.'

Foxe could easily have paid the recklessly extravagant Earl of Pentelow a mere pittance for every volume he bought from him. The man had no interest in books and no conception of what value a collector would place on any of them. He only saw them as a potential source of money to help deal with his continual indebtedness. Foxe, however, did know their value. It pained him to see what must once have been one of the finest libraries in England sold off piecemeal. He was therefore determined to make sure that he could satisfy the earl's constant need for ready cash while selling as few books as he could for the highest realistic price. That attitude had long brought him the trust of buyers and sellers. It had also made his business in rare books one of the most prosperous outside London.

'I expect it will bring you a nice profit too,' Halloran growled. 'What might I need to give you this time?'

'I have to live,' Foxe said mildly. He and Halloran always fenced a little over the price of the books for sale. It was part of the game.

'As far as I can see, Foxe, you live damned well. Servants, a carriage, fine clothes, expensive lady friends. Come on, how much?'

'Three hundred.'

'Never! Ridiculous! No more than a hundred and fifty, and that's generous.'

'Two hundred and fifty then.'

'Two hundred. That's my final offer.'

'Since it's you, Halloran, I'll take two hundred and twenty-five — provided I can persuade the seller to drop his price a fair amount.'

'Done! When can you bring it to me?'

A quick calculation and Foxe decided the earl should receive, say, one hundred and eighty pounds. He would be overjoyed.

By the time Foxe left the alderman's house and its over-excited owner, it was approaching noon. He thought about going home for something to eat, then taking his carriage to the bishop's palace, but decided that would waste too much time. The two small, sweet cakes he had eaten with his coffee at Halloran's house would have to be sufficient. Better to get his talk with the bishop's secretary over with.

Oliver Lakenhurst, the bishop's plump and garrulous secretary, was delighted by Foxe's visit. So delighted that he would have talked until Doomsday had Foxe not taken firm charge of proceedings from the start. As expected, Lakenhurst's actual knowledge of Rev Henry Pryce-Perkins' usual activities proved less than his knowledge of the Pryce-Perkins family. In response to Foxe's questions, he was certainly able to describe in some depth the duties placed upon him as Warden of St Stephen's Hospital. Since it was clear from what he said that these duties were light enough to leave a good deal of time free, Foxe pressed him on what else Pryce-Perkins did to fill his time. Other than suggesting the young warden was 'quite the scholar', Lakenhurst had little to offer.

'What did he study at university?' Foxe asked him. 'Anything other than the usual syllabus for those intending to enter the priesthood?'

'Odd things, as I heard. Early church controversies. Heresies. That kind of thing. That's what the bishop was told by the master of his college at Oxford anyway. Bit weird for someone seeking ordination, I would have thought, but the bishop didn't seem to be bothered by it.'

It was clear that all that mattered to Lakenhurst was that the bishop was unruffled. His own curiosity had stopped short at that point.

'And that's all you know?' Foxe said.

'That kind of thing is well beyond my grasp, or interest, Mr Foxe. I'm not the person to ask. Talk to the cathedral librarian. Pryce-Perkins spent a good deal of his time in the library. He'll be able to tell you more. I'll write you a quick note of introduction —'

'No need' Foxe said quickly. 'I know him well. I've sold him several books for the library and he sometimes comes into my shop as well.'

'Of course. I should have known.'

'There's nothing more you can tell me about the warden then?'

'Nothing. We didn't have much to do with one another. Earl's son and all that, you see.'

'In that case, I see no reason to ask you to stay in Norwich any longer.'

'I can join his lordship, the bishop? Oh, that's quite made my day! Please excuse me, Mr Foxe. I need to prepare to leave as soon as I can. I may even be able to catch the evening coach, if I hurry.'

As Foxe walked homewards, leaving a second person that day overjoyed by the news he had brought them, he was accosted by an enormous fellow with an odd face and a distinctly threatening appearance. Fortunately, the man's expression, which others might have taken for a fierce grimace, was, Foxe knew, his equivalent of a broad smile.

'Hello, Bart,' Foxe said. 'Do you want me?'

'Mistress Tabby send me,' Bart replied. 'She say to go to see her soon as you can.'

'Did she say why?'

'You see her right away,' Bart replied. 'That all she tell me.'

Poor Bart's mind was slow and his speech limited, but Foxe knew just how much Mistress Tabitha Studwell, local Cunning Woman and Foxe's father's beloved mistress, valued him. With Bart watching over her, she could walk unmolested anywhere in the city. The man possessed amazing strength and a fierce devotion to his mistress. At home, Bart worked peacefully tending Tabby's herbs and doing odd jobs. Outside, if anyone had been rash enough to threaten his mistress in the slightest, a low growl and a truly terrifying scowl from Bart would see them scampering off. Offer her violence and you would be lucky to escape with your life.'

'Very well, Bart. Tell her I'll visit her tomorrow morning early.'

'You come 'morrow early,' Bart repeated. 'I tell her. 'Bye Mr Foxe.'

Foxe walked on home feeling somewhat apprehensive. That kind of summons from Mistress Tabby meant she had something vital to say to him. He would never ignore it. He owed her too much. Still, he couldn't help worrying. Now he had three things to worry him. What Tabby wanted; the ominous silence from Lady Cockerton after her maid's visit; and the rapidly approaching time when he would need to face the Catt sisters. It was going to be another sleepless night.

###

Next morning, Foxe reached Tabby's house by the river at half-past eight. He'd bolted down a smaller than usual breakfast and been on his way before anyone could delay him further. He found her working alongside Bart in her herb garden and she motioned to him to go inside. A few moments later, she came in, drying her hands on a small towel.

Tabby never wasted time on meaningless pleasantries.

"I had Arabella Cockerton here yesterday afternoon, Ashmole.' The use of his full name did not bode well. 'I could not tell whether she was more angry or ashamed. She told me you'd sent her maid home with a cold and almost insulting message. I think she realises she's made a dreadful mistake and risks driving you away for good. Unfortunately, she's far too proud to admit it. She asked me to persuade you to change your mind.'

'She demanded I go with her to Bath,' Foxe said. 'Even set a day to leave without bothering to consult me. Treated me like a dog to be called to heel.'

'Oh dear,' Tabby said. 'You are in a temper with her, aren't you, Ash? The trouble is that's she's fundamentally a rather vain and foolish woman. Glamorous, of course, but not so much else.'

'You know how much I hate to leave Norwich, Tabby. And as for expecting me to stop everything else and rush off just to be with her …'

'There we have it, eh? She clearly doesn't know about your hatred of leaving the city and assumes that, if you truly love her, to be with her must be more important than anything else. You see things quite differently. This is going to end in tears.'

'It's not my fault,' Foxe protested. 'I am truly fond of her. I even managed at one time to convince myself I loved her. I can see now I was wrong about that. I do like to be with her, but I have other priorities too. The bishop has asked me —'

'I know all about that,' Tabby interrupted. 'She either doesn't or doesn't care. Being truly fond of someone is a long way short of the kind of abject devotion Arabella expects. She told me she's leaving for Bath the day after tomorrow. Will you go with her?'

'No.'

'Will you follow later?'

'I cannot. I have too much to do here.'

'Ash! Ash! You're getting more like your dear father with every passing year. Pig-headed and set on his own course, though the earth should fall into ruin around him. Like you, he could be cajoled, persuaded, begged, even seduced into doing what I wanted. Never, never commanded. Do that and he turned to stone on the spot. That's it, isn't it. A woman who likes to believe she's an irresistible force has encountered a man who knows he's an immovable object. It's all over between you.'

'Possibly.'

'I knew from the start she wasn't right for you, Ash, but it would have been useless to tell you at the time. You're easily attracted by beauty and glamour, when what you need is steadiness and loving care. What are you going to do about Kitty and Gracie Catt, by the way?'

'I don't know.'

'Strong and decisive in everything but affairs of the heart. That's you Ash. Still, time will tell. I would tell you you've broken Arabella's heart, but that's not true. That organ is made of pure adamant. You've just wounded her pride as much as she has yours. The only heart you've broken is poor Maria's.'

'I'm truly sorry for that, Tabby. I've been feeling wretched ever since she left my house.'

'So you should! None of it was her fault. Ah well, we all have to have our hearts broken a time or two in life, and I dare say she'll recover soon enough. Now, listen to me carefully. There are things about that house in Mancroft Yard you need to know.

'The old woman who died there wasn't a witch. Believe me, I would know. She was just a lonely old woman who happened to like cats. She'd been quite prosperous in her youth and produced a large family. First her husband died, then her children either died or married and moved away. In the end, she and a single servant were the only ones left still living in what had once been her family home. Knowing she was about to join the rest of her family in death, she told the servant where she'd hidden the remnants of her jewels and said she should to take them, along with her two favourite cats, and get as far away from the city as she could. That's why no one could find her after the old woman died. The servant came to see me near the end and told me all about it, hoping I might have something to give her old mistress some relief.'

'Did you?'

'No. It was her time. It couldn't be helped.'

'What about the house ?' Foxe asked.

In her Will, she left it to the parish, to be sold and the proceeds used to help the most needy. Whoever bought it, has done nothing with it since.'

'Why? Why couldn't the new owner simply let it?'

'Because he never tried to. I know that for a fact. The new owner already owned the whole of the yard behind. He must have told his tenant, Holtaway, to encouraged the idea the place was either possessed by demons or haunted. What does that suggest to you?'

'That he wanted to use if for another purpose; something he didn't want anyone from the yard to poke their noses into.'

'That's what I think too, Ash. What it may be, I don't know. It's up to you to find out.'

Foxe sat back and thought for a moment. 'Do you think that young woman went inside for some reason and stumbled on what was going on, so she was killed to stop her talking about it?'

'Very probably. Now, off you go and get back to doing what you do best, which is solving mysteries. Try to stop worrying too, if you can. Fretting never solved anything.'

Foxe rose, gave her a warm hug and a kiss in thanks, and prepared to leave when she stopped him in the doorway.

'By the way,' Tabby said, 'I should steer well clear of women like Arabella Cockerton in future. I doubt you'll even hear from her again. You've made her ashamed and she finds that unforgivable. When she left here, she was working herself up into such a state that little you could do would earn you forgiveness — not even if you lay down in the mud and let her walk up and down your back. Things might change after a few weeks, if you really want to try again, but I wouldn't wager on that happening. My advice, for what notice you'll take of it, would be to move on.'

For the rest of that day, Foxe occupied himself with attending to business matters. He arranged for Charlie to wrap the precious volume of Euclid and deliver it to the alderman's house. After that, he was to go to the cathedral library and ask the librarian, Robert Lavender, whether it would be convenient for his master to speak with him the following afternoon. Meanwhile,

Foxe determined once again to abandon his usual morning walk and visit to the coffeehouse. Instead he would call in person on the two other book collectors to whom he hoped to sell the remaining titles he had brought back from the Earl of Pentelow's library.

He also called into his shop in case Mrs Crombie had been able to gather any useful gossip about either murder.

She had nothing for him about the death in Mancroft Yard, other than that the belief in a homicidal vagrant had wide acceptance. As regards Rev Pryce-Perkins, all most people were discussing were his mother's many scandalous amours, either known or suspected, and the earl's seeming indifference to his countess's conduct. No one seemed to know anything about the dead man. That was a boring subject when there was such a rich field for scurrilous speculation about this mother's activities. Neither of his brothers drew much interest either. One was almost invisibly occupied with the running of the estate and the other thousands of miles away helping to maintain England's growing empire in the face of foreign jealousy.

6

Foxe was now beginning to feel frustrated with the whole investigation into the warden's death. He had earned next to nothing useful from Oliver Lakenhurst; Mrs Crombie wasn't collecting gossip that revealed anything more; and he still had to hear back from Brock. He was quickly running out of potential sources of information.

'Patience!' he told himself. 'Something will turn up in time. It nearly always does.'

At least the previous afternoon had proved successful. By the time he returned home, he had sold all the other books for good prices. When they were paid for, Pentelow would be richer by nearly five hundred pounds and Foxe himself would have made one hundred and twenty pounds in profit. Most satisfactory!

During the morning, Charlie reported that the librarian would be delighted to receive him next day, as requested; then had rather spoiled that news by telling Foxe none of the street children had so far brought him word of what might be going on in the empty house at the head of Mancroft Yard. Thanks to the tales of ghosts and demons, few of them dared to venture near there at night. During the day, they said it stood empty and silent, with no signs or sounds of activity within.

'We'll have to return and search the place thoroughly,' Foxe told the lad. 'There must be some reason why the landlord has taken care to keep it unoccupied. I wonder who it is who owns the place. Do you know?'

Charlie shook his head.

'The difficulty will be to get inside without anyone in the yard noticing. I'll have to think about that. There must be some way of doing it. Any ideas?'

The lad shook his head again.

'No matter for the moment. I have an important task for the street children. Can you pass them my instructions?'

'I'll ask Kate to do it,' Charlie replied. 'She's really taken to you, master. Once she'd got over her tears, all she could talk about was how kind you'd been and what a true gentleman you were. Handsome too, she said. And as for generous … Two whole shillings! That's more money than she's able to earn on the streets most days.'

'Tell her that there are two more shillings waiting for her if she does what I ask,' Foxe said, 'plus three more to hand out. She needs to organise the children to keep watching that house closely, day and night. I want to know what's going on there. Especially who goes in and out. If they see anything suspicious, she must contact me at once. Otherwise, just keep a close watch in place until I speak to her next. It won't be many days probably.'

'If you offered to give her a kiss, I reckon she'd do that for nothing — and walk through fire as well,' the boy said wickedly.

'Don't be impertinent!' Foxe said, though there was no force in his reprimand. 'Just get on your way and do as I told you. Give her a kiss, indeed! I'll give your backside a good kick to help you on your way if you aren't out of here in ten seconds.'

In truth, he was rather flattered by what Charlie had said. Foxe could never encounter any woman young or old, grand or, like Kate, living in the gutter, without trying to win their good opinion. As for Kate herself, wash away the dirt and cheap cosmetics and dress her in decent clothes and she would be a decidedly pretty girl. It broke his heart to see her childhood being ruined in the way it was. She would probably end up like most of the other women forced to sell their bodies to any man with a sixpence to spare. Old by twenty-five and dead by thirty.

He shook such gloomy thoughts aside and turned instead to considering how best to proceed in the matter of Rev Hon Henry Pryce-Perkins. Of course! He still hadn't spoken with any of the old pensioners at the hospital. The man had been their warden for some time — he should have asked Lakenhurst exactly when he was appointed — and lived in the house next to theirs. He led their prayers, morning and evening, and ate with them most days. They must know something of what he did with his time. If they were like most old people with nothing to do but wait for death, they would be as curious as cats. Anything to lessen the monotony of their existence. Why hadn't he thought of them before? He should have no difficulty in getting them to tell him what they knew; especially if he gave them a few shillings to buy tobacco and any other small luxuries they desired.

He thought briefly about sending word to whoever had been appointed as temporary replacement warden, stressing the bishop's request that Foxe should find the killer of the previous holder of that post. Too formal. Too likely to put them on their guard. It would be better just to turn up, hand around a little silver, and let them tell him what they would. If any seemed likely to know more, but proved reluctant to speak in front of the others, he could arrange to see them privately.

He'd go there after seeing the cathedral librarian the next day.

Alfred's report on the inquest held on the murdered girl had provided on or two useful facts. To begin with, the tramp who had found the body and raised the alarm had slipped away long before the constables arrived. No surprise in that.

'Probably expected them to try to pin the murder on him,' Foxe tought to himself sourly. 'I would have done the same.'

Next came the evidence from the autopsy, which had been carried out by an elderly surgeon. He thoroughly annoyed the coroner by giving his evidence in such a low voice the jury complained several times that they could barely hear what he was saying. He declared that the girl had been strangled, as was obvious from the marks around the throat. However, in his view that attack had not itself been enough to cause death. It most likely made the victim unconscious, after which she had been struck several heavy blows to the head; at least three and maybe more. Her skull had thus been fractured in several places. Death could have resulted from any one of those blows. He had found a large piece of wood in the corner of the room, which was what, in his judgement, the killer had used. There were a few blond hairs stuck on a roughened part at one end, along with traces of blood.

'What kind of piece of wood?' the coroner asked. 'Be precise, man!'

'A broken chair leg, sir. Several of the bits of furniture in the room were damaged or broken.'

'An opportunistic crime then,' Foxe mused. 'Whoever it was simply grabbed the nearest suitable thing for a weapon. The strangling didn't kill the poor young woman, so he made sure of it by beating her head in.'

'The surgeon said he found no signs of sexual molestation, sir,' Alfred added, 'though he reported the young woman was not a virgin.'

'Did he make a guess at her age?'

'Around seventeen or eighteen, he thought.'

'Anything else?'

'Not really, sir. He said she wore little or no make-up on her face and her body carried no physical defects. She was well-nourished, but rather short for her age. Oh yes, he said her lower limbs suggested she might have suffered rickets as a child.'

'Hmm,' Foxe said enigmatically when Alfred had finished. 'Much as I guessed myself. Well done, Alfred. An excellent account. Doubtless the verdict was murder?'

'It was. The coroner said the corpse would be buried at the expense of the parish.'

'Thrown into a pauper's grave, that means, with a few murmured prayer given by some harassed curate. Poor child! The final indignity.'

After dinner, Foxe tried to work out a more coherent course of investigation for both his cases. If nothing else, it might serve to distract his mind from the quarrel with Lady Cockerton, and the fact that there were now barely two days before the Catt sisters were due to reach Norwich. He had a few ideas, but there was no pattern to be seen in either murder, which might allow him to move from collecting facts more or less at random to following a clear track to his hoped-for target.

Since sleeping badly had now become something of a habit with Foxe, he rose early once again, drank some coffee and consumed only a single bread roll with butter and jam for his breakfast. Without a clear notion of how to proceed, he simply reverted to habit and set off to walk around the marketplace as usual. He was not due to see Mr Lavender until later, so he might as well stop in at the coffeehouse and glance at the latest London papers.

When he went inside he was annoyed to see what he thought of as "his" table already occupied. But as soon as he realised the person slumped behind a newspaper was his friend Brock, the day felt a good deal better. He sat down at once, eager to hear any news.

'Sorry I haven't come to find you before now,' Brock said. 'Even with Julia's contacts, it's proved deuced difficult to discover much about the late Henry Pryce-Whatever-it-is. Lots about his trollop of a mother, of course. A bit about his supposed father — '

'Supposed?'

'Given the number of men who have enjoyed the mother's favours before her marriage and after, the actual parentage of all of her sons must be uncertain. That woman's the type to bed with almost anyone she comes across. A regular nymphomaniac.'

'Never mind about her, Brock. Did you find out anything about the son who was killed?'

'He was always an odd, withdrawn child apparently. No interests beyond books. Spent most of his time hiding from his father, who kept forcing him outside to do the proper things an earl's son should go. Things like chasing after foxes and striding about with a gun killing anything he came across. The boy was a poor horseman, though. More likely to hurt himself with a gun than kill any peasants or pigeons.'

'So his father decided he would be best in the church and sent him off to university?'

'Precisely. There he proved to be a brilliant scholar. Should have stayed there, probably.'

'Why didn't he?'

'My wife says it isn't the earl who's consumed with ambition, it's the countess. The earl just struts about and flaunts his supposed family links back to William the Conqueror's right-hand man. Proud as Lucifer on the outside, while trying to hide the shame of being cuckolded on a daily basis. You know it's said the moment the marriage ceremony was over, she retired to her room to be fucked by the parson?'

'Come on, Brock! That has to be an invention.'

'It's true! People swear it!'

'People will swear to anything which makes a good tale. Stick to the point, Brock. I'm not interested in yet more wild stories about the countess.'

'The point is,' Brock said, exaggerating every word, the Countess of Westleton has the futures of her three sons decided for them. The eldest, Matthew, is to make a brilliant marriage, double the size of the family's estates, and become Prime Minister. She'll make sure of the marriage, probably by seducing the bride's father. Matthew could well manage the second on his own, since he's obsessed with agricultural improvement. The third definitely won't happen. He has no taste for politics, hates being in London, and never talks of anything but farming.'

'The second son?'

'He'll probably achieve all her hopes, save that of living long enough to become an admiral. I already told you about him.'

'What's his name, by the way?'

'Dillingham. It's his mother's family name.'

'And Henry, naturally, was to be a bishop.'

'Archbishop! He seems to have proved her greatest disappointment. He was happy enough to enter the church. Thereafter, the fellow wanted only to be left alone with his books and his fascination with obscure religions.'

'His what?'

'Old, mostly lost religions. Pagan beliefs. Weird cults.'

'I've been told he studied Christian heresies, Brock.'

'Those as well, I dare say. No one really knows, except that he used to visit the homes of other gentry and ask to search through their libraries. If he found something in one of their books, he'd beg them to lend it to him to study properly.'

'Interesting.' Foxe said quietly. 'I wonder if that had anything to do with the strange people — "like freemasons, but not" — which old Benjamin Gunton mentioned at the inquest. I'm seeing the cathedral librarian this afternoon. Perhaps he'll know more.'

'That's all I know,' Brock said. 'Aside from a few more anecdotes about the countess,'

'I can't believe Lady Julia brought you such pornographic tales,' Foxe protested. 'She's far too much of a lady.'

'No. I got those myself. Talked to some acquaintances who've had business dealings with the Pryce-Perkins family. By all accounts, that estate was riddled with debts before Matthew got involved. His father — supposed father, I should say — left everything to a succession of stewards and land-agents who fleeced him on every side. Even worse, the countess is as extravagant as she is wanton. Buys jewels and clothes all the time and demands they employ a French chef to provide dinners grand enough to outstrip anyone else in the county. I'd guess the parson son was delighted to escape.'

###

The cathedral library was housed in a series of two large rooms in the cloister, one above the other. You entered through a small door which gave no hint of what lay beyond.

Foxe loved visiting the cathedral cloister. He could never quite get used to their enormous size, nor did he think it possible to tire of admiring the magnificent stone tracery, which filled every opening into the cloister garth. The cathedral was huge, but somehow the sheer extent and magnificence of what was, after all, only a walkway, seemed to dwarf it.

Then there were to carved bosses in the vaulting. Hundreds of them. All different and all carved with breathtaking skill and artistry. It seemed a crime simply to walk under then without pausing to admire a 'green man' here and a dragon there. All done to the greater glory of God, he'd been told. Certainly there was no earthly reason to have lavished so much time and attention on merely necessary points of junction between the ribs of the vaulting itself. The cynic in him, never willing to accept the 'official' version of things, dismissed mere acts of faith, pointing out that the bishops of the mediaeval church had been renowned for their love of flaunting their wealth on every possible occasion.

As he approached the door to the library, Foxe decided the reason for constructing the magnificence that was Norwich cathedral hardly mattered. It was there and should be enjoyed regardless.

Robert Lavender, the librarian, greeted Foxe warmly. They talked amicably about books and various titles Lavender hoped to acquire for the library, though he stressed they must be at the cheapest prices. The amount allowed to hm for purchases was extremely limited. Foxe promised to do what he could, but held out little hope in most cases.

Finally, they turned to the main purpose of Foxe's visit.

'I fear I know very little about Rev Pryce-Perkins, Mr Foxe,' Lavender told him. 'An odd fellow, certainly, but the cathedral precincts are full of those. He came into the library a great deal, but rarely spoke, save to ask me to find some volume that was not on the open shelves. At first, his areas of interest were merely unusual. Editions of the early church fathers, especially those in which they denounced various heresies. Some rather obscure historians of the eastern Roman empire when it was centred on Constantinople. Writings on the Albigensian Crusade — that was when the pope ordered the elimination of the sect of the Cathars in southern France. Some volumes we had, others would only be found in a far larger and more academic library than this.'

'You said those were the books he consulted "at first",' Foxe said, proving he had been listening with great care. The librarian paused as if considering what he might be allowed to reveal.

'What I shall tell you now must be kept in strict confidence between us, Mr Foxe. It is not something the dean and chapter wish to become general knowledge, since it would attract quite the wrong type of people to come here and probably reflect badly on the church. There is a special collection. It's kept out of sight upstairs and the book presses are locked. We refer to it only as The Norgate Bequest. Access is allowed only by permission of the dean or the bishop.'

'Do you mean it contains pornography?' Foxe asked, his tone reflecting only the mildest surprise. Such books were common enough in most grand libraries, naturally — the Earl of Pentelow had hundreds, though he probably didn't know it. The only oddity was the thought the cathedral library might have some as well.

'Good God, no!' Lavender exclaimed. 'We have nothing of that kind, I assure you. These are far worse.'

Foxe tried and failed to imagine what those in charge of a cathedral library might consider worse than pornography. Lavender had already said they had volumes in the open shelves containing accounts of various heresies.

'So what does this Norgate Bequest hold?' he asked.

'Elias Norgate was a wealthy wool-merchant, who lived in Norwich in the period of the civil war and after,' Lavender explained.' As I recall, he died in the reign of Queen Anne, about sixty-five or seventy years ago. In his Will, he bequeathed all his books to the cathedral. It was a most generous bequest. His books still form the largest part of our holdings. They have been of great use to the clergy here and are often consulted even today.'

'But there are others you keep hidden away?'

'The bequest came with a strange condition. It was to be all or nothing. If the cathedral did not accept the entire library of books, they were to be sold and the proceeds given to another diocese. Naturally, the dean of the time accepted this condition and the books were brought here. Only then was it discovered that a certain number were quite unsuitable.'

'Could you not have disposed of those?' Foxe said.

'No. I forgot to mention the other condition. The books are supposed to be kept in perpetuity.'

'Quite a dilemma. Pryce-Perkins found out about them and asked for access I imagine?'

'He did,' Lavender said. 'He brought a letter from the bishop saying he was to be given unlimited access to all the books in the library. I doubt that his lordship understood what he was doing. I've never seen him in the library and he's never enquired about its contents.'

'If the fact that you have these unsuitable books is kept secret,' Foxe said, 'how did Pryce-Perkins find out about them?'

'I have no idea. One day, he simply handed me the bishop's note and asked to be taken to look over the shelves where they are kept.'

'I see,' Foxe said. 'Since I have been asked to investigate his death by the bishop himself, isn't it time you told me more about these terrible volumes. What are they about?'

'Alchemy. The Kabbalah. Magic. Witchcraft. That kind of thing.'

'I can see why you keep them under lock and key. Did Pryce-Perkins spend much time with these books?'

'A great deal in the few weeks before his death. I didn't have the courage to ask him what he was looking for.'

'He probably wouldn't have told you the truth if you had,' Foxe said. 'However, I'm very glad that you've mentioned it to me. It fits in with something else I've learned. By the way, do you know if a temporary warden has been appointed?'

'I don't believe so. I was told the vicar of the parish church is taking the prayers and one of the canons is looking after financial matters.'

Foxe was delighted to hear this, though he was careful to say no more. He had already decided he needed to go to St. Stephen's Hospital and talk with the so-called deputy warden — the man who had spoken at the inquest — and as many of his fellow pensioners as possible. He had been going to do it right away. Now he decided it was best left until later. What he had learned from the librarian had changed his whole perception of the warden's death. He needed more time to work out precisely what he needed to ask the old men in the hospital.

Taking his leave of the librarian, Foxe decided he needed time alone. He therefore sent his groom home with the carriage and set out to walk back himself. Walking often helped him think and he had a great deal on his mind. Aside from the two murders, the arrival of the Catt sisters was very close and he still hadn't decided how to respond when they sent word to announce their presence in Norwich. Lady Cockerton's actions had completely altered the circumstances. On the other hand, he still hadn't decided whether his break with her should be temporary or permanent.

For five minutes or so Foxe grappled with that problem. Then he thrust it aside in disgust and turned back to his investigations. He'd told Charlie earlier that he needed to think of a way to get into the house where the young woman's body had been found. Now he also needed to be able to gain entry to the house where Pryce-Perkins had been living. A careful search there might well prove enlightening.

The matter of gaining entry to the waren's house took him barely fifty yards to solve. The other problem, how to search the house where the body had been found without alerting whoever was making secret use of it, was much more difficult. He couldn't send someone else in his place. One poor soul had already died from entering that house. He didn't want another death on his conscience. It was something he needed to do in person.

The more he thought about it, the more convinced he became that there must be at least one person watching that house day and night. Even if whoever was making use of it went only at night — which was what the reports of nocturnal noises and lights suggested — they wouldn't take the risk of their activities being discovered by any casual daytime intruder in search of something to steal. He had to elude their vigilance if getting inside was to useful. If they realised he was becoming curious, they would move whatever as hidden there as quickly as possible. Then he would have no means of discovering their identity.

7

The next day dawned bright and clear with a gently southerly breeze, but all that atmospheric favour was wasted on Mr Foxe. He rose late and barely glanced out of the window at the sunshine. He didn't hear the birds singing in the trees and bushes in his garden, nor see the flowers on the roses. Tomorrow, the Catt sisters were due to arrive and he still had no idea how best to deal with them. Tabby had put it neatly. Foxe was decisive and resolute in most practical matters. When it came to affairs of the heart, he was chronically tentative and uncertain. Like now. As a result, he viewed the coming day with the attitude of a condemned man, who realises that in just over thirty hours he has an appointment with the executioner.

Sheer hunger forced him to consume two slices of cold ham, three breakfast rolls and a prodigious quantity of jam, along with a whole pot of coffee. Then he sat slumped in his chair, too disheartened to decide how to spend his morning.

After maybe ten minutes more of this wallowing in misery and self-pity, he was roused by Molly, the parlourmaid, entering to clear away what remained of his breakfast. At the same time she brought him a sealed note, which she said Bart had delivered to the back door a little earlier.

Foxe turned the note over in his hands and stared at it for a moment, recognising Mistress Tabby's neat handwriting. It was addressed with the single word 'Foxe' and sealed with a rough blob of scarlet wax. When he broke the seal and unfolded the single sheet, he found something closely resembling the prescription a physician might hand to a patient.

TO RAISE THE SPIRITS

The establishment on the corner of St Giles Street and Upper Goat Lane is generally reckoned to be the finest and most exclusive bordello in the city. Mention my name to the madam and you will be admitted without question. Use twice weekly until full vitality is restored.

P.S. By noon this morning, the tide will turn.

Foxe read this note through twice. It was, in his experience, inevitably a sound idea to follow Tabby's advice. He knew of the place she mentioned well enough. It was said to be exceptionally well run, luxurious in it furnishings, and employed only the prettiest and most accomplished young women. It was also fiendishly expensive and screened its customers with considerable care. Yet what did either of those things matter to him? He could easily afford their charges and it seemed the madam had either been forewarned by Tabby, or owed her enough favours, to admit him at once. Perhaps this evening, after dinner, he would walk the short distance to its door and see.

The enigmatic postscript to Tabby's note then held his attention for some time. Despite his natural scepticism, he had several times wondered if the Cunning Woman could actually see into the future. Her ability to see things coming often bordered on the magical. Usually, after they had been proved accurate, he had been able to explain the accuracy of her prophesies as due to a combination of thought and simple observation. There was also the fact that she invariably received news of events before anyone else. Even so, there remained something uncanny about her way of knowing what was to take place, even if it was based on a mixture of early warning and intelligent reasoning.

This prophecy, however, was unusually precise about the time, even if the rest was annoyingly opaque. Why should he be concerned about the tide? Were her words to be taken literally, or merely in a figurative sense? If the latter, to what might they refer? After a few more moments of trying to work it out, he rose and went over to the fireplace to look at the clock on the mantlepiece. It was ten minutes before ten o'clock.

As he dressed in a clean shirt, dark breeches and cream silk stockings, Foxe suddenly recalled that his cousin Nicholas was due to arrive that day. Could that be what Tabby meant by her strange words? To arrive by noon would mean the young man would need to leave his home in Diss no later than nine o'clock and ride at a good pace all the way. It was not impossible, but Foxe thought Nicholas would hardly be so eager to reach Norwich that he would work his horse quite so hard.

Tabby's prophesy actually arrived some ten minutes early. Foxe was sitting at his desk in his library wrapped in his favourite banyan. He was trying to concentrate on a catalogue of rare books for sale which had arrived several days earlier from a dealer in London, when Alfred brought him the morning post.

He recognised the handwriting on the top letter in an instant. Not Lady Cockerton's this time, but Gracie Catt's. His hands shook as he fumbled to break the seal. Surely they had not reached Norwich earlier than they had told him. Was it a summons to join them earlier or notice of a visit that very day?

The contents of the letter proved brief and to the point.

Dear Ash,

We are cancelling our intended stay in Norwich. The leading actress at the theatre in Dublin has fallen ill and Kitty has been asked to take her place. It is a great opportunity for her. We will be sailing from Liverpool in four days time.

Your loving friend,

Gracie Catt

Foxe didn't know whether to shout for joy or pound the desk in fury. For a second time, the two sisters had left him to chase fame and fortune for Kitty, with little more than the briefest of good-byes. For a second time that month, a woman had put her own concerns before affection for him, as if that were the most natural thing in the world. Was he of such little account to them? Was his love no more than a pleasant diversion until something better turned up? Was he just a fool, who was known to be generous with his money?

At that point, Foxe burst out laughing. The truth was that each occasion had brought him relief from a painful dilemma. In the case of the Catt sisters, whether he could stick to his promise to remain faithful to Lady Cockerton and forget all the splendid occasions when one or the other sister had welcomed him to her bed. If he wanted to remain faithful, of course. Her recent behaviour had brought that into doubt. Lady Cockerton's decision to go to Bath had given him a means to escape an arrangement he should not have entered into anyway.

Tabby was right. It was time to rejoice in his unexpected freedom and live as he wished, without being dependent on selfish women. The tide had indeed begun to turn.

Nicholas arrived soon after one. He told Foxe he had left around nine-thirty, but it was such a beautiful day that he had let his horse bear him forward at a steady pace, while he admired the beauty of the countryside along the way. Some of the oak trees had a second growth of shoots whose leaves were tinged with orange. The hawthorn bushes beside the road and in the farmers' hedgerows were beginning to bear their scarlet berries. As he crossed the many patches of heathland, the scent of the gorse flowers was nearly overwhelming, and in cultivated areas, many of the fields showed the barley or wheat was starting to turn to gold, ready for harvest. Everywhere, the bracken was tall and lush and the blackberries carried clear signs of the bumper harvest of berries soon to come. Even as he entered the city, he passed between houses set in gardens in full bloom, with roses everywhere and flowering auriculas set by their front doors. It had been enough to make him forget the bumps, mires and potholes along the way.

Foxe sat with his visitor while he refreshed himself after his journey. For the moment, they talked mostly of trifles and family matters. Nicholas brought loving greetings from his aunt, Harriet, of whom he knew Foxe was especially fond. Foxe explained to Nicholas that he had to leave soon to pursue his latest investigation at St. Stephen's Hospital. Alfred or Molly would show his young cousin to the room set aside for him and help him to get settled. After that, Mrs

Crombie, was full of eagerness to welcome him into the shop and enjoy his company once again.

'What investigation?' Nicholas asked eagerly. 'Has someone been murdered?'

'I don't have time to explain all about it now,' Foxe replied. 'Later I will. Just be patient. I will definitely return home well before dinner. Then we can eat together, and you can explain in detail what has brought you to Norwich.'

'And you'll tell me all about this mystery?'

'If there's time. If not, I'll tell you everything tomorrow, I promise. Just now, I have to visit a group of old men, who may or may not know something that will help me solve a murder.'

###

On most weekdays, Foxe's carriage rolled along at a good pace through the city. He could ride past the marketplace, skirt the great bulk of the castle, and roll down the hill into the cathedral precincts in very little time. Despite being one of the most populous cities in the land, Norwich appeared almost deserted on working days. Only on Sundays and holidays were the streets crowded enough to indicate the number of inhabitants. Since the principal trade of the town was the production of fine cloth, during the hours of daylight nearly everyone of working age was at home, busy witht their spinning wheels, looms and dying vats. The mills which were just beginning to appear elsewhere were unknown in Norwich. Its cloth was hand-woven by home workers, paid on piece-work. There were no new-fangled spinning and weaving machines driven by water wheels. No factories housed in large buildings and sited near a suitably swift flow of water. Norfolk's generally flat terrain was quite unsuited to such innovation and its rivers were slow-flowing. No, the city's fine cloth was still produced as it always had been, by hand

Foxe was greeted on his arrival at St. Stephen's Hospital by Benjamin Gunton, the pensioner who had given evidence at the inquest on the late warden. Carriages drawing up outside the place must have been unusual enough to bring Gunton quickly to investigate who might be inside.

'Come you inside, sir,' he said. 'You come at just the right time, I reckon. We've just 'ad our food, an' everyone is together in the hall — well, almost everyone. Let's say everyone who matters. We all knows of you Mr Foxe, like most folks on this city do, so you needn't waste time explaining who you be and what you be doin' here. Just you ask your questions and we'll do our best to answer. The warden as was were a peculiar kind o' fellow, but kind enough and always see'd we got our few pence of allowance on time to buy 'baccy an' the like. Most of the pensioners don't think as 'ow he deserved to die like 'e did, an' that's God's truth, that is.'

All the time he'd been talking, Gunton had been leading Foxe past the row of tiny houses where the pensioners lived towards the larger building that stood at one end of the row. The two of them entered through a simple doorway and Foxe found himself in a well-constructed, though simple hall, perhaps twenty feet long by twelve feet wide. The kind of hall which was provided in larger mansions for the servants to take their meals. As he would have expected, the only furnishing consisted of a long wooden table, stoutly constructed, with benches at each side. At the head of the table stood a single chair with a high back and armrests. There was still a strong smell of cabbage about the place, and crumbs of bread scattered over the table itself, confirming that the midday meal had not long been cleared way.

'Come and sit you down here in the warden's chair,' Gunton said. 'That way we can all see you an' you can see us.'

Ranged along the table on either side were five elderly men dressed in the distinctive jackets of pensioners. Foxe guessed all were well over sixty years of age. Some probably eighty or more. He had never before seen such a collection of wrinkled cheeks and white beards in one place.

Before he came, Foxe had recalled two things about the elderly. Many of them might be hard of hearing so he needed to speak up; and all were adults with long and busy lives behind them, not dotards or fools to be patronised by the young. He had borne this in mind while considering how best to loosen their tongues and ensure their full co-operation.

He now paid as close attention as he could to the list of names which Gunton reeled off. He knew he would never remember any of these details, try as he might, but he would do his best.

As they began, Foxe was relieved to find that Gunton had been chosen to be the spokesman for the whole group, with the rest speaking only when they had something to add to his answers.

'If'n we all speak at once, sir,' the old man explained, 'it'll all get muddled. Won't do to 'ave people talking over one another and interruptin' all the time. T'ain't respectful, neither.'

The fierce scowl he directed at his fellow pensioners suggested that what was to be avoided was their normal mode of conversation when they were all together.

Foxe now decided to play his trump card right at the start. Turning to Gunton, he passed him a small cloth bag which clinked loudly as he did so.

'Here are a few coins to buy you and your colleagues a little extra tobacco and perhaps a jug or two of good ale. Perhaps you will share them out later.'

The gasps and smiles around the table gave ample evidence that Foxe was now accepted as a most welcome visitor, who should be assisted in every possible way.

'That's right gentlemanly of you sir,' Gunton said, a beaming smile on his face, 'and we all be very grateful. B'ain't we, friends?'

His remark was greeted with considerable approval and muttered thanks on all sides.

'Now, sir,' Gunton continued, 'what is it you wants to know?'

'What kind of a man was the warden?' Foxe asked.

'A scholar and a gentleman, but right strange in many ways with it,' Gunton replied.

'That's right enough', came from one side of the table. ('Real strange.' 'Downright odd, if you asks me.' 'Too clever for his own good.')

'How was he strange?' Foxe said.

'For a start, every Sunday the warden is supposed to preach us a kind o' sermon after our meal. Nothing too long, or most of us would fall asleep.' (You always does, Jeremiah. Snores too.' 'So does you, Henry Tagg, so you needn't be lookin' at me.') Most wardens stick to something simple like a story from the bible or a few words about the importance o' avoidin' strong drink. ('Can't afford it.' 'What was that I smelled on your breath last Tuesday evenin' after that grandson o' yours came to see you?')

'And Mr Pryce-Perkins didn't do that, I take it.' Foxe said, trying to move things along.

'He preached, right enough, but none of us could understand above a quarter of what 'e said. It were all long, complicated words and foreign-soundin' names. 'Gobbledee-Gook, I calls it.' ('All heathen names an' weird goings-on.') That was typical of the man, came o' reading all they books.'

'What books were those?' Foxe asked, suddenly on the alert.

'Lord, don't axe me. He was always reading something. Some days, he hardly put a nose out of his house, save to do his duties. He was always precise about those.'

'Tell Mr Foxe 'ow secretive the warden were Ben,' came a voice from somewhere on Foxe's right. ('Right that is.' 'Real secretive!')

'Never said anything about 'isself, sir, nor what 'e were doin' aside bein' a parson. Kept to 'is 'ouse most o' the time. That wasn't so strange, 'im bein' one o' the nobility an' all that. But 'e didn't go out much either, nor 'ave any callers, 'Id hisself away like. But allus readin', readin', readin'.'

'What about those people you mentioned at the inquest?' Foxe asked. 'How often did they come to see him?'

'Not that often. Mebbe once in a week. Less.'

('That were a 'ermit, that were, that warden.' 'That 'e were an' all. Real 'ermit.' 'Never spent much time with nobody, that didn't.')

Foxe was beginning to tire of the continual Greek chorus of comments from the other old men. He didn't know whether to pay them any attention or not. He therefore tried to hurry things along.

'Can you tell me anything about them?'

'Can't say as I can,' Gunton replied. 'Odd lot. Most of them carried books as well.'

'Why did you say they were like freemasons?'

'Don't rightly know, sir. Just that they talked odd to one another. Like using funny words. Made signs to one another sometimes as well. Like the 'orns you makes when you wants to say someone's a cuckold.'

This time the chorus was silent. It was obvious no one knew any more about the warden's occasional visitors.

'Do you know anything about the kind of books the warden read?' Foxe tried another approach.

('Terrible heathen books. That's what Walter said.' 'Aye, wicked 'e said they was.' 'Not right in 'is 'ead, Walter ain't though is 'e?')

Foxe waited for the chorus to fall silent so that Gunton could answer him.

'I can't say for myself,' Gunton said. 'Nor can the rest 'ere. It's just what Walter said, like.'

'Who's Walter? Which one of your fellow pensioners is he?'

'Walter's not here,' Gunton said. 'Only eleven of us here, you see. Easier that way.'

'Why easier?'

'Walter Parr isn't right in 'is 'ead, no more. Used to be a fine, upstanding man till recently. Now 'alf the time 'e don't recall who 'e is, nor who you are either. Keeps asking who's lookin' after 'is shop, though 'e 'asn't kept that clockmaker's shop in nigh on twenty-five years. You tell Mr Foxe about Walter, Thomas. You were 'is friend.'

A shrunken man, his face almost hidden behind a mass of hair and beard, spoke up from behind Gunton's right. His voice was as shrunken as his body, so that Foxe had to strain to hear him, but he spoke in more educated tones than the others.

'When I was organist and choirmaster at St Peter Mancroft, Mr Foxe, Walter Parr was a churchwarden. A good man too. He and his wife helped many a poor parishioner in their time. Sadly, they were never blessed with children. When Mrs Parr died, Walter was on his own. He gave up his shop because his legs grew too bad to be able to stand behind the counter. That's really why he hasn't come here today. He's none to steady on his feet. At mealtimes, one of us takes him his food so he hasn't got to come into the hall.'

'Mr Gunton here says his mind is going too.' Foxe said.

'I suppose that's true as well, sir. He's become terribly forgetful. Sometimes he'll ask about people who died forty years ago. Why they haven't been to see him. Recently, he's convinced himself his wife has run away with another man and calls her terrible names. He's even starting to forget who I am. Only yesterday, he thought I was Parson Grout, who died at least twenty-five years ago.'

('Tell 'im about all the bible stuff.' 'Aye, tell 'im about all the worryin' about hell-fire an' damnation.')

'Since he can't move about as well as he used to, Walter mostly sits and reads the bible.' Thomas said. 'He always was a very religious man, but even that's become more of a curse to him than a blessing nowadays. He's fixed in his mind on the prospect of Judgement Day and the punishment of sinners. You'll be talking to him naturally enough, and he'll suddenly start shouting that he's going to fry in hell and that the devil is going to take him. He's terrified of dying, I suppose. Once or twice he's even hit out at people.'

'How do you mean, hit out?' Foxe asked.

'If you try to do anything he doesn't like, such as wash his face for him, he'll sometimes lash out with his fists or try to kick you. Usually he's quite docile, but there are times when he'll send you away with bruises.'

'We all try to do our best for him, Mr Foxe,' Gunton added. 'Sweep his room and see he has clean linen an' the like. Even though sometimes he'll curse and swear at you somethin' cruel.'

('Tell the man about the creepin' about.')

That remark from someone in the chorus of old men intrigued Foxe and he cocked an eyebrow at Gunton. Thomas had fallen completely silent.

'We told you ol' Walter's none too good on 'is feet. That's true enough, that is. Most o' the time 'e can 'ardly walk five paces. Trouble is, when the mood takes 'im, he can get a good deal further. If you aren't careful, you'll find him in your room, poking into your things; or halfway across the Close, still dressed in 'is nightshirt.'

'That reminds me,' Foxe said. 'I need to take a look inside the Warden's House, unless it's been cleared out for his successor.'

'No. nothin' 'as been touched, as yet,' Gunton told him. 'We don't rightly know when that new warden will come, see? Then we'll make sure it's all spick an' span for 'im.'

Foxe felt he had learned all he could from the pensioners, so he took his leave of them and followed Gunton to the other end of the row of almshouses. That's where the warden's house stood. It was larger than the others, but still quite a modest dwelling. Far too modest for a member of the nobility.

Gunton unlocked the door for him.

'You needn't stay,' Foxe told him. 'I'll lock up and bring you back the key. It won't take me long to see if anything inside may give me a clue to why the man was killed.'

'My house is next door,' Gunton said. 'Just tap on the door when you're leavin' and I'll come out for the key.'

The front door of the warden's house opened into a narrow hallway and passage, its walls covered with a pale, nondescript paper and hung with etched prints of suitably religious subject. This hallway ended in an elegant sweeping staircase, a little narrow, perhaps, but still able to convey a sense of good taste on a modest scale. To the right of the entrance, there was a modest dining room, beyond which was a small pantry. There was no kitchen, of course. The warden was expected to take his meals with the pensioners in the common dining hall. Looking around, Foxe chose to begin his prowling upstairs.

There he found two modestly sized bedchambers, each with a small dressing room attached. They were furnished nearly identically, with beds hung with curtains of Norwich wool in a good shade of red. There was nothing of interest in either one, so far as he could see.

It was time to return downstairs. None of the upper rooms had given him any clues. He wasn't conducting a real search, of course, opening drawers and poking under beds. There was no justification for such an action at this stage; merely looking about him for anything which might give him an insight into Pryce-Perkins the man, rather than Pryce-Perkins the Anglican priest and warden of St. Stephen's Hospital. He could only hope that the parlour would contain something more informative.

At first, it seemed as if Foxe's hopes would be dashed again. This was by far the largest room in the house. Also the most elegantly furnished and the best lit, with good windows to front and rear. The floor was covered with an expensive-looking Wilton carpet and the room had finer furnishings than the rest. He wondered if Pryce-Perkins had brought things from his family mansion, which he thought better reflected his status as the son of a peer of the realm?

What instantly had drawn Foxe's attention as he stood in the doorway were two large bookpresses of oak on the opposite wall to the fireplace. Sadly on a closer look, he was to be disappointed again. Neither contained anything beyond standard books of biblical commentary, copies of the New Testament in Greek and the Old Testament in Greek and Hebrew. Then there were several books of collected sermons and other theological writing; editions of the standard Classical works in Latin and Greek; and a few volumes containing well-known geographies of the Holy Land and Roman Empire. All dull stuff, to Foxe's mind, but eminently suitable for a young priest of the established church.

Last of all, Foxe turned to the desk. Here he finally struck gold. There were four books set in a neat pile, all bound exactly alike in good leather along with a fifth one, vellum bound. Next to the pile lay an open notebook. Unfortunately, beside some incomprehensible diagrams, everything in that notebook was written in what seemed to be a personal shorthand. Foxe would not make head or tail of any of it.

The book titles, however, were far more informative. One of the four leather bound books contained some of the writings of Dr. John Dee, the famous alchemist and magician at the court of Queen Elizabeth. Two others were also treatises on alchemy. The final one was the most surprising. It was a notorious work by John Toland, an English deist and radical, called *Christianity not Mysterious*. When it had appeared in 1696, it had created a fine furore by its claim that the teachings of the church were nothing but legends and superstition. According to Toland, true Christianity could be recovered by stripping all these away. Then you would see a purely rational religion; one based based on ethical principles, all of which could be reached by the exercise of reason and logic. Toland's name had also been linked to a shadowy work, called *The Treatise of the Three Imposters*, which went so far as to claim to prove that Christianity, Judaism and the religion of the Mohammedans were all deliberate hoaxes; each created to enable their adherants to be enslaved to the will of their rulers.

Not at all matter suitable for a young parson to be reading!

The last book, the one which was bound in cracked vellum, announced its unsuitability instantly by the hand-written name on its spine, *Clavicula Solomonis*. Foxe had never seen a copy before, but knew it to be a treatise on sorcery and magic, originally compiled in Greek in mediaeval times, but claiming to contain the magical teachings and wisdom of King Solomon.

Foxe decided on the instant to take away all the books and the notebook. No good could result from them being discovered where they were. To learn exactly what Pryce-Perkins had been studying would only bring pain to his family and embarrassment to the bishop. Moreover, the four leather-bound volumes had clearly been removed from the cathedral library and the Norgate collection. Each was initialled E. N. on its title page. The source of the vellum-bound volume remained unknown.

All the time he was examining them, an idea had been slowly forming in Foxe's mind. He was beginning to understand how he might use these books to discover the identity of the strange, secretive people with whom Pryce-Perkins had been associating. If he could do that, it must represent a major step along the way to uncovering the identity of his killer.

He therefore returned the house key to Gunton, explaining away the pile of books he held as volumes from the cathedral library, which he would return.

Hurrying home, Foxe hoped to find a way to reach his library without being waylaid by Nicholas, who was hopefully still in the bookshop with Mrs Crombie and Charlie. He needed to hide these inflammatory books and notebook somewhere at the back of one of the cupboards in his desk. That done, he would be free to take his time to think out a plan of campaign using them. He would, naturally, take the leather-bound volumes back to their proper home, but simply to hand them over seemed to him to be a wasted opportunity.

If he could achieve what he had in mind on his return, he could relax for the rest of the day. He would take dinner with Nicholas, then turn to the matter of the young man's future. Explaining about his two current investigations could be postponed to the next day.

8

Neither Foxe nor Nicholas raised any serious subjects during dinner that day. By unspoken agreement, they kept the conversation to family matters and Nicholas's admiration for all Mrs Crombie had achieved in the bookshop since his last visit. Only when they had retired to the drawing room with a bottle of good brandy and some cigars did Foxe raise the subject of the reason for Nicholas coming to see him.

'I've almost finished my period of articles,' Nicholas told Foxe that evening. 'It's been challenging to absorb the intricacies of the law and I've worked hard at it. The other partners have now told me they are willing to allow me to take up a partnership with them in about three months' time, by which time I can count myself fully qualified in all basic legal work.'

'You need the capital to buy into the partnership, I suppose.' Foxe said.

'It's not that, cousin,' Nicholas said hastily. 'My aunt and I live frugally and can raise at least some of the sum ourselves. The rest I can borrow easily, especially since I have been told I can pay in instalments. It's the work the partners do. The partnership deals almost exclusively in drawing up leases for tenant farmers, Wills for much the same people — plus a few local merchants and traders — and occasional sales or purchases of fairly small amounts of land. Worthy and necessary business, but horribly dull and repetitive. Could I spend the rest of my life doing similar work? I'd rather cut my own throat. You and your mysteries spoiled me, cousin. Then I felt most alive, fascinated to be pitting my wits against wrongdoers who used every way they knew to avoid being called to pay for their crimes. To be plain in the matter, I hope to be able to set up on my own here in Norwich — and perhaps be your assistant from time to time, as I was before.'

Foxe was nonplussed. To give himself space to think, he poured himself another large glass of brandy and passed the decanter to Nicholas to do the same.

The two of them were seated either side of the fireplace in Foxe's drawing room. Although the day had been fairly warm the evenings were becoming cool enough for Foxe to have a fire lit there. Its warm, flickering light played on the walls of the room and brought out the deep colour of the cognac they were drinking.

'This is a fine room,' Foxe thought. 'Better furnished and decorated than any in the warden's house I was in earlier today. I wonder what caused young Pryce-Perkins to give up the luxury he must have been used to in the family mansion. Was he truly content? What about apparently turning away from the comfortable certainties of the established church to spend his time wandering amongst the wavering visions and mirages of magic and alchemy? If that came to light, he could say good-bye to preferment.'

With a jerk he pulled himself back to the matter in hand.

'You still believe practising the law is the right course for you?' he asked Nicholas.

'I do,' the young man replied. There was still more than a little of the innocence in him that he had shown when he and his older cousin had first met. True, it was mostly covered over with the veneer of the capable professional man, but it was still there.

'When I was first introduced to legal work, here in Norwich,' he continued, 'it seemed far more exciting and challenging somehow. Most of what I do is simple routine; something to be endured rather than enjoyed. Every day is the same. That's my problem. The practice of law in a small market town hardly changes from year to year — or decade to decade, for all I know. Maybe my view of my future profession became entangled with the excitement of helping you? Do you find your business dull, Cousin Ashmole? I mean your real business, not chasing after criminals.'

Foxe thought for a minute. Nicholas was still naïve in many ways, despite his tall, well-proportioned figure and the deep voice when he spoke. He didn't want to leave the young man disillusioned.

'I did find looking after the shop rather dull, once I had managed to make it run successfully,' Foxe said. 'That's why I count myself fortunate to have found Mrs Crombie to do it for me. To her, it is a continual source of delight and interest.'

'So she told me,' Nicholas said, smiling. 'She was so enthusiastic in her description of the business when I spoke with her this afternoon, you would have thought it the finest, most amazing and unusual bookshop in the whole world. Charlie seemed more subdued though. Doesn't he like being your apprentice?'

'You remind me that I have to deal with the concerns about Charlie which Mrs Crombie drew to my attention only recently. She thinks he will never be truly happy as a bookseller.'

'Is there no aspect of your business you enjoy, cousin?' Nicholas asked. 'Am I hoping for a path in life which does not exist?'

'I still enjoy dealing in rare books,' Foxe told him. 'Partly because I love books for their own sake, especially old ones. Partly, I suspect, because it involves a good deal of research and discovery to unearth them. There are also continual decisions to be made about the amount to pay the sellers and the price to set for purchasers. There are few of us who are serious exponents of the skills involved in doing that. We compete all the time, naturally, though we know each other well and are generally on cordial terms. It is not like simple bookselling, you see. There you learn what your customers want and make sure you can provide it. I never know from week to week what I might have to sell, while my customers are far more demanding than the gentlemen to whom Ms Crombie sells the latest books on Natural Philosophy or Theology; or their wives and daughters who are mostly interested in whatever novels are the most talked about in fashionable circles. Men buy novels too, of course, and some ladies are any man's equal in matters scientific or philosophical, but our society tends to act to confine each to their traditional sphere.'

Nicholas looked glum. 'So you think practising law in Norwich would be much the same as it is in Diss, even if I were to establish my own practice?'

'I consider it very likely. Unusual business, like that generated by the needs of the city government or the diocese, is usually put into the hands of a few firms who have enjoyed a monopoly of such work for many, many years. The merchants are the same. They come to rely on certain trusted legal advisers, with whom they've done business many times before. Changing to someone new, a person whose honesty and competence they had not already proved for themselves, would be seen as a considerable risk. That's why I'm warning you that setting up your own practice here would be far from easy. I fear you would be stuck with simple, repetitive task like the conveyancing of property, and little else. If you are set on it, I will help you all I can. However, Norwich is already well supplied with lawyers. None would welcome the arrival of another competitor.'

The look of misery on Nicholas's face at these last few words almost caused Foxe to try to take them back, though he knew them to be true. He had begun by inheriting an established business from his father. He had never needed to fight for the right to be what he was. Nicholas's future was far more uncertain. Nothing was to be gained by minimising the difficulties he would face.

'Cheer up!' he said, with as much liveliness as he could. 'All is not lost. An idea has just come into my mind which may solve most of your problems and one of mine as well. Meanwhile, stay here for a few weeks and help me with my latest investigation. I need a little more time to reflect on my idea before sharing it with you. I don't wish to raise false hopes, especially if more considered reflection reveals major faults in the entire concept. You may not even like it.'

'At least you have an idea worth considering.' Nicholas said. 'I have none.'

Since both were tired, though for different reasons, they soon decided it was time to retire for the night. Any idea in Foxe's mind about following Tabby's prescription to raise his spirits would have to be set aside for another day.

Over breakfast next morning, Foxe honoured his promise and began telling Nicholas about the murder in the haunted house and the strange death of the Warden of St. Stephen's Hospital. As he did so, Nicholas forgot his troubles and became absorbed in the twists and turns of both cases.

Foxe's mind must have been working hard while he slept, for he had woken with a firm idea of his next steps. He would spend that morning returning the purloined books to the cathedral library and attempting to convince the librarian to do as he would ask and let him offer some of them for sale. At the same time, he would send Nicholas on an important errand to Mancroft Yard, and Charlie to seek out Kate Sulyard and hear what, if anything, the street children had been able to observe.

Charlie needed no detailed instructions about the task he was to undertake. Nicholas, on the other hand, definitely required a fuller explanation.

'I need to know who is the owner of the supposedly haunted house at the head of Mancroft Yard,' Foxe told him. 'Charlie can point it out to you before he leaves to find the leader of the street children. Go into the yard and ask for a man called John Holtaway. He's a carpenter who lives and works there and seems to be a kind of unofficial spokesman for the other residents. Tell him you're moving to Norwich with your wife and family and wish to rent a substantial property. Try to look rather less prosperous than you do right now. See if Alfred can find you an old hat of mine to wear without a wig. If Holtaway asks you, invent some suitable work for yourself. A clerk to some merchant would do very well. It's important that you convince him you need somewhere large but cheap, so you'll be willing to overlook the rundown state of the property.

'And this Holtaway will tell me who I need to approach about taking a lease?'

'Eventually, I hope he will. He'll probably start by warning you about the place's reputation for being haunted. He'll also point out that a woman was murdered there recently. It's got to look realistic when you dismiss his warning. Perhaps you could say something to the effect that those drawbacks to the place must surely lower the rent substantially. Few people would be willing to consider it at all, so you think it likely the landlord will be pleased if someone comes who is willing to rent the place in spite of them. Use your imagination. Whatever he tells you, keep insisting that you won't leave without learning the name of the landlord. Declare stubbornly that you feel sure you'll be able to convince him to let the place to you, if you can only manage to speak to him face to face. If you persist, I'm sure Holtaway will tell you in the end. I expect him to be reluctant, but I can see no reason why he should persist too long in refusing.'

'I've never done anything like this before,' Nicholas replied nervously. 'Why can't you go yourself?'

'I don't want whoever's using that property in secret to know of my interest. Holtaway already knows me and I'm too well known to be sure of escaping detection even by using a disguise. If whoever it is in there at night suspects an interest on my part, he'll disappear in an instant and find somewhere else to set up whatever it is that goes on in there. Then I'll never be able to find him again.'

'I understand that,' Nicholas said slowly, 'but even so —'

'You wanted a challenge, didn't you?' Foxe told him. 'Something different instead of all the routine. Look on it as a challenge at the start of a new life.'

'Very well, I'll do it. I'll go to find Alfred on the instant.'

'You're not used to having servants are you?' Foxe said drily. 'Ring the bell and let him find you.'

With Charlie and Nicholas given their instructions and sent on their way, Foxe could leave the house himself. Once again, he'd not been able to take his usual walk around the Market Place, so he determined to walk to the cathedral library instead.

Unfortunately, Foxe found the walk less pleasant than he had expected. The great Market Place and all the streets leading to and from it were too thronged with market traders, street vendors and shoppers. Was that day perhaps one of the infrequent holidays sanctioned by the city government? Yes, that was it. Today was the start of the assizes. The world and his wife were taking advantage of a day free from labour to watch the parade of dignitaries assembling to welcome the king's judges to the city. He could only hope the librarian would still be in his usual place.

Most of the way, Foxe was jostled and forced to press himself against the walls of several buildings by the sheer press of people. He also felt half deafened by the constant chatter of voices. Foxe's spirits didn't lift until he finally left the streets about the marketplace and started down the hill at the edge of the huge castle mound. Ahead lay Norwich's glorious cathedral, its spire seeming to brush the clouds. Who could fail to be impressed every time by the looming gates into the Close and the sudden calm as you passed into the cathedral precincts?

Once again he passed through the richly decorated doorway and entered the stupendous space which was the cloisters: that truly mind-numbing combination of carved stonework to each side and a ribbed vault enriched by stone roof-bosses carved, with the most exquisite craftsmanship, into scenes and faces and fabulous beasts. He never grew tired of admiring it.

Foxe walked the full length of one side of the corridor, finally coming to the door to the cathedral library. To his considerable relief, he found it open and the librarian at his desk inside.

Presented with the books Foxe had brought him — the four leather-bound volumes only, since the vellum one clearly belonged elsewhere — the librarian was torn between anger and disappointment. Anger that books had been removed from the library without permission; disappointment that such an outrage had been committed by a man of the cloth. It took some time for Foxe to calm him enough to enquire whether these volumes were typical of those which formed part of the Norgate bequest.

'Certainly,' Mr Lavender said, 'though they are probably some of the most reprehensible of its titles. I never realised Pryce-Perkins was reading matter of this kind or I would have felt compelled to speak to the dean about it.'

'I can appreciate now just how unsuitable many of the books left to the catedral by Mr Norgate are,' Foxe said, 'and why you have to keep them locked away.'

He was preparing the ground carefully for what he was going to suggest next.

'It will probably shock you to know,' he went on, 'that I have learned Rev Pryce-Perkins was in touch with a group of people with similarly devilish interests. They were even invited to his house in the Close.'

Mr Lavender could only nod his head in stunned agreement.

'It may also be that one more of them had a hand in his death.'

Lavender gasped and raised his hands in horror at the thought. Devil-worshippers and murderers in the cathedral precincts! The mere idea appalled him.

'Not surprisingly,' Foxe continued, 'these men operate in secret. I need to flush them out to discover whether there lies the solution to this terrible deed.'

'Quite, quite. Flush them out,' Lavender echoed, his eyes still wide with shock.

'To do that I need bait. They are like wild beasts, who must be lured into the daylight.' Foxe feared he was applying the hyperbole with too large a brush, but the librarian appeared to be taking it all in.

'Bait,' came the echo.

'What I have in mind is to offer some of these books for sale, without, of course, saying where they come from. The people I seek will be attracted by the opportunity to acquire such rare volumes. They will contact me and I will be able see who they are and question them.'

'Sell the books?' Lavender bleated. 'but the terms of the bequest …'

'Elias Norgate died in the time of Queen Anne, you told me. The most recent of these books was published in 1696. That's almost seventy years ago. Did he leave any children?'

'Only one, as I understand, though he may also be dead by now. He became an adherent of the Jacobite cause and a Catholic, so he was forced to flee to France when the Old Pretender's attempt on the throne failed in 1715. So far as I know, he never returned.'

'So if he had any descendants they would also most likely be in France and living as Frenchmen? In that case, I can hardly imagine they would know or care what had become of their grandfather's, or great-grandfather's books.'

It was time to play his trump card.

'Selling what you call the most reprehensible titles would remove them from the church property and bring you what might be a significant addition to your funds for new books at the same time. Will you support me if I take my suggestion to the dean?'

Lavender hesitated, then gave his reply in a firm and decisive voice.

'Better still, Mr Foxe, I will put the idea to the dean myself. I have dealt with him for many years now and understand the best way to secure his approval. These books have laid a blight on the library since they arrived, sometimes attracting persons of the most dubious character to enquire after them. They are worthless, hidden away and quite unsuitable for study. If they could serve as both bait to secure the conviction of a foul murderer and yield some money —'

'Quite a lot of money,' Foxe added quietly, 'less my commission, of course.'

'— to purchase books far better suited to the library's purpose in educating the clergy of the diocese, that would be better than burning them, which is the treatment they richly deserve. Leave it to me, Mr Foxe. I will convince the dean and then select the books best suited to your purpose.'

Thanks to the librarian's fairly ready acceptance of his plan, Foxe now set out to walk home again in the happiest of moods. However, he had barely left the Close for Tombland when he was hailed by a man he recognised as one of Alderman Halloran's two footmen.

'My humblest apologies for stopping you in the street like this, sir,' the man said, 'but it seemed foolish to ignore such a piece of good fortune. It will also save me a long walk to your house and back.'

'What is it then?' Foxe said rather coldly. He didn't want to encourage such presumption in future.

'The alderman has sent me to ask you to call on him as soon as possible, sir. Today, if that is convenient.'

Since they were little more than a hundred yards from the alderman's house, Foxe thought he might as well to there right away. It was still barely past noon and the streets would be at their most crowded. It was odd that Halloran was not taking part in the judges' procession with the mayor and most of the rest of the city's corporation.

'I'll go there right away,' Foxe said to the footman. 'You go ahead and tell Alderman Halloran I'm on my way.'

He had no intention of walking along in the company of a servant.

9

'It's lucky my man caught you,' Halloran said, as Foxe was shown into his library. He was standing leaning one arm against the mantlepiece, dressed in a plain morning gown. He must never have had any intention of taking part in the procession.

'I'm surprised to find you haven't accompanied the mayor,' Foxe said. 'The judge's procession is a somewhat special occasion after all.'

Halloran looked sheepish. 'I had a bad attack of the gout yesterday and sent a message warning the mayor that I might be too unwell to take part. Feel much better today, to be honest, but my wife and nieces have set their hearts on going to the grand ball in the Assembly House tonight. I'm saving myself to go with them. All that walking in procession today would probably bring on the gout again. To be honest, I always find it a great bore anyway. Only attend because it's expected of me. Are you going to the ball Foxe? I know Lady Cockerton is in Bath, but you don't usually find it hard to provide yourself with feminine companions.'

Foxe had actually forgotten all about the ball, just as he had forgotten the assizes opened today. Lady Cockerton would certainly have reminded him and demanded that he should be her escort, but she was doubtless enjoying other balls and other men's company in Bath.

'I have an unexpected visitor just arrived,' Foxe replied, glad of a convenient excuse. 'My young cousin, Nicholas Foxe. I could hardly drag him to a ball the day after his arrival.'

'Young Nicholas? Do ask him to call on us while he is here,' Halloran said. 'He was a great favourite of the ladies on his last visit, especially my elder niece, Maria. He will find her quite grown up since he came last. She'll soon be eighteen, you know. Hard to believe, isn't it?'

Halloran told Foxe to take a seat and sent for some refreshment for them both. Foxe tried to explain that he really ought to return home right away, but Halloran waived all that aside.

'I always take some light refreshment at this time of day,' he said, 'and I've already told them to bring enough for two. To save you a long, slow walk back, I'll tell my groom to have the chaise ready to take you home later. He'll know the best route to avoid all the crowds. I've asked you to come because the mayor's been pestering me to tell him what progress you've made on that murdered parson. The fellow's quite in awe of the bishop and imagines his lordship is expecting regular reports.'

'That seems most unlikely.' Foxe replied. 'If he's busy attending on the king and meddling in politics, I'd be very surprised if the bishop has given it another thought.'

'You forget this Pryce-Perkins fellow is the son of an earl. Even bishops try to keep on the fair-weather side of peers of the realm.'

This was a good point, so Foxe gave Halloran a detailed summary of what he had been doing and what he had discovered so far. He ended with a brief explanation, for Halloran's ears only, of how he planned to lure Pryce-Perkins's secretive friends into the open.

'I won't tell the mayor that last bit,' Halloran said when Foxe had finished. 'Not fully anyway. I'll just say you're working to lure them into the open. If he asks how — which I doubt he will — I'll say you're keeping the details to yourself for the moment, for fear of alerting them. By the way, what are these unsuitable books about which the cathedral librarian's been hiding away? Not pornography, surely!'

'Mostly alchemy and magic,' Foxe said. 'Works of Hermes Trismegistus and that sort of exotic religious mysticism. Raising demons. Plenty of people collect books of that kind. Personally, I think it's all mostly nonsense.'

'Dangerous nonsense though, Foxe. Undermines respect for the church and the proper social order. I'd love to see the bishop's face when he finally learns one of his favoured circle was secretly dabbling in heresy and blasphemy. He'll likely feel it's a good thing the man's dead. Even so, I'm sure it won't change his determination to see the murderer face justice. He can't ignore the killing of a priest, especially one which took place in the cathedral precincts.' He paused, while two servants brought an array of food and a jug of ale. Then he suddenly exclaimed, 'Oh my heavens! What will the earl do when he knows?'

'Try to keep it quiet, I imagine,' Foxe said drily, 'which is what the bishop will do as well, I shouldn't wonder. They won't be nearly as keen as before on seeing someone in the dock, in case the whole story gets into the hands of the public. They might also be tempted to call off any further investigation, were it not for the fact that there seems to be a whole group of people out there who know what Pryce-Perkins was involved in. The only way to ensure their silence will be to discover who they are and threaten them with prosecution for blasphemy.'

'Do you think the dean will agree to your plan?'

'I hope so. It's the only way forward that I can see.'

'Tell me if he proves awkward,' Halloran said. 'I don't know him personally, but I am acquainted with people who can probably put the case to him in suitably forceful terms. I'll also ask the mayor to mention it when he writes to the bishop. He's most eager to be able to report satisfactory progress to his lordship. Thanks to you, Foxe, he'll be able to do so. Well done.'

'Don't let him get too excited. We haven't found these people yet, let alone persuaded them to tell what they know. It's just that I had an investigation a while ago, where a member of a similar group was so eager to obtain a rare book that he killed the man who had it.'

'Very well. Our current mayor tends to be either wildly excited or deeply depressed. There's no middle ground with the man. Anyway, enough of that. There's something else that has arisen, and I think you may find it interesting.'

At this point, one of the alderman's maids came in with a tray carrying a large jug of beer, together with bread and cheese and some slices of ham. The two men therefore broke off their discussion and rose to go to the side table to help themselves to whatever they wanted. While they ate, few words were shared, the occasional comment being confined to remarks about the weather and other small talk. Only when they had finished did Halloran return to whatever it was that he wanted to tell Foxe.

It now looked as if the alderman was ready to begin on a lengthy tale. Normally, Foxe would indulge him, but that day he was eager to return home to discover how Nicholas and Charlie had faired with the tasks he had set them. Still, he didn't have to walk back now.

Halloran must have sensed his concern.

'Don't worry about the time, Foxe. This won't take long and I'll have my man take you home, as I said. Did you hear about the young woman's body that was found in what is said to be a haunted house, not far from St. Peter Mancroft?'

'I did hear about it,' Foxe said calmly, not giving anything away.

'I hoped you had,' Halloran continued. 'Though it seemed possible that, with this investigation for the bishop, you had missed it. What I'd be interested in is your reaction to something which happened to me only yesterday in my capacity as a magistrate. The dead girl's father came to see me with a remarkable story.'

Foxe waited, not trusting himself to make a response. He hoped, at least, he was going to learn who the murdered girl had been.

Halloran swept on.

'The man's name is Mr Cuthbert Custance. Naturally, no one had connected him with the dead woman. It was entirely by chance that he was able to identify her as his missing daughter.'

'Surely, the body had already been buried?' Foxe objected.

'Yes, it had, and in quicklime too, as is often the case with unidentified paupers. People still fear that they might carry some epidemic. As you surmise, seeing the body was impossible. What gave her away were the clothes she had been wearing.'

'How did this Mr Custance manage to see those?' Foxe said. This was getting more and more strange.

'Entirely by chance. The day before yesterday, the dressmaker who had made them was walking past a used-clothes dealer in the market and noticed them laid out for sale. Since she hadn't made them very long ago, and they had been expensive, she was amazed to see them there. Her first thought was that they must have been stolen. Her second was that they had proved unsatisfactory in some way. In either case, they should be returned to the Custance household. The dead girl — her name was Grace, by the way — was a good customer. The dressmaker brought them from the dealer on the spot, then took them to Custance's house yesterday morning, eager to offer to alter them in any way if they hadn't been as required.'

'Did she ask the dealer how they had been acquired?' Foxe asked.

'Not then,' Halloran said, 'When she got to the house, she found all in disarray. Grace Custance had eloped almost a week earlier. The young blackguard concerned —'

'Never mind that now,' Foxe interrupted. 'You can tell me that later. You will recall that today I'm in a hurry to get back to my guest.'

'So you are,' Halloran said. 'I'll try to be brief. The father recognised the dress, petticoat and bodice right away. Hoping to discover where his daughter might have gone, he went at once to the market, taking the dressmaker with him to point out the stall where his daughter's clothes had been.'

'Did he find out how the clothes had come to be there?' Foxe asked.

'Eventually. The dealer was reluctant to tell him for what proved to be an obvious reason. However, impatient demands to know, backed up by the offer of a few coins, weakened the woman's resolve sufficiently for her to explain that she had bought them from the undertaker; and that they had been taken from the corpse of the girl found in the haunted house. I'm sure you can imagine the father's response to such terrible news.'

Foxe merely nodded.

'The man came straight to me to lodge a charge of murder against a certain Richard Benbow, the fellow with whom his daughter had eloped. The hue and cry is already out to find the wretched fellow.'

'It's not Custance's daughter,' Foxe said.

For several moments Halloran was struck dumb.

'Not his daughter, Foxe?' he managed to gasp eventually. 'How can you say such a thing?'

'I saw the body.'

'But … But … How could you have seen it? You assured me you would concentrate entirely on the bishop's request to find who murdered young Pryce-Perkins.' Between shock and indignation, the alderman's face had turned an ugly mottled colour and he seemed to be struggling to get his breath.

'Don't get so excited,' Foxe said calmly. 'I'll tell you all about it, if you stop looking at me as if I were one of your servants who had spilled wine all over your most prized book. You'll also be very glad I knew about it and was curious enough to make a few enquiries. With luck, I'm about to reveal a serious criminal enterprise that's active in the heart of the city. May I have another glass of beer before I begin? This talking is thirsty work.'

A maid was summoned and returned swiftly with another jug of the alderman's best ale. After consuming no less than two glasses, Foxe dried his lips and prepared to explain.

'The story is this,' Foxe said, 'and it'll make it clear why I'm sure the dead woman wasn't this Miss Grace Custance.'

He began by explaining how he had been alerted by the street children and had arrived at the scene of the murder soon after the constables. Then how he had managed to go to where the corpse was lying and take a close look at it.

'The hands gave it away,' Foxe said. 'The body didn't have a lady's soft fingers and palms. Rather, they were rough and hardened in places, showing that their owner had been used to a fair amount of manual work. Not truly heavy work, you understand. Not the chapped and reddened knuckles you would find on a skivvy or a kitchen maid. The closer I looked, the more I became convinced the dead girl had been something like a parlourmaid, or a lady's maid in a prosperous, but not especially wealthy household. I also found tiny scars where she had repeatedly pricked her fingers, probably while sewing.'

Halloran frowned, but said nothing.

'Tell me about this fellow Custance, who claims it must have been his daughter,' Foxe went on.

'Surely a man would know his own daughter,' Halloran said. 'Am I to believe he lied to me? He recognised the clothes, Foxe. He knew who had worn them.'

'But he didn't see the body, did he?' Foxe objected. 'Had he done so, I agree he could not have failed to identify it as his daughter — if that's who it was. I don't dispute they were his daughter's clothes, only that she wasn't wearing them.'

'Who was the dead woman, then?'

'I have no clear idea at this stage.'

The two men sat and looked at one another. Halloran as if still somehow hoping that Foxe was wrong, and there was no mystery to be solved once Richard Benbow was apprehended; Foxe equally certain he was right. He just needed to convince Halloran of that, if the next stage in his plan to discover the killer were to stand any chance of success.

It was Halloran who broke the silence.

'What should I do about this man, Custance?' he asked. 'He's convinced his daughter is dead and the man she ran away with is the killer. If I tell him he's wrong, purely on the basis of what you've told me, either he won't believe me or I risk giving him false hope. Then, if you turn out to be wrong, he'll suffer even more than he has so far.'

'Say nothing, please.' Foxe replied. 'We'll soon know definitely whether the daughter is alive or not. If I'm correct about the murdered girl — and I'm almost sure I am — Miss Grace Custance will reappear in perhaps a week's time, alive and well and duly calling herself Mrs Benbow. It's a long way to Scotland and back again, but that's the only place where she would be able to marry without her father's consent. I'm hoping when she does return she'll be willing to tell me to whom she gave her dress. That at least will make a good start on identifying the dead girl.'

'Won't it tell you for certain?'

'Not for certain. The dress may have been sold before the dressmaker saw it in the market. But there's an even stronger reason why I want you to act as if we've never had this conversation. As much as I want to find who killed the girl in the haunted house, I also want to catch whoever has been giving rise to the rumours of ghosts and devils. If he, or they, think we're running safely down the wrong path, they'll probably be bold enough to start their activity again. It's the only way to catch them.'

Sensing that Halloran was on the brink of agreeing to do what he asked, Foxe explained about the property not being put up for rental and the strange nocturnal lights and noises he had been told about.

'It seems most likely to me,' he concluded, 'that the girl went inside for some unknown reason, stumbled on whatever was going on, and met her death as a result. If I can get inside myself, preferably when no one else is there, I may be able to discover what she found and begin to trace it back to the gang or individual involved.'

'So you want me to say nothing about this outside this room?'

'Precisely. Continue, in your position as magistrate, to try to find Richard Benbow, but don't do more that your duties require. As I said, I'm certain he'll be back soon enough and it will be plain to everyone he has no case to answer. You can't face a charge of murdering a person who isn't dead. Above all, please don't say anything to the mayor. We both know he can't be trusted to keep a secret.'

'Very well. Foxe, the alderman said. 'You're usually right in these matters. Just so long as I don't have to offer poor Mr Custance what may turn out to be false hopes.'

Travelling back home in the alderman's chaise, Foxe was torn between satisfaction and concern. Despite his recent confident words on the next stage, he had, as yet, no clear idea how he was going to get inside that house without anyone finding out — especially whoever the criminals might have set to keep watch until people lost interest in that poor girl's death.

###

Foxe arrived back home to find Nicholas and Charlie both eager to tell him what they had discovered. Nicholas in particular was bubbling with excitement over his success at Mancroft Yard.

'I found John Holtaway and told him the tale about wanting to see if I could rent the empty house, as you suggested,' he told Foxe. 'At first, he was unbelievably suspicious, especially when I calmly dismissed his tale of hauntings as mere superstitious nonsense. I'd thought about how best to deal with that response as I was walking there, so I had my answer ready. I told him I was a clerk in lawyer's office and had become interested in tales of ghosts and the like while preparing documents for the prosecution of a murderer. The fellow had tried to convince the court he had been driven to do what he did by the vengeful ghost of his uncle. According to him, the victim had strangled his uncle the year before in order to claim an inheritance.'

'Very inventive,' Foxe said dryly.

'I thought so,' Nicholas replied. 'I added that we suspected the jury might be swayed enough by this fantastic tale to accept the idea the killing was justifiable homicide. I therefore made a study of such manifestations in the past and was able to provide the lawyer handing the case with sufficient evidence to convince them that no ghost — even if it existed — could take away a man's free will. I then suggested he should point out to the jury that the defendant's tale had been copied from the plot of Mr William Shakespeare's drama *Hamlet*. It worked and the fellow went to the gallows.'

'It sounds as if you enjoyed yourself a great deal,' Foxe said. He longed to tell Nicholas to get to the point, but was reluctant to quench his enthusiasm too brutally. Nicholas had arrived from Diss in a most downcast mood. Here he was today, full of life and vigour. It would be cruel to brush that aside.

'Next Holtaway wanted to know why I was interested in such a large house. I was ready for that objection too. I explained that I had married two years before and my wife had proved amazingly fertile. She had already presented me with two sets of twins and was now pregnant again.'

'Did he believe such an unlikely story?' Foxe asked.

'He swallowed it down like a hungry fish seizing a tempting worm,' Nicholas said. 'Shook my hand and congratulated me most warmly on my good fortune.'

'Did he ever tell you who actually owns that house?' Nicholas had been given enough time to enjoy telling of his success, Foxe felt. He'd also been lucky to have had to deal with a fairly simple-minded artisan. A real criminal would never have swallowed such fantastic stories.

'He did,' Nicholas said in triumph. 'It's a Mr Richard Hatchard, a goldsmith and jeweller, with premises in Cockey Lane. Do you know the man?'

'I think so,' Foxe said. 'If I'm correct, he was always a reclusive fellow. A sound tradesman, though, and a skilful engraver. Never much given to social contact, though. He and his wife kept themselves to themselves. I don't think he had any children either — or, at least, none who survived to adulthood. Hatchard is an old man though and I believe he has more or less turned oversight of his business over to his wife.'

'Cousin Ashmole,' Nicholas said. 'There is one matter that puzzled me. I finally wrung the name from him, but Holtaway still did his best to dissuade me from approaching the owner of the property? Surely it was nothing to him whether I managed to rent it or not?'

'I've been thinking the same thing,' Foxe replied. 'Our Mr Holtaway requires careful watching. Now, Charlie. What have you to tell me?'

The apprentice's story was much simpler. For the first few days after the murdered girl had been found, the street children had seen no activity at all in or around the haunted house. They had, however, noticed two men who were constantly loitering in the street nearby. One would be there during the day and the other at night.

On the third day, the daytime man was there as usual, but, as it was getting dark, the night-watcher arrived with two other men. All three went up to the front door of the house and let themselves in. For a while, all was silent. Then a series of strange thumps could be heard, followed by a brief rattling. It sounded so like heavy footsteps accompanied by the sounds of chains that several of the children became really frightened. Kate remained firm though and held the group together.

After a while, the noises stopped, only to begin again after a short break. This time, they were accompanied by flickering lights. It was too much for the younger children and they ran away. Only Kate and one other stayed where they were.

'Did anything else take place?' Foxe asked.

'Not until much later,' Charlie explained. 'Until then the same noises continued. They weren't continuous. There would be perhaps fifteen minutes of the thumping and rattling, followed by a lengthy gap. Neither Kate nor her remaining friend, another girl, had pocket watches, of course. Nor could they tell the time. They simply judged how long had passed by to the chimes from the tower of St Peter's church. They had just heard it strike three when the men came out again. Now they were carrying small leather bags, which they tried to hold close to their bodies. Two of them headed off into the Hay Market and the other crossed the Market Place in the direction of Gentleman's Walk.'

'What do you make of it all, cousin?' Nicholas asked Foxe when Charlie had finished.

'That Kate Sulyard is a remarkably brave and resourceful young woman, who deserves a better life than she has. I shall have to see if I can do anything about that.'

'Not that! The thumps and rattles.'

'These are definitely not ghosts. That's for certain. These are men doing something in secret in that house. That's what I've been thinking all along. I just need to get inside to see what that is.'

'How are you going to do that, Master?' Charlie said. 'The children said the place was being watched day and night.'

'I expect it's being watched from inside the yard during the day as well, Foxe said. 'Our Mr Holtaway may well have a hand in that. Whatever's inside, someone is taking great care to make sure it stays secret. Yet we know there is at least one way to get in unnoticed. Both the murdered girl and the tramp managed it.'

'Unless the girl was spotted and followed inside by her killer,' Nicholas objected.

'That's possible, I suppose,' Foxe agreed. 'Sadly we don't know what time of day it was when she went there. From what Charlie has just said, there doesn't seem to be a watcher at night when the men are inside. However, none of that is relevant What I have to do is think of a way to get in and out without being seen. It may have to be at night.'

10

The evening passed without incident, though not without a good deal of plotting and planning on Foxe's part. The trouble was that he could go no further in the investigation into Pryce-Perkins's murder until he learned whether the dean had agreed to let him sell some of the books. In the meantime, he would fill the gap by trying to make progress on the body in the haunted house.

He explained all of this to his friend Brock.

'Have you considered talking to Mistress Tabby about your investigations?' Brock said.

He and Foxe were sharing a table in their favourite coffeehouse, both of them leaning forward and keeping their voices low to avoid being overheard. Truth to tell, there was so much general chatter going on around them it was highly unlikely any of the other customers could have heard what they were saying anyway, unless they came very close. Still, it did no harm to be cautious.

Foxe looked slightly puzzled.

'She knows about almost everyone in the city, Foxe, including tradesmen, shop-keepers and even some artisans. She also knows their families and a good many of their servants. Lots of people visit her house every day, looking for cures, charms and who know what else. She's bound to have some knowledge of the Custance household. Why not ask her about them?'

'I think I may be losing my wits,' Foxe said, his tone cross. 'It never occurred to me. You're right, of course. However, she probably doesn't know any more about the Pryce-Perkins family than I do.'

'I wouldn't be so certain,' Brock replied, waving to a waiter to bring more coffee. 'It doesn't do to underestimate Mistress Tabby. You of all people should know that.'

Foxe merely nodded to acknowledge the point. Why had he not taken such an obvious course of action? Tabby should have been almost his first port of call.

Of course, he had spoken with her not very long ago, but only on the painful matter of Lady Cockerton. Perhaps there lay the answer. He'd somehow linked Tabby with Lady Cockerton. When he managed to push Arabella Cockerton's demands and tantrums out of his mind, he'd shut Tabby out at the same time. That must stop right away. He'd visit Tabby at once, before he returned home.

'There's another thing about Mistress Tabby you ought to consider as well,' Brock added. 'Now don't take this wrongly. I have the greatest respect for the Cunning Woman and what she does. But the fact remains that she's likely to be more aware of everyone in this city with an interest in the occult that almost anyone else. She isn't the only Cunning Person, is she? Not all of them are as benign as she is. I've heard of people who think they've been bewitched or cursed. Most of them go straight to Mistress Tabby for help to remove or counteract the spell.'

Foxe held back the angry words that had been on the tip of his tongue. Brock was right. All Cunning Folk had some acquaintance with the dark corners of their art and how to lay curses on people. They couldn't afford not to, even if like Tabby, they rejected any idea of dabbling with curses and calling up demons to force them to obey you.

'You're probably right,' Foxe said, 'but I'm sure anything she knows won't be more than superficial. Tabby has more sense than to get involved with such nonsense.'

'I did a little more digging into the matter of the earl's household myself,' Brock added, after another lengthy pause. 'Didn't find out much though. They're an odd family. Both the earl and the second son, the naval fellow, are proud as Lucifer. The captain, however, is currently in the Mediterranean with our fleet. Commands a frigate, I'm told, which is highly unusual at his age. Shows he's seen as a star commander. Mad bugger, though. Takes huge risks. So far, his luck has held. Won't do so forever.'

'What about the eldest, the heir?' Foxe asked.

'Matthew, courtesy title of Lord Dalling. Only happy on the land amongst the pigs and the sheep. Too busy making changes in the management of the estate to take notice of anything else. Nothing there, as far as I can see. Want me to do anything else?'

'Just keep your eyes and ears open' Foxe replied. 'Something may come along. Didn't you say something about ordering more coffee a few minutes ago? Better get on with it.'

Brock aimed a playful slap at his friends face, which Foxe easily avoided.

'Wake up, Foxe!' he said. 'I did that minutes ago. Look, here it comes. Do pay attention.'

###

'Sit down Ash.' Tabby said. 'Shall I ask Bart to bring you something to drink, or are you still awash with that filthy brew they hand out in the coffeehouse and pretend is actual coffee?'

On leaving Brock, Foxe went directly to Tabby's house to try to make up for his earlier mistake of ignoring what she might know. She greeted him without surprise, stopped what she was doing and took him into her small parlour. Then she sat down almost opposite him, as if preparing for a lengthy conversation.

'Nothing to drink, thank you, Tabby dear,' Foxe said. 'What I want to ask you about is — '

'What do I know about Grace Custance and her household, and whether I can make an educated guess at whatever group it was that poor Pryce-Perkins had got involved with,' Tabby said at once.

Foxe hated it when Tabby did this, interrupting his carefully thought-out approach and making it obvious she had anticipated whatever it was he had come to ask. Was it second sight? Or did she simply keep a far closer watch on his activities than felt entirely comfortable?

'Am I correct?' she asked, looking a picture of innocence.

'Bloody —! Sorry, Tabby. I swear you do that purposely to unsettle me. Of course you're correct, as you know perfectly well. Tell me what you know, please. Is it all about witchcraft?'

'Which I never practice, as you well know,' Tabby reprimanded him gently. 'Whatever else I may be, I am not a witch, nor ever have been. If I happen to practice a certain amount of intelligent anticipation …'

'Get on with it!' Foxe muttered. 'You've had your fun.'

'What a bad-tempered fellow you are today, Ash,' Tabby said. 'I've half a mind to send you on your way until you're in a better frame of mind …'

A noise like a low growl came from Foxe, which proved enough to bring her back to the topics in hand.

I know nothing about such matters, Ash, save that they exist and many people believe in them. They come to me to have curses removed. All nonsense, of course. They've suffered some misfortune they can't explain in any other way. I usually suggest a sensible way of dealing with their problem, mumble a few meaningless words and send them on their way happy.'

'So you can't help me?'

'Not with that. Did you want anything else?'

'What can you tell me about the Custance family?'

'There I can assist you,' Tabby said. I presume you want to know about the daughter.'

'Yes, please.'

'Grace Custance is a pretty and accomplished young woman, but no great catch in the marriage market. She may be Mr Cuthbert Custance's only child, and the apple of his eye, but the family's business cannot afford to equip her with an especially generous dowry. Nonetheless, her father seems to be obsessed with the idea that she can marry into some far wealthier family, particularly one with a fine mansion and many acres of productive farmland.'

'Not very realistic, surely?' Foxe commented. 'Families like that look for marriages to increase their wealth, not the spend it.'

'As you say. Not realistic. Still, maybe by luck or sheer persistence, Mr Custance persuaded a certain Peter Bridgemere, only son of Mr Eldon Bridgemere of Maisley Hall, to pay court to Grace and ask her to marry him.'

'I don't know the Bridgemeres, Foxe said. 'Who are they?'

'Middle-level landed gentry,' Tabby replied. 'The father managed, by a combination of hard work and ruthless cunning, to extend what had been a mediocre estate at best. The word is that his son is too indolent to continue the process.'

'Go on,' Foxe muttered.

'I shall, despite your uncertain temper today. The problems confronting the marriage were two-fold. Grace hated Peter Bridgemere on sight. She'd also managed to fall in love with someone else; someone her father decided was neither worthy of her nor wealthy enough. A certain Richard Benbow. His father is a glazier and maker of stained glass.'

'So it's this Richard Benbow she's eloped with and who her father claims has murdered her?' Foxe said. 'The glazier's son. Perfectly respectable profession.'

'As you say, a perfectly respectable. Since Richard is the only son, he'll inherit the business one day. He's also said to be strikingly talented in the business of making fine stained glass for church windows, with commissions for his work all over East Anglia.'

'Not a likely suspect as a murderer it would seem.'

'Cuthbert Custance always did have a tendency to act without thinking,' Tabby said, her voice heavy with disapproval. 'The man's a complete fool! His daughter would have led a wretched life tied to that lazy dolt he wanted her to marry. Worse, the fellow would be almost certain to quickly undo all his father's work and reduce the Bridgemere estate to penury. Richard Benbow is full of ideas and energy. With the right wife to support him, his course in life will be steadily upwards.'

Foxe's mind had been working rapidly while Mistress Tabby had been talking and had presented him with a possible solution to at least part of the mystery of the dead woman.

'Do you know whether Grace Custance had a personal maidservant?' he asked.

'It's quite likely,' Tabby replied, 'though I can't say for certain she did. Her father indulged her in nearly everything after her mother died. The poor fellow tried to make up for that loss by turning her into a grand lady. Sadly for both of them, she grew up to be appropriately decorative, but far too active in mind and body for the kind of life most women amongst the gentry lead. Why don't you ask him?'

'He's convinced he knows who killed her. It's Richard Benbow. I did send my manservant yesterday to ask if I could speak with him, but he received a very terse and direct answer. "Tell your master not to interfere where he's not wanted." It seems I'd best leave him alone.'

'Grief and worry do terrible things,' Tabby said. 'You can only pity the man. He lost the wife he loved most dearly. Now he thinks he's lost his only child as well. All he wants to do is lash out at whoever did this to him. You're right to stay clear, Ash. Do you want me to see if I can find out anything useful for you?'

'Yes, please, Tabby, if you can. Get the maidservant's name if possible. Unless it's clear she's alive and well, I suspect it was she who was wearing her mistress's clothes and met her death in that house.'

'Wouldn't Mr Custance have recognised her?'

'He never saw the body, only the clothes. I did. It was a pretty girl with fair hair, whose hands revealed she had been a servant.'

For a few moments there was silence between them as the shadow of a life needlessly extinguished fell across the room. When it passed, Tabby was ready to move on.

'About this group of fools young Henry Pryce-Perkins seems to have been involved with,' she began. 'As I said, I can't help you there. Just because people call me a cunning woman, they think I waste my time with old spells and the trinkets of witches. You, at least, should know me better than that, Ashmole. What I do, whether with herbs or words, has the sole purpose of helping to heal people in body and mind. True cunning folk deal with practical applications of what others claim is magic. To my mind, there's nothing magic or supernatural about any of it. My herbs heal because I've learned which plants nature has endowed with the power to affect human beings in specific ways. I've also learned through long experience the amazing ability the mind has to affect the body. Just as grief and melancholia can cause you to waste away or suffer some fatal disease, so hope and belief can do the opposite and bring healing where know-all physicians claim the situation is beyond curing.

'The kind of men you're seeking deal only in theories and dead book-learning. They think they're discovering hidden knowledge, when they're only digging amongst the pathetic remains of previous generations of people with the same delusions. Who are they? Almost certainly prosperous merchants or tradesmen with time on their hands, a taste for inventing mysteries and conspiracies, and considerably more learning than sense. You'll need to rely on your own ideas to seek them out, Ash. The secrecy with which they surround themselves is an essential part of the game they're playing.'

If Foxe was disappointed, he made sure not to show it. When Mistress Tabby spoke in that way, he knew better than to argue. Nor had he missed the rebuke in her words. He therefore began to rise to take his leave.

'Sit down,' Tabby said. 'I haven't finished. I've said all I'm going to say about magic and witchcraft, true, but I have some news for you. News about Arabella Cockerton, I had another letter from her yesterday.'

'I didn't know she was such a friend of yours,' Foxe said.

'She isn't. She only writes to me because she knows I'll tell you what she says. It's part of her silly game of trying to take revenge on you for not doing as she bid. Now she's written to tell me that her estranged husband has had the grace to die. Probably from the pox, she thinks, given his habits. Anyway, the man is dead and she is properly a widow.'

'Does she think that makes a difference?'

'It definitely will. Her husband had, it appears, had a new Will prepared recently, probably knowing that he had little longer to live. In that Will, he left all his wealth to various male friends with whom he doubtless shared his bed. However, death took him before he was able to sign it. As a result, the previous Will, drawn up when they married, remains in force. Arabella Cockerton is not only a widow, but a wealthy one as well. Sir Ralph Cockerton had made a considerable fortune from the trade in slaves.'

'An abominable business, if you ask me,' Foxe said. 'I'm surprised she wants such tainted money.'

'My guess is that she hopes you will want it too,' Tabby said. 'It shows how little she came to know you. The purpose of the letter, I imagine, was to make clear what a prize is slipping away from your grasp. Unless, of course, you approach her with sufficient humility and contrition, promising never to disobey her wishes in future. What a wasps' nest you managed to stir up in her heart, Ash! Didn't some poet or playwright say hell possesses no fury equal to that of a woman who thinks she has been scorned?'

'I did nothing to Arabella. My only sin was not to put her first in everything.'

'The worst sin of all in her eyes. Now, don't let it upset you, Ashmole dear. I realise that this was probably the first time you attempted to go beyond the most superficial of relationships with a woman. Sadly, you've had your fingers burned as a result. It happens to the best of us. Life is like that.'

'I asked her to marry me and she turned me down on the grounds that she was still married to that man who's just died. I was fool enough to believe that was the only reason. Did she really care for me so little as now appears, Tabby?'

'You've got it wrong, Ash,' the Cunning Woman said. 'All this cold fury shows she cared for you rather deeply. Probably still does. What's getting in the way is her pride. She's hoping to make your suffer as she is suffering.'

'In that case, she has failed,' Foxe said sadly. 'Don't worry about me, Tabby. It's true I've felt badly hurt by what has happened. I wouldn't be human otherwise. But it's also come with a sense of relief. I was about to make a bad mistake by marrying her, you see. I did love her and she was — is— one of the most desirable women I've ever encountered. But that's all. Being tied to her would have been like owning a wonderful thoroughbred horse. Something to be maintained at dreadful expense and shown off to impress everyone. It was like the time when I tried to dress as the most fashionable man in Norwich. That cost me a great deal of money, some envy and some derision as well. After a time, I felt the drawbacks exceeded the benefits, so I stopped. That's how it would have been with Lady Cockerton.'

'Will you try to explain to her?'

'No. I'm sure it would only provoke her more. I'll leave her to get on with her life. Her letter to you has explained something that was bothering me though. I couldn't work out why her attitude to me seemed so changed. Now I know. She's got her own wealth — or soon will have — and feels it entitles her to make more demands. The money went to her head. She'll probably realise it very soon, but, as far as I'm concerned, it's too late. I'm moving on. I am sad about Maria Worden though. When poor Maria was sent to see me, I couldn't avoid sending her back to her mistress with the message I did. She's devoted to her mistress and clearly felt hurt badly by what I told her to do. I've felt wretched about that ever since.'

'It wasn't the poor girl's fault this has happened, nor yours either, Ash. Sending her to you with a letter was pure cowardice on Arabella's part. I expect she suspected what your response might be and couldn't bring herself to face you. Maybe she wanted her new freedom to extend to finding a lover of higher status than a bookseller in Norwich?'

'Good luck to her. That kind of snobbery rarely turns out well.'

Well, that's that then. I shan't hurry to reply to Arabella,' Tabby said. 'Her anger will burn itself out in time if it isn't fed. I wonder if she'll return to Norwich, or if her inheritance includes a grand property somewhere else? We'll probably never know.'

11

Next day, after what had felt like a long period of frustration and limited progress, both of Foxe's investigations took several definite steps forward.

He received a message from the librarian at the cathedral to say the dean had agreed to the sale of whichever books the librarian judged to be superfluous to the true purpose of the collection; and that the proceeds could be spent on adding books of greater value to the clergy of the diocese as a whole. Foxe should therefore come at his earliest convenience to collect the first batch of books and discuss the matter of his commission.

Foxe was eager to make a start on laying out his bait to discover who might be members of the group of men whom the pensioners had seen visiting Pryce-Perkins after dark. Of course, it was quite possible that they had nothing whatsoever to do with the warden's eccentric tastes in reading matter. If he was to be honest, the link he was banking on was nothing more than a guess, based on his experience in the investigation into Dr Danson's death, coupled with Gunton's description of them as being like freemasons. The old man might have seen something totally innocuous and allowed the subsequent murder, and his imagination, to turn these men into figures of much greater. significance than they deserved.

Still, the theory which he was now hoping to turn into practical action was the only course which Foxe could see towards discovering the reason for the murder of Pryce-Perkins, and then the identity of his killer. If this failed; if the only response he got to spreading the word about the titles the librarian would give him was from collectors already known to him, or, even worse, silence, he was facing a dead-end.

At least, thanks to some hours of thought and discussion with Nicholas, he believed he had come up with an idea that would let him enter and leave the haunted house unseen and unmolested.

After breakfast, Foxe determined once again to forego his usual visit to the coffeehouse and set out immediately in response to the summons from the cathedral librarian. Foxe invited Nicholas to accompany him, but received the vague response that he was going to spend a little more time with Charlie in the stockroom. After that, he intended to take a walk around the city to visit a few of the better class of shops. Foxe should not be concerned if he did not return until it was almost time for dinner. What the purpose of this extended perambulation of the city streets might be he left unexplained. The questioning look Foxe directed at him also produced no response.

Very well, Foxe thought, if he wants to make a mystery of it, let him. Maybe he simply needs to be on his own for a while.

'Alderman Halloran asked me to invite you to call on him too,' Foxe said. 'You might include that in your travels.'

The only response was a grunt.

Mr Lavender, the cathedral librarian, handed Foxe six books, all concerned with heretical or esoteric subjects. Amongst them were three of the four from the library Foxe had found on the warden's desk.

'I judge there may be at least thirty or forty more which should be sold,' Lavender said, 'but you said you wanted to put them up for sale in small batches.'

'Too many books on similar subjects for sale at the same time is going to invite unwanted questions about the source,' Foxe said. 'If possible, it would be best to ensure none of the books on offer can be traced back to the cathedral. Also, putting them on the market gradually should help get the best prices.'

'I heartily agree with both of those notions,' Lavender said. 'The last thing we need is some interfering busybody seeking out the terms of the original bequest and making trouble. Now, about your commission …'

Their negotiations on this potentially awkward topic were mercifully brief. Foxe had anticipated pleas of the special claims of church property and the dire need the library had for funds for new purchases. He therefore stepped neatly around such pleading by stating at the outset that his usual commission on book sales was thirty percent of the selling price. However, on this occasion he was prepared to accept twenty. A minute or two of polite bargaining reduced this figure to fifteen, which was what Foxe had privately decided at the outset. Both parties were thus satisfied, hands were shaken, and Foxe left to walk for what seemed the hundredth time up the hill by the castle, across into Cockey Lane, and thus back to the marketplace and thence home.

The crowds that had been such a nuisance on the opening day of the assizes were long gone and the streets had resumed their usual weekday appearance of emptiness. He thought at one point he caught a brief glimpse of Nicholas entering a shop selling expensive millinery at the far end of Gentleman's Walk, but it was too far off to be certain. May be his aunt had given Nicholas a commission to place an order for a new hat for her. That might account for his reticence to explain the precise purpose of his walk around the city. He might have felt embarrassed at confessing he needed to find a milliner's establishment. Besides, that might not be the only task his aunt Harriet had laid on him. If they were all of a domestic or personal nature, he wouldn't want to risk provoking Foxe's amusement.

Dismissing from his mind what was no more than idle curiosity, Foxe stepped out smartly across the market, weaving his way between the stalls as he did so. Unlike most gentlemen taking such a route, he had little fear of pickpockets. Almost all who pursued that light-fingered game amongst the many buyers and sellers were street children. None of them would ever steal from their greatest friend and benefactor.

Once he had carefully placed the books in his own library, Foxe set out again, pausing only to drink a glass or two of small beer to quench his thirst on what was turning into a warm day. This time his destination was the theatre, close by the street where his house stood.

At one time, Foxe had been a constant and warmly welcomed visitor both to the theatre and the actors who worked there. Besides, not a few young and aspiring actresses had proved gratifying in their eagerness to share his bed for a night or two in the hope of a nice present afterwards, and a quiet suggestion to the theatre manager that he might be overlooking the extent of their talents. Since Foxe was also a long-term patron of the theatre, and a contributor on several occasions to appeals for extra funds, all meant that a succession of managers viewed maintaining his goodwill to be more important than an occasional poor performance by an actress whose hopes exceeded her talents.

An observer might have noted that Foxe spent quite a long time in the theatre that day, and that several members of the company were summoned to speak with him. They might also have found some significance in the broad smiles and occasional bursts of laughter that accompanied these actors' return to their own duties. Finally, a young actress, pale, thin and possessed of a mass of white-blond hair, was summoned to the manager's office. She stayed there for almost forty-five minutes, then drifted back into the depths of the theatre looking pensive. Those who knew her would have expressed considerable surprise that she was called to see Mr Foxe and the manager. That she had stayed so long would have astonished them, for she was one of the youngest and least experienced of the present company. A few, possessed of dirty minds, would have doubtless jumped to the conclusion that Mr Foxe's tastes had suddenly settled on someone young and androgenous. Susie Hirst — for that was the young actress's name — had more than once dressed in shirt and breeches to play a small role usually taken by a lad of fourteen or fifteen. Dressed in that way, she had appeared entirely convincing on stage and off. That too would have surprised those whose explanation for Mr Foxe's actions were confined to his sexual tastes. He had always seemed to favour ladies with fine figures rather than the boyish and skinny.

When Foxe left the theatre, both his heart and his purse were considerably lighter. Most of his plan was now in place. It only remained to explain fully to Nicholas and Charlie the parts they were to play in the enterprise. Then it could go ahead.

On his way home, he decided to call into the shop and see whether Mrs Crombie had managed to pick up any more gossip which might be useful. He was also curious to know what Nicholas was up to. What was he doing that necessitated leaving the house right after breakfast and not returning until well into the afternoon? Despite his determination to accept Nicholas was free to do as he wished, Foxe's curiosity could not be so easily quieted.

In terms of gossip, Mrs Crombie had little to offer him.

'People have moved on to other topics,' she told Foxe. 'With nothing new happening with regard to either murder, they are no longer news. Some of my customers seem already to have nearly forgotten them. The only hint of useful information for you came from a gentleman who was here with his wife, both of whom wished to use our circulating library. He enquired about books on the layout and planting of gardens. I had only one or two to show him, but he spent all the time that his wife was upstairs choosing novels paging through each of the volumes slowly. I imagine he was committing the information he required to memory, for he purchased nothing. The moment his wife returned, he thanked me for my help and left with her. He didn't even have the basic courtesy to ask whether he could re-shelve the volumes he had been inspecting. Just left them on the counter and walked away!'

'Would you have allowed him to re-shelve them?' Foxe asked, his face a picture of polite curiosity.

'Of course not! I have a simple system for arranging books, but all system would be destroyed if you allowed people to return books themselves. What I mean is that it would be polite to offer.'

Foxe was amused, but was careful to keep his expression neutral.

'What did this sadly impolite man say?' he asked.

That earned him a sour look.

'I happened to mention the death of Rev Pryce-Perkins,' Mrs Crombie said, 'while he was standing at the counter. His response was to say that the man got what he deserved.'

'What did he mean by that?'

'Exactly what I asked him, Mr Foxe. I didn't want to appear too curious, so I simply said that I found his words puzzling.'

'Did he give you an answer?'

'Not really. All he did was quote the old proverb. You know the one. "If you sup with the devil, you'll need a long spoon." After that, he wouldn't say anymore.'

Foxe thought for a moment about that enigmatic reply.

'I've always taken that saying to mean something about taking care if you dabble in dangerous matters,' Foxe said slowly. 'That getting too close to certain things risks being caught and drawn into serious trouble. Especially things judged to be wicked or likely to bring you or others harm. I wonder what the fellow knew that made him say that? Could he possibly have been aware of Pryce-Perkins's odd taste in topics of study?'

'Maybe,' Mrs Crombie said. 'I couldn't prise any more out of him.'

Foxe couldn't really decide whether what she told him was useful or not. In one sense, it added nothing to his knowledge. On the other hand, it seemed to indicate that the warden's taste for the kind of knowledge generally judged to be forbidden or even dangerous, was more widely known that he had imagined.

'Have you seen much of my cousin?' he asked, after a few moments thought. 'He's been rather left on his own these past few days.' Foxe could dangle a tempting bait as well as any angler.

'He and Charlie spent almost all day in the stockroom yesterday,' Mrs Crombie said. 'I believe Charlie was showing him that old printing press he's been learning how to use. He was also eager to talk about the latest books Mr Lavender has sent him for repair. That young man is becoming quite skilled in working with old, damaged books. He's only really happy when he's doing something with his hands, Mr Foxe. Have you thought any more about what I asked you about his future?'

'I have been rather preoccupied with other matters to tell the truth,' Foxe said. 'I had intended to approach a bookbinder before now. A good many of our wealthier customers like to buy old books unbound, then have them finished to match the other volumes in their libraries. A shelf of leather-bound volumes, all matching, makes a suitable display of wealth. I'm convinced few of these fine gentlemen ever open the books they purchase. They're more interested in fox hunting and shooting pheasants than improving their minds. If we could offer them a binding service, as well as selling them the books, it might prove profitable. Shall I make enquiries along those lines?'

'Please do,' Mrs Crombie said. 'But best not to raise Charlie's hopes unless you know they can be fulfilled.'

'I'll do it as soon as I can,' Foxe said. 'I have a lot on my mind, so please keep reminding me until I do. By the way, I thought I caught a distant sight of cousin Nicholas in Gentleman's Row a short while ago.'

'He's been invited to dine with Alderman and Mrs Halloran and their nieces, I believe. I expect you'll be included in the invitation, Mr Foxe. It didn't arrive until after you'd left the house this morning. As soon as he read the invitation, Mr Nicholas came to consult me about suitable small gifts to take for Mrs Halloran and the young ladies. I suggested perhaps a pair of gloves or some ribbons. He became quite a popular visitor with the Halloran ladies when he was here before.'

Foxe grinned.

'He'll be pleasantly surprised when he meets Miss Maria and Miss Lucy again. As you know, Maria is almost nineeen years of age and quite the beauty. Lucy is not quite her equal in that respect at sixteen, but she's even more full of mischief than she was. The alderman and his wife are inordinately proud of them both.'

'Is Miss Lucy still convinced she is going to marry you, Mr Foxe?'

'I hope not,' Foxe said. 'My wicked ways may have appealed to her at one time, but I doubt that the alderman and his wife would consider me a suitable husband for either of their nieces. Unlike my fine, upstanding young lawyer cousin, perhaps. Though he lacks a suitable fortune yet, I fear.'

'Unlike yourself,' Mrs Crombie said. Now it was her turn to throw out a baited line. 'If you could choose, which one of them do you think would make you the best wife?'

'Lucy, without a doubt. Maria has the sweetest nature and is, as I said, uncommonly pretty, but she would probably try to reform me. Lucy has that look in her eye that promises any husband an exciting life, if only he can match her sense of fun and independence with his own. But enough of such idle speculation. I may not even be included in the invitation.'

Of course he was, as he knew very well he would be. He also found another invitation on his desk which he received with almost as much pleasure. This one was to visit Mrs Katherine Danson, whose late husband's murder had been fairly recent amongst Foxe's investigations. She now wished to speak with him about selling her husband's large book collection; books which included many on precisely the same subjects as those he was about to offer from the cathedral library.

Mrs Danson's request could not have arrived at a better time. There would be no problem in letting potential buyers know that the bulk of the books on offer came from the library of the late Dr Danson. The cathedral's volumes could be slipped in amongst them and sold without mention of their different source. Even better, explaining he would be likely to have many books on offer over the next few months, all on topics relating to secret knowledge and supposedly hidden wisdom, would be an irresistible lure for the people Foxe wished to tempt from the shadows. He would go to see Mrs Danson as soon as she might find it convenient. Letting word circulate amongst collectors of rare volumes of that nature would take about a week, if not longer, so the quicker he could have a catalogue available of at least some of the books the better.

If the prospect of success in his hunt for the people with whom Pryce-Perkins was involved was uppermost in causing his excitement, Foxe was far from blind to the considerable profit he would earn at the same time. With the volumes he had just sold for the Earl of Pentelow, the sales would add many hundreds of pounds to his wealth.

Foxe would be the first to admit that there had been several past occasions when he had allowed himself to become distracted in the course of an investigation. It was an easy trap to fall into. Information didn't arrive in any kind of order, let alone at the time when you wanted it most. Tempting byways invited exploration, and it could take time, and waste considerable effort, before you found they took you only to dead ends. If that hadn't happened to him on this occasion, it was mostly because he still had little or no evidence to point him in any obviously fruitful direction.

The sensible thing to do, therefore, was to step back, review what little he knew, and establish a rational plan for the next stage.

Regarding the killing in the haunted house, he knew little more than he had at the start. The body had still to be properly identified. Cuthbert Custance's belief that it was his daughter was obviously wrong and could be ignored. Maybe Mistress Tabby could provide him with the name of the servant who disappeared from the Custance household at the same time that Grace Custance eloped. Equipped with a name, he could start a search for her current whereabouts. A failure to find her should then suggest the body was hers.

The other route forward necessitated entering the house unseen and undetected by any observer. His plan to achieve that was now fully developed in his own mind, but was going to take a few days to be ready. In the meantime, the less interest he was reported to be taking in that property, the better.

Things were moving at last in the other matter occupying his mind, the death of the Warden of St. Stephen's Hospital. Sadly, his plan for the next steps there must also take time to prepare, then execute. Book collectors were not noted for speed in their lives, especially not the ones Foxe was most keen to bring into the open. He would make a small start by placing an advertisement in the two Norwich papers announcing the forthcoming sale of the late Dr Danson's library. That should stir some interest, even if he was not in a position to start selling for at least a week, maybe longer. As he recalled, Danson had kept a meticulous list of his books. That would make the business of producing notification of the titles to be sold, together with brief details of the books and their condition fairly simple to undertake. If he wrote it out, Charlie could print it on the old printing press in the stockroom. He still wouldn't offer too many at one time, of course. That could drive prices down as the supply of books for sale exceeded any possible demand. These were the kind of books which would only appeal to a small number of dedicated collectors.

That left only one thing: to go to see Mrs Danson as soon as he could, agree terms and collect her late husband's list of the books he owned.

However, first there were some matters to be settled with Charlie and Nicholas about his plan to gain entry to the haunted house. Nicholas was not at all satisfied by his role as principal lookout at the front of the property. He kept pressing for the opportunity to do something more active, despite Foxe assuring him many times that being forewarned of any potential interference with events within was crucial to the success of the whole enterprise. In the end, he accepted his role, but not without a degree of muttering and many mutinous looks. The reality was that Foxe wanted him to be protected from any problems to his future career, should the plan go awry and the authorities get involved.

Charlie's main task would be to assemble the street children, make sure they knew what to do, check certain of them were properly dressed in the costumes the wardrobe mistress at the theatre was making for them, and then creep into Mancroft Yard himself to keep watch from the rear. Foxe would have given him the opportunity to be directly involved in entering the building, but making him a look-out as well might, he hoped, go some way to smoothing down Nicholas's ruffled feathers.

Foxe himself would see to all the remaining preparations. He'd already been to the theatre and set that part of the plan into action. He would also enter the property to conduct the search, taking only a small group with him to provide the diversion he had planned. Once inside, they would open the shutters of their dark lanterns. Then they would be ready to provide what Foxe hoped would be a theatrical performance of a truly spine-chilling nature. All that was left was to find a suitable night when there was no performance in the theatre. He also needed to set Charlie two important additional tasks.

'Send a message to Kate and the street children to make a careful watch on when there are people in the house at night and when it's empty,' Foxe told the boy. 'I need time to make a thorough search without fear of anyone discovering me inside. We can only be sure of that if we begin our little performance when whoever is busy in that house by night is there.'

'I understand, master,' Charlie replied. 'I think Kate said they were there almost every night, but I'll ask her to make certain.'

'The other job I have for you is critical. Can you find if there's anyone known to the children who can unlock an outside door for us to use and lock it again behind us. Then, after those inside have left, see it stays open so I can come out again?'

'Bound to be, I'll wager,' Charlie said. 'Not everyone does their thievin' in the streets by daylight. Most of the rest will break in to houses by levering a window open or something. Still, there must be someone as knows about pickin' locks. Don't you worry, master. I'll find you a proper burglar.'

12

The dinner with the Hallorans proved a great success. Foxe was always a popular guest, bringing gifts of books for Mrs Halloran and Lucy and new songs for Maria. She was most accomplished on the pianoforte and possessed a sweet soprano voice. As a result, no evening with guests in that house was ever complete without Maria and Lucy giving an impromptu concert. The younger sister was becoming proficient on the transverse flute. Her naturally lower-pitched voice, not yet mature enough to be deemed contralto but heading that way, blended well with her sister's in duets.

Foxe couldn't help noticing over the dining table the warm, almost ardent looks Nicholas kept directing at Miss Maria; nor the way she acknowledged his attention with shy smiles and becoming blushes. He was certain Mrs Halloran had seen these exchanges as well, and perhaps even approved. Nicholas had been a great favourite with her during his previous visit. Now he was on the verge of obtaining a partnership in a law firm, that proof of his diligence and professional status must count for something with her. The only problem might be his apparent lack of fortune. Foxe silently determined to improve matters in that direction by pointing out that Nicholas would, in time, receive a substantial inheritance when his mother's grandfather, still alive at ninety-two years of age, finally passed to his rest. It was unlikely to be a fortune, but it should be more than enough for Nicholas to be able to offer any wife significant comfort and security. He might also remind the Hallorans that Nicholas was his own closest relative. Since they knew Foxe was a rich man, this might also count in the young man's favour. Nor should they forget that successful lawyers charged high fees. All in all, her niece might do far worse, should their obvious attraction deepen into something more. The girls' father was apparently destined to remain abroad for some time to come and had only his income from his role with the East India Company. At least, Foxe had never heard of any other family wealth.

As they travelled home that evening in Foxe's carriage, Nicholas could talk of little else than Miss Maria's graceful beauty and her obvious musical talent. His gift of a pair of fine doeskin gloves had also proved a success with that lady.

Foxe, suspecting beforehand that Miss Lucy, two years younger, might be in danger of being overlooked, had made certain to arrive equipped with an even more generous present for her than usual. It took the form of a splendidly bound copy of the latest translation of the travels of Marco Polo, together with a collection of flute sonatas newly composed by Johann Quartz. As a result, the evening was marked by great good humour in both the hosts and their guests.

Since, next morning, Nicholas once again left with no more than a vague suggestion that he would probably be gone for most of the day, Foxe found himself entirely at leisure until it was time to go to Mrs Dansons' house. Another wealthy widow, he thought. I'm beginning to collect them. It's probably a sign of approaching old age.

He had just completed his breakfast and was about to get ready to resume his normal habit of taking a walk around the Market Place, followed by a visit to the coffeehouse, when Molly brought him a message delivered by Bart, Mistress Tabby's servant.

'She asks you to call on her,' Molly said. 'It seems she has a name you wanted her to discover, along with a few more items she says will be of interest to you. She will be at home all day.' Foxe, eager to make any kind of further progress in his investigations, decided on the spot that visiting Mistress Tabby was more important even than writing out an initial list of books he would put up for sale to act as the means of luring Pryce-Perkins's shadowy visitors into the light.

Foxe found the Cunning Woman in her garden, weeding with great care between the plants, few of which he recognised. As usual, Bart was nearby. He had drawn two buckets of water from the well and was sprinkling it gently over some shallow dishes of earthenware which held various seedlings.

'It never does to use a hoe to remove the weeds in this garden,' Tabby told him. 'You may lose something useful that way. This, for example, has grown here all by itself. I didn't plant it, yet it must stay, since is a useful preventative against the itch.'

She held up a small plant with a mass of tiny white flowers amongst reddish leaves. To Foxe's eyes, it was just an insignificant tuft of leaves of the kind you would walk upon without a second thought, yet Tabby picked a small sprig of it and placed I carefully into a basket of similar bits and pieces of nondescript stems and leaves which was beside her on the ground.

'If I lived anywhere but in the city,' she continued, 'it would be easy to walk in the fields and coppices to find all I need for my medicines. Yet, even here Nature bestows a little of her bounty for those with eyes to find it and the patience to take their time with mundane tasks. Come, let us go inside, Ash, for I have things to tell you. Bart will bring us some refreshing tea made from the leaves of the mint plant.'

As usual, the two of them sat on simple, wooden chairs in Mistress Tabby's kitchen, with the sharp smell of something simmering on the charcoal cooking-range tickling Foxe's nose. Tabby washed the earth from her hands, took the bowl of dirty water and poured it gently over the roots of a large bay tree which stood in a sunny spot just outside the back door. A few moments later Bart came in, washed his hands clean in a similar way and busied himself making their refreshment, which included slices of what Tabby told Foxe was tansy cake along with the mint tea.

'Grace Custance's maidservant was called Annie Beechey,' Mistress Tabby said. I can also confirm that she has gone missing. Everyone assumes that she accompanied her mistress when she eloped, but I think that's most unlikely. Others say she probably realised Mr Custance would suspect her of complicity in his daughter's flight and dismiss her anyway. In fact, my sources tell me, Annie disappeared a day before her mistress did. That may argue foreknowledge or there may be some other reason for her going. Either way, Miss Custance is said to have treated it as of no great consequence. There's no real proof that Annie Beechey was a particular favourite. She was simply one of the household servants, obtained like the rest, from the Overseers of the Poor.'

'It sounds very odd to me,' Foxe said. 'How did she come to be wearing her mistress's clothes? That is, if the body in that house was indeed that of Annie Beechey and not Grace Custance herself. Why did she go into the place at night, despite the tales of ghosts and demons? Maybe all this has nothing to do with the murder anyway.'

'That is for you to discover, Ash,' Tabby said. 'I have done my part. If the girl came from the Overseers, she was most likely an orphan, so she'd hardly be seeking refuge amongst her family.'

'I'm still convinced it wasn't Grace Custance in that house,' Foxe said. 'The dead girl's hands were those of a servant, not a pampered daughter. Perhaps it wasn't this Annie Beechey either, neat though that would be. If so, I wonder where she is now?'

'If anyone can find her, you can, Ash,' Tabby said, her eyes bright with amusement. 'Stop feeling sorry for yourself. There's no reason whatsoever why events should be arranged exactly according to your wishes. Things are what they are. Send out those street children you rely on so much. They'll find her, if she is still to be found above ground.'

'I will,' Foxe replied. 'If I only had the Second Sight like some people I know …'

'It would likely be of no service to you whatsoever. It isn't something you can call up whenever you wish. Occasional insights into future events come when they come. They cannot be commanded.'

'If you say so, Foxe replied, sulking a little. 'You haven't heard any more about Pryce-Perkins, have you?'

'No, or I would have told you. Now, forget about your murders for a little while. I have had another letter from Lady Cockerton.'

'She has suddenly become a most assiduous correspondent,' Foxe said sourly.

'I wish heartily she wasn't,' Tabby replied. 'I haven't replied to her last letter. There's no reason at all for her not to write to you directly. I suspect she's afraid of what you may say in reply.'

'Even so,' Foxe said, 'I imagine whatever it contains is meant for my ears.'

'It was. But when you hear what it contains, I think you'll share my view that this letter will prove to be the last. The lady is going to Italy.'

'Italy! Whatever for?'

'For the same reasons most wealthy people give for deciding to go there at some point in their lives. To see the many famous buildings and works of art. She writes that she has met a group of people in Bath who are planning to make the trip together. They have invited her to join them. Being about to be possessed of a significant amount of money, she has decided to accept their invitation. She says she will return briefly to Norwich in a week or so, but only to set her affairs in order and organise for the lease on her house here to be sold to someone else. Then she will depart for London to join the others. They expect to be away for at least a year, possibly more.'

'I wonder if she expects to leave Norwich for good?'

'That is my guess. Apparently, Maria, her maid, is to remain in Bath, where she has already found a position with another fashionable lady.'

'In a way, I'm relieved,' Foxe said. 'If Lady Cockerton was still residing in Norwich, I would be bound to encounter her from time to time to our mutual discomfort. I'm also happy that Maria has found a new mistress.'

'Relief clearly isn't the emotion Lady Cockerton is hoping her news will cause you to feel, Ash. She says that you will doubtless be envious of her visiting the home of so many great libraries, as well as paintings.'

'How little she knows me.' Foxe said with a laugh. 'I didn't want to travel to Bath, because it would mean being away from my home city for several weeks. Why should she imagine I would feel envious about going all that way to Italy, then staying away for a year or more?'

'There's more. Right at the end of her letter, she adds a sort of casual postscript. It seems she has prevailed upon a certain Major Garrod of the King's Horse Artillery to join the group as her particular escort. He is currently on leave from his regiment and now intends to resign his commission to be her companion and protector during her stay abroad. Much as Lady Julia persuaded your friend Capt. Brock to act in her case.'

'She expects me to suffer pangs of jealousy, I suppose,' Foxe said. 'To reflect that it could have been me instead of this Major Garrod. Pah! All it causes me to think is that it has taken that lady next to no time to find someone to take my place in certain other respects as well. It sounds as if she is also fool enough to imagine he's making the trip for any other reason than with an eye on her fortune. Rich widows attract fortune-hunters like dead meat attracts flies.'

'On which matter,' Tabby said. 'I hope you are making use of the prescription I sent you.'

Foxe agreed that he was, though not quite as often as she had suggested. In truth, he'd been far too busy with other matters. Now he realised one of the greatest advantages of his previous dealings with women. He'd always been able to increase or decrease contact to fit in with whatever else he was doing at the time. Commitment to one meant fitting in with their needs, which might clash wit his own.

###

As he waited for a suitably dark night for his entry to the haunted house, Foxe quietly continued with what needed to be done on his other investigation. The moon was waning and would become a new moon in less than a week. That would ensure almost total darkness. He wondered what the phase of the moon had been on the night of the murder itself. Probably a half moon or larger, he estimated, and thus more than enough to provide a good light for the murdered woman to find the house and determine to go inside.

Right now, however, it was time to call on Mrs Danson. Fortunately, the lady was often at home, so it proved easy to make a suitable appointment. One o'clock in the afternoon of that day had been set as the time for Foxe's visit.

It felt odd to be returning to the Danson house after what must be a period of six months at least. On the outside, nothing had changed. He hardly expected it would have done. Inside was another matter. A neatly dressed maidservant let him in and asked him to wait in the hall while she told her mistress he had arrived. No butler now. Looking around, Foxe noticed at once that the hall had been subtly altered, so that it looked brighter and more welcoming than before. Was there less furniture than he recalled from his previous visits? He thought so, though he couldn't be certain. Something had definitely been changed to make it feel more spacious. What furniture there was now chiefly consisted of chairs and glass-fronted cabinets, all in mahogany rather than oak. Somehow, it gave a distinctly feminine feel to the place.

Mrs Danson received him in her drawing room. There too she had clearly been at work. The heavy oak panelling on the walls was gone, replaced by pale wallpaper. Again the furniture was lighter, more gracious than before. It too was mahogany, in place of the previous oak. There were fine landscapes pictures on the walls, where there had been portraits of gloomy looking ancestors, and several new mirrors helped add to the brightness of the whole interior. Whatever else she had done about the house in the short time she had been its owner, she had obviously spent freely in the hall and drawing room.

The lady herself, even in the dark days following her husband's murder, had maintained a calm approach to what had to be done, holding up well even under the suspicion of being somehow involved in her husband's death. Then had hardly been the time to remark upon it, but Foxe had not failed to notice the undeniable attractiveness of her person, despite the dull clothes of widowhood, and the liveliness of her personality. Mrs Katherine Danson had always been a pleasure to deal with.

Now, having abandoned black bombazine in favour of the muted colours of half-mourning, she was transformed. She wore an elegant day dress of luminous purple damask over a pale lilac petticoat heavily embroidered with tiny sprigs of spring flowers. The result was a delightful ensemble, one well calculated to set off her fine complexion. It also made the most of what he could see was her pleasingly soft and gently rounded figure.

Foxe rated himself a connoisseur of female beauty, and he was startled by the change since he had seen Mrs Danson last. In her own quiet, grey-eyed way, she had laid aside what had previously held her back and revealed herself to be a woman of some beauty.

She greeted Foxe warmly and they soon concluded terms for the sale acceptable to them both. The late doctor's book catalogue was handed over, with clear instructions about which books were to be sold and which left behind. She also shared with him her plans to continue transforming the house she had inherited into something much less sombre and scholarly in its interior arrangements and furnishings.

'Like most men,' she said to Foxe, 'you have always been in control of your own wealth and expenditure. Women must rely on their husband's or father's generosity for the funds to do what appeals to them. Dr Danson was not in any way parsimonious in my allowance, but he reserved the vast bulk of his wealth for his purchases of books and other personal interests. This house had been fitted up to suit him long before I arrived. There was no question of him even considering any significant changes.'

The hand she swept in an elegant gesture to indicate the library to which they had moved was sufficient to make her meaning quite clear.

'For a time, immediately after I was freed from unjust suspicion — thanks mostly to your efforts and faith in my innocence …' Foxe found himself bathed in a radiant smile which set his heart in something of a flutter, for he was of a most susceptible nature. ' ... I felt disposed to sell this property and everything in it and move to live elsewhere. I'm not quite sure what changed my mind. Now I feel determined to live here and see this gloomy place transformed into the kind of home I have always desired. Is that so very silly of me, Mr Foxe?'

'Not at all,' Foxe replied warmly. 'It is your house now and you must do with it as you wish. But doesn't the prospect of needing to handle all your own affairs seem at all daunting to you?'

'Not in the least,' Mrs Danson replied, calmly earnest in this as in all matters. 'I shall seek help where it is needed, of course, but I am quite confident that I shall manage very well. I hope you will become a suitably frequent visitor here to observe the changes and give me your opinions. You are a person I have learned to trust under most trying circumstances. I should not wish to lose your friendship and counsel through any waywardness on my part.'

At that precise moment, Foxe could imagine few more pleasant prospects than spending time with Mrs Danson. He therefore gave her his warmest assurance that he would hold himself honoured to enjoy her friendship and trust in the future.

It was quite foreign to Foxe's past experience to find himself attracted to a woman for any reasons beyond the most obvious and earthy. The effect on him of barely an hour in Mrs Danson's presence was nearly as surprising as it had been pleasant, and he walked home in something of a happy daze as a result. The potential income from selling Dr Danson's books now assumed little more than minor importance in his mind compared with the opportunities the sale would offer him to visit the widow to collect more volumes and keep her in touch with how things were proceeding.

Since his plans to advance further on the long road to discovering who killed Rev Pryce-Perkins were now well under way, it was time to concentrate on the other matter and learn what was going on in Mancroft Yard. There was still a sliver of the old moon at night, but that would not be enough to give more than a glimmer of illumination. He would go forward with what he intended, either that night or the next. He'd waited long enough.

13

Nicholas shifted his feet and moved slightly further back into the shadow of the doorway in which he had been standing for the past thirty minutes. He felt stiff and bored. The clocks of several churches had chimed the half hour a few moments ago, making enough noise for him finally to let out the cough which he had been suppressing for what seemed like hours. Not that the sound should have mattered. On both sides, the street appeared totally deserted. Still, such an obviously human noise, however soft, would be bound to draw attention, perhaps even from whoever was inside the house across the roadway and slightly to his left. When he, Charlie and his cousin Ashmole had arrived, they had all been concealing as much of themselves as possible under dark cloaks. The street children were already waiting and one of them explained that three men had entered the house just before the clocks chimed midnight.

After that, Charlie had crept silently through the archway into Mancroft Yard, where he would conceal himself to watch the rear of the house. Nicholas himself had chosen this spot in a suitably recessed doorway, and Ashmole had slipped away to collect the others outside the stage door of the theatre. As for the street children, they had silently melted into the shadows all along the street. Nobody could now approach the house without being seen.

It was a warm night, close and humid. The sky was a mass of dense clouds, so it was far too dark to see more than a few yards to either side. A few moments ago there had even been a distant rumble of thunder, and lightning had flickered over the rooftops to the south. Now, it seemed, the storm had either subsided or drifted away somewhere else.

Nicholas started. What was that? There it was again! The sound of someone — perhaps two or three people — trying to approach without being heard. When they drew within a few yards of him, he could see them. Not clearly, but well enough to be able to make out their number. There were four figures, all small, slipping along close to the wall on the opposite side of the street. The tallest one was heavily cloaked and hooded, while the others seemed to be wearing shawls or close-fitting garments of a dark colour. On their heads, all wore some kind of caps, tied under the chin with — surely not! — what appeared to be tufts or short horns above their ears.

After that, he could see no more. They had pressed themselves close to the wall on either side of the door to the house where it was darkest.

Nicholas wondered if the tallest, cloaked figure could be a woman. There had been a crisis earlier in the evening when word was brought to Ashmole that the actress due to play the major role during the night was too ill to take part, probably as a result of eating a tainted pie. For a while, it looked as if the whole thing would have to be postponed and Charlie had been sent to tell the street children of the change. However, he had returned after barely ten minutes, grinning all over his face.

Whatever he had whispered to cousin Ashmole had first resulted in no more than a shake of the head. Charlie had persisted, however. Finally, he and his master had left the house together. By the time they returned, at almost ten o'clock, Ashmole had told his cousin they were proceeding as planned. Nicholas could only assume that they had found a last-minute substitute for the sick actress.

Now three more figures emerged from a patch of dark shadows to Nicholas's right. These were tall, yet wrapped in dark cloaks like the first group. As they approached, what was clearly a lad of about fifteen years of age came out of the shadows and also pressed himself close to the front door,

As he did so, the thunder rumbled again, sounding far closer this time. A pause, then the sky was lit briefly by sheet lightning, revealing a mass of dark, boiling clouds to the south. Unless they veered away to follow the river towards Yarmouth, the city was in for a sharp storm very soon.

When the figure by the door stood back, Nicholas could see the way into the house was now open. All the figures, large and small, slipped inside and the door was closed and locked behind them, still in total silence. Finally, the lad walked back to his hiding place as silently as he had come.

Nicholas peered at what had been claimed to be an empty, deserted house. That is what it still appeared to be, though, by his reckoning, there now at least were eleven people inside. The place was as dark and deserted as ever. Only once, soon after he had taken up his position, had Nicholas seen anything. Then it had been a brief glimpse of a light behind one of the dormer windows in the roof. Those, he presumed, were attics. All the windows on the lower two floors had stayed completely dark.

Nicholas reckoned later that he had spent at least another ten minutes straining his eyes and ears, but neither seeing nor hearing anything to indicate what might be happening inside the house.

After that, everything started to happen at once.

It began when a bolt of lightning hurled itself earthwards out of the clouds now massed above, bathing half the city in blinding light and striking the weathercock on the top of the nearby St. Stephen's Church, so that it sagged over and crashed to the ground in a twisted mass of red-hot metal. At the same moment there came a sound that suggested the very firmament was being torn in two, instantly followed by a peal of thunder which shook the whole area and must have shattered a good number of windows. As it faded away, it was accompanied by sounds of falling glass on all sides.

This display of fury from the heavens had startled Nicholas into bewilderment. He had scarcely recovered his wits before an unearthly scream from within the house turned his legs to water. On and on it went, then died away into a series of moans, accompanied now by various thumps and crashes. Then there were more rumbling noises, this time interspersed with more groans and wails of distress.

Not to be outdone, the sky produced another bolt of lightning, more jagged this time, followed by another crash of thunder immediately overhead. As the sounds gradually died away into silence, a single word, screamed in a powerful female voice, rooted Nicholas once more to the spot.

'Murder!'

Now there was a great deal of noise from inside. Cackling and moaning, a revolting noise like someone choking, then the unmistakeable sound of hurrying feet, with a dragging noise at the same time.

The front door rattled and shook, then flew open and two men emerged, dragging the limp body of a third between them. Once outside, the largest of the three managed to heft the limp figure onto his shoulder, then staggered away along the street, weaving from side to side as he did so. His other companion ran off in the opposite direction , stumbling on the uneven surface but clearly not willing to slow down for anything. Everyone's faces were chalk-white and their eyes wide with terror. The third man had either fainted or was too overcome to stand or move on his own.

Immediately, most of those who had arrived earlier came out and hurried off in the direction of the theatre. They were less furtive now but still remained covered by the cloaks they had arrived wearing.

Lights were beginning to appear in houses on all sides as people, roused by the strange noises, came out into the street to discover what was going on. The street children quickly ran amongst these new arrivals and Nicholas heard the words "ghosts" and "devils" being passed from mouth to mouth. As a result, as quickly as they had appeared, all the onlookers disappeared back into their homes, shutting the doors firmly behind them.

At this point, Nicholas, mindful of the instructions he had been given, stepped up to the front door of the house to wait for his cousin, still somewhere inside. He was there for maybe five minutes only, before Ashmole appeared and the two of them set off towards the theatre. Ashmole to dispense praise and rewards, and Nicholas still hoping to discover what precisely had taken place inside.

As they did, another series of lightning flashes and roars of thunder announced the arrival of torrents of rain, so that they didn't linger at the theatre once Ashmole's immediate business was settled. And though they hurried the few hundred yards homewards as quickly as they could, both arrived drenched to the skin. Charlie, equally sodden, joined them as they arrived.

###

These three met soon after in Foxe's library. They had managed to dry themselves and put on fresh clothes, while Molly, already roused from sleep from the fury of the storm, got busy in the kitchen heating water to make a suitably warming and reviving pot of tea. While they waited, Nicholas, Charlie and Foxe got as close as they could to a small fire that had been earlier lit in the grate by Foxe's instruction. It wasn't a cold night, but waning excitement and wet clothes had made them all feel chilled enough to crave extra warmth.

Nicholas and Charlie were desperate to hear what had taken place inside the house. Foxe, wishing to keep matters straight in his mind, made them tell their own stories first.

They began with Nicholas, who swiftly explained all he had seen from his vantage point across the road. When he had completed his tale, Foxe checked again that he had seen no one else watching the house before the strom began and the events inside took place.

'No one,' Nicholas assured him. 'It was completely quiet. There was nobody about at all until the noise brought the curious onto the street.'

'What happened then?' Foxe asked him.

'The street children appeared and ran amongst the onlookers saying something about ghosts as devils. That was enough to send everyone running back inside again as fast as they could.'

'Excellent!' Foxe said. 'I knew I could rely on them.'

'Before these neighbours were alerted, you saw nobody watching from inside any of the houses nearby?'

'There were none that I saw.'

'Good. For my plan to work, it's vital that there be no suspicion of trickery being involved,' Foxe said. 'Now you, Charlie. What did you see?'

'Nothing at all before that great crash of thunder,' the lad replied 'As far as I could tell, everyone in Mancroft Yard was asleep. I didn't even see a cat.'

'Go on.'

'When that terrible scream came, I almost jumped out of my skin. Fair made me think about ghosts, it did, and I knew it wasn't anything supernatural. The sound seemed to echo round and round the yard and I heard windows opening. Two or three folks came outside with candles to see what was going on. Then, when they heard the next crash of thunder and heard the cry of "murder!" they bolted back inside as fast as they could. No one came out after that. Too terrified of what they might see.'

'Nothing afterwards?'

'Only a couple of minutes later. Then the back door of the house flew open and that fellow what calls himself mayor of the yard came rushing out as if he had all the devils in hell on his heels.'

'John Holtaway,' Foxe said. 'I was pretty certain he was mixed up in this.'

'Why did you think so?' Nicholas asked. 'He seemed a nice enough fellow to me.'

'I saw him very soon after the body of that poor young woman had supposedly been discovered. He was very reluctant to answer any of my questions. He also did his level best to convince me they could handle things on their own. It was very obvious that he didn't want me to be involved in any way. All he did, of course, was convince me of the opposite.'

'Hold on a moment,' Nicholas said. 'I'm feeling lost. The story you said he told you seemed perfectly sensible, didn't it?'

'Only if you took it all at face value,' Foxe replied. 'All that about the unknown vagrant who found the body, then conveniently disappeared. I was convinced it was a tissue of lies from start to finish. Was I really expected to accept that a vagrant, who was a total stranger to the place, came into the yard in the dead of night when it was pitch black; managed by some miraculous means to discover the house is empty; then decided to find a place to to sleep inside? Every vagrant I've ever encountered avoids entering houses at all, except to steal. This one opens a locked door and settles down for the night in the middle of one of the principal rooms. Next morning, the same fellow wakes to find he's been sleeping next to a corpse, so he hurries outside to raise the alarm, then vanishes before anyone can even see what he looked like. Does that sound like the truth to you?'

'When you put it like that,' Nicholas said, feeling like the greatest fool imaginable, 'it's no more than a fairy story.'

'Exactly. Someone had spent time dreaming it up before raising the alarm. It might have worked with those idiots of constables. Unknown vagrants are constantly being accused of everything from petty theft to multiple murders. Saves everyone a good deal of trouble and hides all manner of laziness and incompetence. I felt quite put out that Holtaway could imagine it would work on me as well. Still, as the old saying goes, give someone enough rope and he'll hang himself.'

'So you said nothing?'

'I merely nodded and tried to look convinced. His entire manner was wrong too. Think about it. A young woman has just been found, murdered, in the house right next to your own. Yet Mr Holtaway told me about it as if it was a regular occurrence. He was entirely calm. No sign of being in the least upset by what had happened. It was as if he'd been talking about yesterday's afternoon tea.'

"Do you think he knew who you were?" Nicholas asked.

'He knew who I was and all about my interest in rooting out crime. That was clear,' Foxe said.

'Everyone in this city knows about Mr Foxe,' Charlie added. 'It would only be odd if he claimed to be different.'

'Everyone may know who I am,' Foxe said, 'but I've taken good care over the years to try to make sure few if any of them know about the investigations I've carried out. At first, I played the empty-headed, fashionable fop, who dressed outrageously and had no interests beyond clothes and bedding as many women as I could. Then, when that was no longer quite believable, I suddenly reformed my ways, started to dress much more soberly, and built up my business, generally sticking to one mistress at a time. The only people who know all about my activities in bringing criminals to justice are the rich merchants who run this city and pay for my efforts — and criminals. Which category would best fit our Mr Holtaway?'

The other two stared at Foxe, ashamed of their own gullability.

'When I seemed to be taken in by his act,' Foxe went on, 'Holtaway made his worst mistake. He tried to elaborate on his tale to make absolutely sure I was convinced. I was, but only that he was a liar.

'You'll have to explain it to me,' Nicholas said. 'I'm in awe of the way your mind works.'

'He spun me a long yarn about the house being occupied previously by an old woman, who everyone believed was a witch who called up demons. Then he embellished that with rubbish about a landlord who was content to accept the house was now impossible to rent. Yet, when I went inside I could see the place was only a little dusty. The furniture was good, nothing was broken down or showing signs of rot, even the windows were intact and the shutters neatly drawn back. All this in a house which was supposed to have been unoccupied for several years. And what kind of landlord accepts a house cannot be rented, yet leaves good furniture, carpets and even china ornaments inside, where any half-competent thief could make off with them?'

He paused for breath and to pour himself another dish of tea. It had been a long night and his eyes were feeling sore and gritty. Still, a glance at the other two was enough to show him it would be cruel to stop his narrative right now.

'Imagine an old woman, alone save for an equally ancient servant and several pet cats. The kind of poor old soul whom ignorant people mark down as a witch. What kind of house would you expect to find she lived in?'

'A tumbledown cottage,' Charlie replied at once.

'And how would you describe the house at the head of Mancroft Yard?'

'Old, but still a substantial property for all that. Three floors, maybe ten or twelve rooms inside at least,' Nicholas said. 'With some exterior modification, it would make a good property for a prosperous tradesman and his family.'

'Not where you would expect to find an old, old woman living alone,' Foxe said. 'Not unless she was wealthy. Wealthy old ladies are described in many derogatory ways, but I've never heard of one being labelled as a witch. It's the poor who still believe in witchcraft. Those who are better off scorn such out-dated ideas. The witch story and the haunting was invented. Why? To stop the poor folk who live in the crowded, wretched tenements crammed into Mancroft Yard from being curious about whatever is going on in that house. Now, I have brought that fiction to life.

By doing so, I'll wager I've left Mr Holtaway and his fellow criminals as puzzled as they are anxious. Hopefully, they won't connect any of this with the curious Mr Foxe either.'

'Do you think they'll be back?' Nicholas asked.

'I'm banking on it,' Foxe said. 'I've seen what they're doing in that place. It's worth far too much to them for a mere ghost and a few devils to make them abandon it.'

He held up his hand to stop any more questions.

'Before you start asking me any more now,' he said firmly, 'I'm more tired that I have been in years and I can see young Charlie's eyes drooping. It's high time we all got some sleep. The dawn will be here very soon. My tale will wait until tomorrow. No! No more now. Go to bed, both of you. I'll finish what I have to say later. Come here again at one o'clock tomorrow afternoon. Now off with you!'

###

Foxe kept his promise. Once the three of them were together again next day, he explained what had taken place inside the haunted house

He began by reminding them how it looked, late that previous afternoon as if the whole affair would have to be postponed until the actress, who was to play the role of the murdered girl, recovered from her illness.

'That was when you sent me to tell Kate Sulyard and the street children they wouldn't be needed,' Charlie interrupted, 'and Kate offered to play the role herself.'

Foxe nodded.

'I admit I was very dubious,' he said. 'However, everyone else was ready and all thought she would only have to stand still and make some ghostly moaning noises. I arranged for the theare's most experienced actress to apply white make-up to her face and powder her hair. For costume, she could wear her own shift.'

Kate-the-budding-actress had other ideas. She declared her own shift was too soiled and skimpy to serve the purpose. She wanted something better. She was therefore dressed in a plain white gown, far too large for her, which flapped about her legs when she moved. She and the theatre's actress then took it outside and smeared it with mud and greenish matter, until it looked like a winding-sheet from a grave. Kate's face was made white, and also streaked with green and yellow. Her eye-sockets were darkened. The effect was gruesome, even in clear light. In the yellow light from a dark lantern, especially one held low down, she resembled nothing so much as a partially-rotted body risen from its tomb.

The two male actors who were taking part dressed themselves all in black and hid their faces behind cloth masks. Their role was two-fold: to supply indistinct but threatening noises and lift Kate up so that she would appear to be hovering in mid-air. Four street children were dressed as demons. Once inside the house, they would move silently up the stairs and hide close to the first-floor landing. Their role was to dart out once anyone inside passed them, heading for the front door, and stop them going back upstairs.

'Kate was magnificent,' Foxe said. 'There was no time for me to do more than tell her she was to represent the ghost of the murdered girl. We would stage her tableau in the hallway, close to the room where the body was found. We would also be sure to leave a path open to the front door. We wanted anyone inside to run away, so I could examine the rest of the house undisturbed. Kate just nodded and said she understood. Then it was time to get into position, moving some chairs so the actors could conceal themselves. Kate and they had dark lanterns. At a suitable moment, the lanterns would be uncovered, so that Kate would be illuminated from below.'

'How were you going to bring the men inside downstairs to see your tableau?' Nicholas asked.

'The actors had lengths of chain wrapped in cloth to prevent any noise until it was needed,' Foxe said. 'At my signal, they were to rattle the chains, while I stamped and thumped on the floor. We hoped that would be enough. Those in the house probably knew the tale of ghosts was all fiction. Hearing noises from below, especially uncanny ones, they would have to find out what was going on. It might be burglars or someone from a rival gang — or even the constables come to arrest them.'

None of this had been needed. The bolt of lightning and that initial noise of thunder had shaken the windows and brought any work upstairs to a halt.

Kate, sensing an unrivalled opportunity, took a deep breath and let out a truly terrible scream.

'My hair stood on end, truly it did,' Foxe said. 'I could see her do it, yet I still had trouble believing any human throat, let alone one belonging to a fifteen-year-old girl, could produce such a dreadful sound. We heard noises from upstairs at once, something like tools being dropped, then the sound of feet descending the stairs. Whoever it was seemed to be in a hurry. Even so, they were still hesitant to approach too closely.'

'How many people were coming down?' Nicholas asked. 'Could you tell?'

'Just one person at first. A young man. The moment he stood on the landing, peering down into the hall below him, the actors lifted Kate up and opened their lanterns. Kate then appeared in a flickering, ghostly light. I expected her to do what I'd asked, which was nothing. Just to stand and let herself appear like the spirit of the dead girl. What she actually did was far better.'

By this time, Nicholas and Charlie were hanging on Foxe's every word, their eyes and mouths wide open with excitement.

'What? What did she do?' Nicholas whispered, when Foxe paused in his narrative to take a breath. 'Don't stop there!'

'There was a second thunder-clap at that point,' Foxe said. 'Once again, she made best use of this unexpected help from Nature. She raised her arm, pointed at the man on the landing, and screeched "Murder!" at the top of her voice. Then she followed it up with the most horrible choking and gurgling noises. The actors, as quick-witted as she, began muttering "murder!

murder!", interspersed with cackles and moans. It was enough to make even the strongest, most sceptical person's blood run cold.'

'And the man on the stairs?' That was Charlie.

'He stood stock still for a long moment and I saw — and smelled — him fouling his breeches as he did. Then his eyes rolled up in their sockets and he fainted away, falling head-long down the stairs to lie in a heap at the bottom.

'I was just on the point of moving forward to see if he'd hurt himself badly, when I heard more feet on the stairs and two men came rushing down into the hall. By this time, the actors had closed their dark lanterns and lowered Kate so she could conceal herself behind a handy curtain. Even from there, she made those awful choking noises, mixed with moans and howls. In the darkness and confusion, it was impossible to be sure where the sounds were coming from. They seemed to echo about the space, interspersed by the cackles and yells of "murder!" from the street children disguised as demons.

'The two men glanced round briefly and ran for the door. Of course it was locked. One had a key, but his hands were shaking so badly it took half a dozen attempts to get it into the lock. Then they glanced at each other, darted back to pick up the prone man, and were outside as fast as their feet would carry them.'

'You didn't see Holtaway?' Nicholas queried.

'No. Thinking about it afterwards, I realised a house like that would have a separate set of stairs for the servants, probably ending close to the kitchen. He must have come down those and rushed directly to the back door, abandoning the others to whatever they might find. Our Mr Holtaway obviously puts self-preservation far above loyalty to others or helpfulness in a crisis.'

'We saw — or rather I saw — the actors and Kate come out. What did you do?'

'I was certain no one was going to return that night, so before they left, I gave a few moments to congratulating Kate and thanking the others. The actors were fulsome in their praise of what the girl had done. They begged me to bring her to the theatre as soon as possible and let the manager see what she could do. According to them, Kate's a born actress whose talent should not be wasted a moment longer.'

'Will you do it?' Nicholas asked.

'Definitely. That poor child is prey to every kind of harm and disease in the life she is being forced to live. I imagine the actors will be telling the manager all about her already.'

'I don't think she can read, master,' Charlie said. 'That might be a problem.'

'A problem easily remedied with a few guineas from me to pay someone to teach her.' Foxe replied. 'Besides, if I ask the manager to take her on, I doubt if he'll refuse. I've long been an excellent patron of his theatre and he owes me more than a few favours. Provided Kate agrees, I will see that it happens.'

'Did you find out what was going on inside the house?' Nicholas said. All this business about the young tart was hardly to the point.

'Easily,' Foxe replied. 'There was nothing obvious on the ground floor. I never imagined there would be. Nor in the bedrooms on the first floor. Plenty of beds there for our imaginary vagrant to use rather than lying on the floor. The only problem was that none of the beds had a mattress. I soon found out why. They'd been taken up into the largest attic above and stacked against the walls to muffle the noise from the two coin-stamping machines I found up there.'

'Counterfeiting!' Nicholas gasped. 'No wonder it had to be so secret.'

'It looked to be taking place on a large scale,' Foxe continued. 'Aside from the two machines and several sets of dies, I found bags of shillings and sixpences. They'd also tried their hand at florins and some Spanish silver dollars. When they fled, they left all the evidence behind. They must have a small army of people passing these coins into circulation all over Norfolk. I expect the Spanish coins are destined to be taken abroad, though some of the merchants in towns like Great Yarmouth and King's Lynn will probably accept almost anything they're led to believe is silver.'

'Were they good counterfeits?' Nicholas asked.

'See for yourself.' Foxe tossed him what appeared to be a silver sixpence. 'A little too light, if I'm any judge, but otherwise good enough to pass muster as a well-used coin. Anything too shiny and new would immediately be suspect. My guess is they're mostly lead and tin, with a small amount of silver added to produce the right colour. There might be a bit of copper as well. I'm no expert in such matters.'

'But a good silversmith might be,' Nicholas said. 'He'd also have access to the necessary metals.'

'He'd also have furnaces for smelting, and the skill to make the stamps for the front and back of the coins. Especially if he was known to be a skilled engraver.'

'Hence the house being left empty,' Nicholas added. 'Buy why keep it furnished?'

'Partly to allay suspicion if anyone managed to get in or look through the windows. Mostly because he'd want to move his machines every so often just in case people grew tired of the tales of ghosts and started to become too curious. Then he could let the place again and move on.'

'So what now?'

'Whoever is behind all this will either want his men back at work or set them to moving everything elsewhere. I've told the children to continue to keep a close watch and let me know the moment they see any signs of renewed activity. Next time, with luck, we'll catch everyone involved inside and hand them over to face the gallows, as they richly deserve.'

14

When he was occupied by an investigation — or, in this case, two — Foxe easily forgot all the other things he should be dealing with. As a result, day-to-day business and household matters, too long set aside, became urgent and caused him unnecessary problems. He therefore took the opportunity of what felt like a natural pause in both his topics of investigation to catch up with less interesting, but no less important, matters.

Regarding the business in Mancroft Yard, the timing of his next step depended on when, and how, whoever was behind the counterfeiting enterprise managed either to restart operations or chose to try to remove what was inside that property to another location. In the case of the murdered Warden of St. Stephen's Hospital, there could be no further progress until book collectors began to respond to Foxe's advertisements in the principle papers and the printed sale catalogues he had sent out.

Foxe therefore turned his thoughts to the futures of the two young men for whom he believed he had some responsibility. He spoke with Charlie about the possibility of learning more of the art of bookbinding. Finding the lad enthusiastic about the idea, Foxe set about making arrangements for him to spend Monday to Thursday with an established bookbinder, returning to help Mrs Crombie on Fridays and Saturdays.

Nicholas was sent to talk with Alderman Halloran about finding a legal position in Norwich. Ever since the dinner party at the alderman's house, Nicholas had talked of little save his desire to find more demanding legal opportunities in Norwich, perhaps in handling the legal affairs of some of the prosperous merchants and bankers who lived there. No mention was made of the chance to call on Miss Maria from time to time, but Foxe would have been a dullard had he not understood the real attraction of a move to the city. Nicholas had also been invited to escort Mrs Halloran and her nieces, while they went walking in Quantrell's Pleasure Gardens, on two occasions now. Since the alderman's wife was no more blind or foolish than Foxe, it was clear that Nicholas's interest in her elder niece was not an unwelcome development.

The young man had no great fortune at present, but would inherit from his grandfather and was heir presumptive to the uncle. The one who had so eagerly welcomed Nicholas's departure when he himself remarried. So far, that union, like his previous one, had not been blessed with any offspring. Moreover, his young wife proved to be somewhat sickly, though tenacious so far in clinging to life through every period of illness. The uncle had also begun to display obvious signs of dropsy. Since he was already in his sixties, he might yet make her a widow before her own ailments proved too much for her. When he died, Nicholas should inherit a house and a small estate, together with a substantial amount of money invested in consols. His uncle had long been a parsimonious man, so his savings would probably represent a goodly sum, even allowing for whatever provision was made for the widow during her lifetime. In time, Nicholas would be an obviously eligible young man, and, if anyone could open doors for him in his legal career it would be Halloran.

Foxe also took time to visit the manager of the theatre, before taking young Kate Sulyard to see him. He'd had his servants help to wash her and dress her in the new clothes he had arranged should be made to replace the gaudy rags which proclaimed her former profession. Clean, well-dressed and with her hair newly arranged under a demure bonnet, Kate was transformed as she walked beside her benefactor to the theatre. There the manager would decide whether she was truly a born actress.

He invited the girl to get up on the stage and say something. There were no nerves. No hesitation or protests that she didn't know what to say. She took to that stage as if it was her own, destined domain, filling the auditorium with a voice loud enough to be heard in every corner. Far from being frightened by the various additional exercises the manager asked her to undertake, she appeared to be enjoying every moment. So much so, that several of the established actors left off what they were doing to gather around and provide her with an audience in embryo.

After that, there could never be any doubt of the outcome. Kate was warmly welcomed into the company. Foxe undertook to pay for her board and lodgings until she was able to earn her own living, as well as paying for reading and elocution lessons, and the matter was sealed. As the manager said afterwards, it was a change for Foxe to be providing the theatre with a new actress, rather than borrowing one for a few nights.

At last, with all these other duties dealt with, Foxe could turn his attention back to his investigations. Letters had begun to arrive from book collectors asking to inspect various of the volumes Foxe was offering for sale. Demand for the titles had already proved lively amongst Foxe's regular customers. These he had already contacted in person. As a result, almost a third of the initial batch of books available had already been sold at more than satisfactory prices. Foxe was an old hand at the game of bargaining. Few people ever managed to convince him to sell them books at prices below those he had determined in advance. That should always be the outcome of the bargaining process. You tried for a higher price and the customer tried for a lower one, then you agree on a figure close to what you knew before you were prepared to sell them for.

So many new enquiries now came that Foxe had to send messages to both the cathedral librarian and Mrs Danson to arrange for him to collect fresh stocks. At the same time, he told them of the sums of money already raised, leaving both of them eager for him to collect all of the books they were willing to sell.

Mrs Danson invited Foxe to take tea with her when he collected more books from her late husband's library. It proved an extremely pleasant occasion for them both. So much so that they stayed talking until the hour for dinner approached. Mrs Danson naturally invited Mr Foxe to stay to dine with her. Foxe politely accepted the invitation. The dinner and more conversation afterwards meant that it was dark by the time Foxe took his leave, so that he had to send for two linkmen to light his way homewards.

On the way, a rough-looking fellow tried to rob this gentleman who was foolish to be out so late. He soon regretted his foolish action. As he threatened Foxe with a knife, the linkman to the rear lunged forward and drove his fist full into the man's face. That allowed a moment for Foxe to extract the small pistol he carried from the pocket of his coat. When the man, now recovered, saw the gun he lunged forward again, only to be thrown back by the discharge of a ball into his shoulder. It was time for him to leave, obviously, and he turned away, clutching his shoulder. The other linkman sent him on his way with a powerful kick on the backside, which sent him sprawling, face down into the mud and filth of the street. The retching and spitting noises they heard as the first linkman spun his rattle to summon a constable showed that the footpad's open mouth had encountered a pile of dung.

'Must be a stranger,' the second linkman said. 'The regular footpads 'ave got more sense. Serve 'im right, if you asks me, Mr Foxe.'

Then, with the wounded robber being led off to the bridewell, Foxe and his escort proceeded calmly on their way.

Sadly, the use of books as bait to discover Pryce-Perkins's night-time visitors was not going to plan. None of the local book purchasers so far had been people unknown to Foxe beforehand; nor had any admitted to knowing Henry Pryce-Perkins. Those from further afield admitted to no earlier links with Norwich at all. By this time, almost all the books had been sold. The few left were not, in Foxe's estimation, very likely to attract the kind of people he was looking for. The late Dr Danson's library had contained many books on magic and similar exotic matters, but many of them were scholastic tomes and deadly dull. Not knowing the subject himself,

Foxe had selected the initial books to list according to age and title. He had clearly gone badly wrong.

During all this activity concerning book sales, word also reached Foxe that fresh events had taken place at Mancroft Yard. The street children reported that two men had arrived, quite openly, at the empty house and had been joined by Holtaway when they went inside. Enquiries later amongst the denizens of that place revealed that one of the two men had been the landlord himself, and the other was Dr. Zabek, a notorious local quack doctor, magician and seller of universal nostrums.

'Zabek came an' exercised the 'ouse,' one of the children explained. 'Wandered round mutterin' spells 'an burnin' bunches of 'erbs and the like.'

'I imagine you mean exorcised,' Foxe said gently.

'Tha's what I said, weren't it?' the child replied indignantly. 'Exercised it — only you speaks more lah-di-dah than I does. Threw out any ghosts an' devils an' such. Only the word is it's goin' to take Zabek at least two more visits to do the job proper, like.'

You couldn't fault Dr. Pietr Onesiphorous Zabek — or Thomas Huggins, as Foxe knew his real name to be — for making the most of the opportunity to earn extra cash.

Two more visits, Foxe reflected. Then a day or so to persuade the frightened men to return to their nightly labours within, or to start to dismantle the stamping machines and move them elsewhere.

Either way, Foxe was determined to be ready for them.

During this second enforced delay, an unexpected development occured which at first seemed to be another setback, rather that the breakthrough it proved to be. Foxe received a message from Mistress Tabby to go to talk to her at once about a young man she'd been asked to treat.

'My conscience has troubled me a good deal in this matter,' Tabby told Foxe, when he arrived later that day. 'The only reason I decided to tell you about this young man is a medical one. If he is truly the one was been mixed up in the death of that girl in Mancroft Yard, I suspect he needs to lighten his conscience by confessing what he's done before he has any hope of recovery.'

Foxe had hurried to Tabby's house as soon as he had got her message. There he had found her in an unusually sombre mood, clearly uncertain whether she was doing the right thing.

'If murder hadn't been involved,' she told him, 'I would have said nothing. I am a healer, not an instrument of the laws of this land, many of which strike me as both unduly harsh and useless for the purpose for which they were passed. In the end, I decided murder can never be condoned or treated lightly. Even so, I need a promise from you before I will speak further about what I know.'

Foxe had never seen Tabby like this. He had always assumed that she was secure in her decisions and thoughts about the world. It was lesser people like himself who fretted and worried about what was best.

'Tabby dear,' Foxe said. 'You know I will do my best to agree if I can, whatever it is you ask of me. I trust you like I trust no one else. If it helps, let me say that I try to serve the ends of justice, tempered by mercy as much as is possible. I am neither the slave of the law, nor blind to its defects.'

'Then you will promise me that, in this case, healing comes first?'

'Without hesitation. But that must include the healing of wrongs done to others as well.'

After a pause, Tabby took up her tale. She had, she told Foxe, been contacted by a woman desperately worried about her son. Apparently, he had told her he worked as a watchman in a large warehouse. He started his work at about ten o'clock at night and finished when the first daytime workers arrived at six next morning. If seemed to be a job which paid him well, so she had swallowed her concerns when he left his previous work with a local whitesmith to take up this role.

Two days previously, very early in the morning, two men had brought him home. According to them, they had found him lying on the ground when they began work. They had no idea what was wrong with him, but they thought it might be a fever or something of that kind. He was shaking all the time and seemed unable to speak. He had also fouled himself.

His mother cleaned him up as best she could, then put him into his bed and tried to keep him warm. For a whole day, he lay like a dead man, saying nothing and refusing to eat or drink. Eventually, she got him to drink some small beer and eat a little bread dipped in milk. He also began to speak again, raving on and on about a ghost he had seen, and how it had come to drag him off to hell and eternal punishment. What this punishment was for he would not say. All he kept assuring his mother was that he hadn't meant to do it. Then he would fall back into a kind of delirium and none of his words would make sense.

'The poor woman is desperately worried,' Tabby said. 'The only thing she could make out in his other ravings is that he thinks he has been cursed. That's why she came to me.'

Throughout her narrative, Foxe's own conscience had been troubling him more and more. All he'd planned to do with his elaborate charade in that house was frighten the men inside into leaving and staying away long enough to allow him to search the place properly. He'd never imagined it could produce such a terrible effect. Kate's performance, coupled with the unexpected storm, had been far more potent than he had intended.

'My guess is that this is the young man we saw in the haunted house that night,' he told Tabby. 'The one who fainted at the sight of young Kate's performance as the ghost. He may thus be the one who killed that poor young woman. If he's telling the truth in his delirium, that was unintentional, which would make it manslaughter rather than murder. Sadly, counterfeiting itself is a capital offence, though he might receive mercy on account of his youth. Do you know how old he is?'

'Seventeen, according to his mother.'

'If it comes to court, I would do my best to see he didn't face the hangman,' Foxe said, 'but the sentence is not in my hands. However, if he is judged to be suffering from madness and unfit to plead, his fate would be far worse. Even death must be preferable to being sent to Bedlam and chained up. If you aren't mad when you arrive at that awful place, just being there will drive you out of your wits in a few weeks.'

'I may be able to convince him he's not cursed and doomed to hell,' Tabby said, 'though that's a job for a parson, not for me. I can certainly give him herbs that will calm him. For the rest, my reason for calling you is simple. If you can, I want you to persuade him to tell you everything. After that, I must rely on your mercy and good sense. If he must face a court of law, so be it.'

Foxe assured her he would do his best. It was probable that this poor young man in fact played a very insignificant part in the business going on at Mancroft Yard. Only the possibility that he had brought about the young woman's death made Foxe believe he had to answer for what he had done.

After more discussion, the two agreed on a course of action. Tabby would go to see the young man and treat him as best she could. Then, if he seemed to be sufficiently recovered, she would tell the mother that her son had to confess what was troubling him so greatly, and that Foxe would be the best person to hear what he had to say. After that, the outcome would depend on what Foxe could learn from talking with him.

###

By now, Foxe was eager to tell Halloran about the things he had discovered in the house at Mancroft Yard. The moment he left Tabby, he therefore hurried to Halloran's house in Colegate hoping to find the alderman at home. It would have been more sensible to have made a proper arrangement. It would also have avoided what proved to be an extra walk and a good deal of wasted time. Not only was the alderman not at home, his butler informed Foxe that the entire family had left to take advantage of the better weather and undertake a short regime of sea bathing at Cromer. The alderman considered it to be a sovereign remedy to ease his periodic attacks of gout. Mrs Halloran and the young ladies had accompanied him for the sake of their general health. The sea at Cromer, being turbid and cold, was considered ideal for the purpose.

Foxe trudged home deflated. He felt he was now entirely blocked from making progress on either of the mysteries facing him. His initial offering of books had failed to produce contact from anyone who might conceivably to part of the group with which Pryce-Perkins had been involved. Notice of the second set of books offered for sale had only just been sent out and the newspaper advertisement would not appear until the weekend. He'd purposely refrained from his normal habit, when selling large numbers of books, of placing discrete announcements in the principal London papers. The collectors he wished to bring into the open had to live in Norwich. Attracting London collectors and dealers would sell the books more quickly but defeat their use as bait.

In addition, his plan to capture all those working in the haunted house was also necessarily in abeyance. That had to wait until he could be sure everyone involved would be inside the house, and that was not yet.

To make matters still worse, it was a close, airless day. The sort of day when smells hang in the air for hours, and are constantly increased by whatever had caused them in the first place. Foxe toiled up the hill beside the castle with his nose filled with the aroma of horse dung, enriched by the scent of sheep pellets liberally scattered by a large flock on its way to the market. There was a little relief when he turned into Cockey Lane, but the Market Place stank almost more than he could ever recall. It's aroma was compounded of horse and cattle dung, blood from the butchers' stalls in the Shambles, human sweat, and offal and fish guts from the many fishmongers' stalls on the west side of the great open space.

Rather than approach that particular stench any closer, Foxe took a diagonal path amongst the stalls. That meant being bombarded with constant attempts by the various stallholders to sell him things, as well as being jostled by persons of every degree, some of whom had plainly avoided soap and water for many months. One especially ragged old man blocked Foxe's pathway and shouted his demands for alms full into Foxe's face. The sight of a mouth filled with rotted stumps of blackened teeth, coupled with a blast of fetid breath mixed with onions, very nearly turned Foxe's stomach completely. The outpouring of oaths and curses that arose when he pushed the beggar out of his way was a small price to pay for the chance to breath fresher air.

By this time, Foxe felt so dispirited he would have rushed into his house to wash his face and hands and change his clothes. What stopped him from doing so was the sight of Mrs Crombie waving from the shop window to attract his attention.

The moment Foxe entered his shop, Mrs Crombie was beside him, bubbling over with excitement and stumbling over her words in her eagerness to tell Foxe what she knew.

'Mr Foxe! Mr Foxe!' she said. 'She's back! Miss Custance is back! Though now I must remember to call her Mrs Benbow. Mrs Lofting told me this morning. She lives almost opposite the Benbows, you understand. She said the former Miss Custance and her new husband arrived back last night, probably from the King's Lynn coach. Young Benbow's parents came out to welcome them and they all went inside.'

'I knew she would return,' Foxe said calmly. 'although she's taken long enough to do so. Do you know where she's staying? I need to talk with her as soon as I can.'

'Apparently, Mrs West and Mrs Starling both saw her this morning making her way from the Benbow house towards her father's place. Sadly, they were too far distant to be able to see what happened when she got there. Do you think he will forgive her?'

'I have no idea,' Foxe replied. 'That's none of my business anyway. My guess is she and her new husband must be staying with the Benbow household for the present. I need to send someone there with a message asking if I may talk with her as soon as possible.'

'Does that prove the poor young woman murdered in that house at the top of Mancroft Yard was her maid?'

'No. Not really, though for the moment I can't imagine who else it could be. It had to be someone who was either given that expensive dress or managed to steal it. Mrs Crombie, why would a young woman give away an almost new dress? Can you tell me that? We'll assume it fitted properly. Otherwise, she'd simply summon the dressmaker to alter it until it did.'

She thought in silence for several moments.

'The only reason I can think of is that she didn't like it.'

'Wouldn't giving it away imply something more than simple dislike?'

Mrs Crombie thought some more.

'You're right, of course, Mr Foxe,' she said. 'She would have chosen the fabric herself and approved the style, all before the dressmaker began. There would then have been several sessions to try it on. Plenty of opportunities then to have it altered if she changed her mind. To be honest, I'm stumped.'

'So am I,' Foxe said. 'However, it's pointless to waste more time on speculation when I hope soon to be able to ask her myself. Was there any other useful gossip? What you've just told me is the only positive thing I've heard today.'

'No, nothing. Everyone has exhausted all the gossip about the two murders. Well, there was one thing. That charlatan Zabek has been telling his audiences how he's been wrestling with the most determined demons in that house. He says he thought he'd sent them packing on his first visit, but when he returned yesterday to be sure, they were back in force. He had to summon up his most powerful spells to throw them out again. After that, he'd sprinkled a potion he sells — "Zabek's Curse Blocker" he calls it — along the window-ledges, on the thresholds and on the hearths. That, he tells people, will keep Satan himself out, let alone some feeble witch's curse or a paltry ghost. I believe he charges two shillings and sixpence for a bottle.'

'And sold a good many yesterday, I don't doubt,' Foxe said, laughing. 'You really have to admire such brazen impudence. Good evening, then, and many thanks for the news of Mrs Benbow.'

Grace Benbow agreed to meet Foxe next morning, but did so with ill-concealed hostility. Foxe thought her pretty enough save for the scowl on her face. Blond hair, a good complexion and a well-proportioned, if stocky, figure. There was enough of a resemblance to the murdered girl to suggest that clothes which fitted one wold look well enough on the other. Were they more or less the same age? The dead girl, as Foxe remembered her, had probably been barely twenty years of age. Grace Benbow, for all the prosperity of her upbringing, looked decidedly older. Maybe twenty-five or even a year or so more.

Mrs Benbow obviously had little time for polite preliminaries. Instead, she launched at once into the attack.

'I only agreed to meet with you because it would have been grossly discourteous to refuse,' she said. 'However, Mr … um … Foxe, was it? If you have come from my father, you had best leave at once. If he now regrets his cruelty and coarse words on the subject of my husband and myself and wishes to make an apology, he can come to me in person to beg forgiveness, not send you as an intermediary.'

The calmness with which Foxe received these angry words should have made Mrs Benbow realise she was barking up the wrong tree.

'I have come on quite another matter, madam,' Foxe replied. 'I can assure you that I have never met your father, nor spoken with him on this or any other subject. Your family business is no concern of mine. I have come to talk to you about a dress.'

'A dress? Since when do fine gentlemen such as yourself concern themselves with dresses?'

'It is a lengthy tale and a sad one,' Foxe said amiably. 'It is also one which may perhaps be related better sitting down, rather than standing before each other like prize-fighters about to start trading blows.'

Mrs Benbow was clearly startled by Foxe's words and suddenly, even painfully, aware of the impolite manner with which she had treated him so far. Perhaps there had, after all, been some truth in her father's recent description of her as having the manners of a workman. That she also had the morals of an alley-cat she rejected fiercely.

She at once invited Foxe to be seated and called for a servant to bring coffee. Then, all hostility forgotten and now seeming both younger and more curious than perplexed, she asked Foxe to explain what he had meant.

'I believe that shortly before you left your father's house,' Foxe began, 'you gave one of your dresses to someone. It that correct?'

'Certainly. I gave it to my maid, Annie Beechey.'

'May I ask you why you did that? I believe it was quite new and made of expensive cloth. Not very suitable garb for a servant.'

'You seem uncommonly interested in this matter, Mr Foxe,' Grace Benbow said. 'I can only imagine that Annie has got herself into some kind of trouble and, finding the dress in her possession, you have assumed it had been stolen. I assure you it was not. My father demanded that I should have that dress made. He wanted me to wear it when we attended the upcoming Mayor's Ball, intending that a certain gentleman of his acquaintance should see me and decide that I would make him a most suitable wife. Mr Custance, I fear, had aspirations to see me marry into the gentry, aspirations which I in no way shared. I told him whom I wished to marry, but my husband, though at least his equal as a tradesman, was not good enough in his eyes. He forbade him the house and tried to force me to wed against my inclinations. That dress, though it suited me well and was, as you said, of superior quality, came to represent in my mind all the unpleasantness and misery I had suffered for refusing to obey my father. You may think I could have defied him anyway, since I am four-and-twenty years of age, but I knew that if I tried to wed in this city, he would hear of it and be sure to come and spoil the occasion in any way he could.'

'So you and your husband-to-be ran away,' Foxe said.

'Left in secret, rather, since my husband's family have been in favour of the marriage from the start. We went only as far as King's Lynn, where I stayed in the house of an acquaintance of the Benbow family for the time necessary to fulfil the terms of the bishop's special licence and establish residency in the parish. We were then married and spent a few days longer travelling to Ely to see that ancient city and its magnificent cathedral. We returned to Lynn, before coming back here. I never expected Annie to wear that dress herself, but it should have been worth a good amount if sold. She was my only friend in my last weeks at home and I had no money to give her. My father did not believe in generosity or in giving me a personal allowance. Anything I wanted, I had to ask him for. Then, if he agreed, he would give me the exact amount and demand that I show him my purchase afterwards.'

'I'm afraid it looks as if this Annie Beechey did wear the dress, though in strange and most unhappy circumstances. It was found on the body of a young woman cruelly murdered in an empty house at the top of Mancroft Yard.'

This news struck Grace Benbow with the force of a speeding coach. She stared at Foxe, open-mouthed, then burst into questions.

'But … But … why was she in such a place? What business had she there? I cannot believe it! Poor Annie. I told her to leave a day or so before I did. I even wrote her an excellent character. I knew my father would have dismissed her at once with no character to help her find fresh employment. But … murdered! I cannot … will not … believe even he would stoop so low.'

Then she burst into helpless tears.

As she was struggling to recover herself, waving away the maidservant who had rushed in at the sound of crying and directed furious looks at Mr Foxe, a fresh question obviously arose in her mind.

'Was that … Was that what my father was raving about last night? Was that why the magistrate came to this house earlier and demanded to see me along with my husband? They thought I had been murdered?'

'Your father certainly did,' Foxe told her. 'Since it took time for the news of the death to reach him, the body had already been buried. Fortunately, the dress had been kept by the clerk to the coroner's court. That, and the description of the murdered woman given by the surgeon who examined the body, were enough. He at once instigated a prosecution against the man you have married on a charge of wilful murder.'

'All is now explained,' Grace Benbow said, 'including his wild accusations that my husband and I had contrived to make him appear a fool. No happiness that I was still alive and well, you note. Not a word of relief on that count. Oh no! Just anger that he had been proved mistaken.'

'I saw the poor woman myself,' Foxe said 'shortly after she had been found. Various people know I have sometimes been able to bring criminals to justice, so I was called to the house before the body was removed. I was convinced from the start that the dead women had been a servant. Her hands told me as much. She may have been wearing fine clothes, but she was never a lady. I guessed she must either have been given that dress or stolen it somehow. It looked as if it had never been worn before.'

'It hadn't,' Grace Benbow agreed. 'And this poor, murdered woman looked like me?'

'There was a definite resemblance,' Foxe sad. 'Quite enough for the description given by the surgeon to have convinced your father. I believe he had even applied to the church authorities to have the body exhumed and transferred to the family plot. I would have told him of my doubts on the matter, but it was made clear to me that my interference was unwelcome.'

'That was typical of the man. Few men are as stiff-necked and reluctant to admit their mistakes as Mr Custance. Will you please describe the woman as you saw her, Mr Foxe? There is a great mystery here. I doubt that Annie Beechey could have managed to fit into that dress.'

'It was a woman of about your years, or slightly younger,' Foxe said, treading warily. 'Blond hair, blue eyes, a good complexion. Much the same height as you, I imagine, and possessed of a good figure. What convinced me she was a servant were her hands, which showed signs of hard work, and her countenance which I judged too coarse to admit of being what the dress proclaimed her to be.'

'I see you are accomplished and experienced in judging members of the opposite sex, Mr Foxe,' Grace said, smiling for the first time. 'She may indeed have been a servant, but she was definitely not Annie Beechey. Annie is nearly thirty years of age, shorter than me and a good deal plumper, and her hair is almost black. If it was indeed my dress, as my father clearly believed, I have no notion how this poor girl came to be wearing it.'

'Could he have been mistaken?'

'Oh no! He supervised every stage in its completion personally. If he said it was my dress, that's what it was without doubt. Annie must already have sold it. When did the killing take place?'

'On the night of the day you left home,' Foxe said. 'How long before that did you give Annie your dress?'

'But one day. Could she indeed have sold it, and this woman purchased it, in that brief space of time?'

'It might be possible. I came here expecting the mystery of the identity of the murdered woman to be solved. Now, instead, I have another one.'

15

Foxe walked home after his meeting with Grace Benbow in a thoughtful mood. The information she had been able to give him had thrown his plans for tracking down the murderer at Mancroft Yard in complete disarray. There was, perhaps, a certain satisfaction in confirming who the victim had *not* been, but it was a meagre return for a morning's effort. And, though he now knew Annie Beechey was still alive, her former mistress had no idea of her whereabouts. Given the passage of time since she left the Custance household, the maid may already have been able to secure fresh employment in the city or outside. All Grace Benbow had been able to suggest was that she thought Alice's parents lived in a yard somewhere in King Street. One with "a funny name like Messing."

It was not even as if he didn't have a great many other matters in front of him. Set in with the rest, Foxe told himself, confirming the dead girl's name and story was unlikely to take things much further. He wouldn't ignore it though. To leave loose ends gave Foxe great offence. Instead he would recruit extra help to follow up that part of the search, while he turned back to more substantial matters.

It took Foxe only a slight diversion from his homeward-bound route to bring him to the theatre. There he sought out the manager and asked if he might borrow the services of Richard and Jeremy for a few days. Foxe had first brought them to the theatre, since when the two had proved to be a most substantial asset to the place, saving the manager considerable effort and reducing his anxiety to a level which was manageable. He was therefore hardly likely to deny Foxe's request. The two young men were sent for immediately and presented themselves at the manager's office within a few moments.

While Richard and Jeremy were indeed separate people, it was quite impossible not to see the pair as a single entity in all practical terms. Call one and they both came. Seek out one and you would find the other as well. Within the theatre, people referred to them as the twins. No one knew whether they were actually twins, or just brothers, or perhaps lovers. Nor was their surname — or surnames — known to anyone; assuming they shared a family name, or had ever had one of their own different from the other's. Foxe had never known them as anything but Richard and Jeremy, not even in the days when they lived amongst the street children. They simply were, and always had been, inseparable.

They stood before Foxe now, smiling as they listened to the manager, who said he had been asked by Mr Foxe — indicating him by a theatrical sweep of the hand — to allow them to assist him. Since there were no performances for the moment, he had agreed. Was this acceptable to them also? That was met with vigorous nods of both heads.

A meaningful glance from Foxe now sent the manager out of the room. At once the atmosphere changed as "the twins" rushed forward to pump Foxe's hand and express their joy at seeing him again. It was he who had rescued them from life on the streets, when they were only thirteen or fourteen. He had secured them steady employment at the theatre as general hands, progressing to becoming scene-shifters and handymen as they grew and their muscles developed. Now, some six years later, they were sturdy young men, both a little below average height, but more than capable of taking on almost any tasks requiring strength and precision. They were quiet, respectful and quick to learn. Indeed, on some occasions they had even played walk-on parts, just as long as they could remain together. There was another reason they could not be parted. Jeremy was a deaf-mute, unable to speak or hear the loudest sounds. Over the years, with Richard's tireless help, he had learned simple lip-reading, but for the most part he relied entirely on Richard to act as his ears and mouth. Between them, they communicated by a series of rapid gestures of eyes, lips and fingers, impossible for any outsider to understand. Indeed, so quick and unobtrusive were the movements that many people refused to believe that some form of telepathy wasn't involved.

Foxe now told them what he wanted them to do, while Richard listened intently, flickering his fingers constantly as he conveyed Foxe's requirements to Jeremy. They were to seek out Annie-Beechey, starting by discovering where her family lived and asking them. Once they had found her, they were to question her, then follow the trail of the dress she had been given, starting with the dealer to whom she had sold it. With luck, the dealer would be able to tell them enough to let them locate the purchaser. They should not approach whoever it proved to be. Foxe would do that — assuming she was still living. They were to return and tell Foxe the exact sequence of events, from the point where Annie was first given the dress, to the person who had last bought it. He would give them each three shillings now, to make up for the loss of their wages from the theatre, with three more if they brought him the information he needed.

In truth, they would have done it all for nothing, had Foxe asked them, but he had learned long ago that to presume on someone's gratitude for past favours usually led to problems in the future. Foxe was always generous with his money. That way, no one ever felt taken for granted or reluctant to help him again, should he need it.

With that task completed and the twins eager to start on what he had set them to do, Foxe returned home in good spirits. Once again, his cousin Nicholas was abroad in the city on some business of his own and not expected to return until late in the afternoon. By this time, Foxe's curiosity about what his cousin was doing had become intense. However, he reminded himself sternly that Nicholas was a visitor and an adult, not a child who must account for his absences and actions. He would doubtless explain all when he was ready. Until then, Foxe would continue to need to exercise the virtue he found hardest and least pleasant – patience.

###

The next morning, while taking breakfast with Nicholas, Foxe's hopes and sense of progress were further heightened by a message which came from a Mr Gamaliel Ransome, saying he wished to examine certain of the books he understood Mr Foxe was offering for sale. He might be interested in several volumes now and perhaps more in the future, should Foxe have more to offer. He also explained that he had been commissioned to act on behalf of a group of gentlemen of similar interests. Then he ended the note by saying he had told the messenger to wait for a reply, and hoped it would be possible to present himself at noon that day.

Foxe told Alfred to tell the messenger that it would be entirely convenient to meet at noon, as requested. Then, to Nicholas's great amusement, he rose from the table and danced a jig on the hearth rug, singing "The fish are biting! The fish are biting!" in a very respectable tenor.

'Are you certain, cousin Ashmole?' Nicholas asked, once the jig was over and Foxe had explained the reason for his glee. 'Might not this be another approach by people you have dealt with before; and the mention of further purchases merely added to induce you to lower your prices in the hope of more sales to come?'

'O ye of little faith,' Foxe responded. 'Do you think I would not recall a man with the preposterous name of Gamaliel Ransome? This is what I have been waiting for. I feel it in by bones. I am as certain of it as I am that you are sitting there acting the part of a sceptical lawyer. Now, I fear I shall need to see this gentleman on my own and in private. You do not startle the mouse whose nose is already sniffing the cheese in the trap — '

'Have no fear, cousin,' Nicholas said. 'I have several matters to attend to and will probably be out for most of the day. Mrs Halloran has once again invited me to escort herself and Miss Maria on an afternoon walk in Quantrell's Gardens. Miss Lucy, I understand must stay behind for her flute lesson.'

Foxe merely nodded, careful not to reveal his satisfaction at discovering the probable cause of Nicholas's frequent absences.

Sadly, Gamaliel Ransome failed to live up to the exotic nature of his name. Foxe had a vague notion that Gamaliel had been some kind of Hebrew rabbi. This Gamaliel, however, looked more like a prosperous publican. He had red hair, a snub nose, and pale, watery eyes, and his stature indicated a lengthy period of good living. Not only that, his manner of dress was that curious blend of the conventional and the unusual which denotes men who wish to appear dashing, yet lack the courage to depart too far from the norm .

Foxe had decided in advance that the best way to deal with him would be to treat him as a normal customer, while staying alert to any remark which might provide an opportunity to bring up the killing of Pryce-Perkins He brought out the books Mr Ransome said were of interest to him and talked easily about the beauty of their bindings, the unusual nature of the typeface used in some of them, or the venerable age of the edition, exactly as he would with any other customer. Foxe represented each book as a once-in-a-lifetime opportunity for the discerning collector. Mr Ransome responded as most customers did. He wrinkled his nose in apparent disgust, discovered flaws on all sides, and hinted that he knew of all manner of booksellers elsewhere who were offering superior versions at far lower prices.

Thus it went on until Foxe began to fear that he would make no sales, and that nothing short of a series of direct and probing questions was going to reveal the hoped-for link to the group who had been seen to visit Rev Henry Pryce-Perkins by night.

The breakthrough came when Foxe brought out one of the only two books in the group chosen which had come from the cathedral. *The Tractatus Hermeticus et Gnosticus Aegyptorum* was a small, undistinguished volume. It was bound in cracked and soiled vellum and printed with such lack of skill that it would be hard to read. That is always provided that anyone would be willing to work through its two hundred and more pages of closely spaced text. It had apparently been printed in Padua in 1506, though even the date was hard to make out. Foxe had it in his mind to ask perhaps a guinea for the wretched thing. He then expected to be bargained down to fifteen shillings or even less.

When he saw this sorry volume, Mr Ransome's face lit up with every appearance of joy.

"*The Tractatus!*' he exclaimed. 'I can scarcely believe it. We were resigned to losing all access to it when our dear Brother Henry died. The copy he had borrowed from the cathedral library looked very much like this. It was also, so far as we all knew, the only accessible and complete volume in England. It is priceless, Mr Foxe. Priceless! We tried to purchase the cathedral's copy, but that proved hopeless. They would not sell. They were also so reluctant to allow their copy to be borrowed, that Brother Henry told us he had been forced to give a most solemn undertaking to return it, undamaged, within two weeks. If he failed to comply, he would be banned from using the library ever again. Our gratitude to him for obtaining it for us to examine knew no bounds! Yet here, in my own hands there is a copy offered for sale! I still cannot fully believe it.'

'The price must reflect its rarity and importance,' Foxe said smoothly.

'That I quite understand,' Ransome replied. 'We are not wealthy men, Mr Foxe, but we will be willing to raise a substantial amount between us, if only it is not offered as a price entirely beyond our reach.'

In an instant, Foxe decided to respond exactly as if he had known all this from the start. Mr Ransome had already said enough to prove that he and his group had dealings with Pryce-Perkins in the recent past. Those dealings were either entirely innocent, as he was starting to suspect, or this man was possessed of an amazing level of cunning to skirt around the whole matter of murder as if it were of no importance whatsoever.

'It may be rather more expensive that you imagine, Mr Ransome. I had half a mind not to bring it out, suspecting that only the wealthiest of my customers could hope to acquire it. As you say, it is uncommonly rare. I have never seen another copy.'

This latter statement was completely true, though Foxe suspected that the other copies, however few in number, had been thrown away as worthless.

'Indeed, Mr Foxe. That must be the case. "*The Egyptian Explanation of Gnostic Hermeticism*". Could there be a better subject to those, like us, interested in seeking higher knowledge, far beyond the childish stories and platitudes of religions designed for the masses? This book is transforming, Mr Foxe. A distillation of the ancient wisdom that the Catholic Church sought to eradicate for ever by branding it heresy. We ourselves would not have understood its vital importance without the guidance of Brother Henry'.

'He had met it before?' Foxe asked, trying to keep his words as innocent as possible.

'I doubt it, sir, for all his great learning and studies on the topic of those areas of knowledge condemned as heretical by the early church. He knew of it certainly. But I seem to recall that he said something of his amazement and elation when he found a copy in the cathedral library. I will need to consult my brothers in our lodge, but I feel confident we could raise at least one hundred guineas. If that might prove enough.'

The concern on the Ransone's face made Foxe feel he would be ashamed to take advantage of these men's delusions to the tune of such a huge amount.

'Let me take a few days to consult the person for whom I am acting, Mr Ransome. If you are willing to tell me a little more about your lodge and what it does, I might be able to secure a lower price for people like yourselves, who would cherish it and appreciate its real worth. Knowledge is beyond price, Mr Ransome. It must not be sullied by crude attempts to use it for mere monetary gain.'

'You never spoke truer words, Mr Foxe. I will tell you whatever you wish to know about our lodge. We are not a secret society. If we take modest pains to remain hidden from the majority, it is only to avoid the approbrium and ignorant prejudice we would face otherwise.'

'Why should that be, sir?'

'Simply because we chose to reject all orthodox religion in favour of something more lofty and spiritual. The teachings of Thrice-Great Hermes have been known and studied since the days of the Pharaohs. It was only when the Jewish people sought to be rid of their Roman conquerors that they turned to the notion of a divinely-inspired leader; a messiah who would lead them in the longed-for uprising to secure freedom and salvation.

'These understandable, if misguided ideas, were taken up by the followers of one of these supposed messiahs. They began to translate them into something universal, far away from the struggle for Jewish freedom from the Romans. The ancient tribal god of the Jews had been modelled on the tyrants of Persia, complete with demands for total obedience, without questioning of any kind. It was this notion, translated from a struggle against the chains of slavery, which became a supernatural need for salvation from the chains of sin. The heavenly tyrant remained, along with a saviour messiah, who could abate his murderous wrath against all who disobeyed his edicts. His — '

'All most interesting I'm sure, Mr Ransome.' Foxe was starting to believe the man was quite capable of talking on the topic for many hours. 'So your group — you and your colleagues — are scholars of ancient philosophy. Not either magicians or alchemists?'

'Heavens, no! Those matters are as much based on ignorant superstition as today's religions.'

'Wasn't it odd that a minister of the established church was interested enough in such matters? Interested enough to become an active member of your lodge?'

'He was forced to join the church by his family, he told us His father might be counted amongst the nobility, but he was weighed down with almost insupportable debts. All the result of generations of arrogant display on the surface and every kind of corruption and excess beneath. There was not even sufficient wealth for the heir to pay off more than a small fraction of what was owed. Yet the family pride was such that most forms of making a living were ruled out. Only the military and the church were deemed acceptable. The middle brother was sent to sea and, fortunately, proved to have a talent for nautical matters. Brother Henry had no interest in anything save reading and study. He was therefore told he was to join the church, where he could do both to his heart's content while supported by the tithes of a suitable rectory. Should he suddenly discover a taste for more sensible pursuits, he could use his connections and the lustre of the family name to secure a suitable bishopric. Indeed, to do any less would confirm his family's opinion of him as a worthless member, best not spoken about.'

Foxe nodded his head. 'So all you do is study this ancient wisdom. May I ask to what end?'

'It is an end in itself, Mr Foxe. It enriches our lives. Nothing else is needed.'

'I was told your Brother Henry received secretive visitors by night. That's what a witness said at the inquest. He described these visitors as being "some sort of freemasons". I take it that, by that description, he meant to suggest a secret group who would not want their activities known.'

'What nonsense!' Mr Ransome said, giving way to a healthy burst of belly laughs. 'If we went by night, it was because all of us have to earn out livelihood by day. I am a cloth-dyer, Mr Foxe. Others are also involved in the cloth trade. Then there are grain and coal merchants, a maltster, two shoemakers and members of several other trades. We went in the dark because the sun sets early in autumn and winter.'

'You know that Pryce-Perkins was murdered?'

'Sadly, that is so. We are all hoping his killer is soon brought to justice. Why he should have suffered such a fate, I have no idea. He was a man of peace, as we all are. All we could imagine was that someone, learning of our interests, so misconstrued them as to believe he was involved in some form of satanic worship. Yet even that is surely no excuse for murder, is it? I fear human aggression and human ignorance have long been close companions. Do you not agree?'

There it was. Foxe's single hope of finding some reason for Pryce-Perkins's murder in his membership of a secret society had gone. The worst that could be said of these people was that they were misguided and gullible. They were clearly not murderers. In an odd kind of way, Foxe felt their naïve belief in ancient mysteries touchingly eccentric. It was about as far removed from witchcraft and sorcery as you could get.

By the time Mr Ransome left, he had purchased four books for the total sum of three pounds, sixteen shillings and eightpence. Foxe had also determined, inwardly, that the longed-for *Tractatus* should be handed over for the sum of ten guineas, the remainder having been paid by an imaginary benefactor on hearing something of the group and its aims. He was only willing to charge that much because the bulk would go to the cathedral library, His own commission of twenty-one shillings he would use to pay for reading books for those street children who wished to become literate.

###

Foxe had instructed the servants at Halloran's house to let him know the moment the alderman and his party arrived home from Cromer. The next morning, therefore, a message came that they had arrived home at around dinner time the previous day. The alderman had an appointment with the mayor that morning. He was now expected to return at around one o'clock.

At one-thirty, Foxe's carriage drew up outside the house in Colegate and Foxe hurried to use the knocker to announce his arrival.

Alderman Halloran seemed fit and rested after his few days away with the family. He responded to his visitor's polite enquiry about the sea-bathing with a wry smile.

'I'm not sure that the word pleasant is the best one to use of sea-bathing, Foxe. Up early in the morning to drink a large glass of foul, salty water from the waves. Then a period of being expected to jump, stark-naked, from the steps of the bathing machine into six or seven feet of swirling, icy water, after which a couple of burly attendants repeatedly hold you under until you fear you are going to drown. The best part is being wrapped in dry towels, while the horse drags the machine back up the beach. Somehow your feel warmer than you ought to and your skin tingles all over. After a light meal, you must then take a bracing walk along the cliffs, often in a freezing wind. Even on warmer days than we have been having, the German Ocean manages to be deuced cold. However, you didn't rush here to talk about the joys of sea-bathing. Have you ever tried it, by the way?'

'Certainly not!' Foxe replied vigorously. 'If I need to get exercise and tingle all over while naked, I prefer the method that involves a warm bed and a naughty woman.'

'Of course,' Halloran laughed. 'I should have known that. Have you caught Rev Pryce-Perkins's killer yet?'

'Unfortunately, I'm beginning to feel I'm not going to succeed there.' Foxe had now lost his grin and his jaunty manner. 'My last hope was to find the group the old men said had visited him in secret. The ones Benjamin Gunton called "something like freemasons, only different".'

'Did you find them?'

'The day before yesterday. I think I could best describe their representative, Mr Gamaliel Ransome, as a frustrated preacher, and the group as a whole, as he described them, as deluded but harmless eccentrics, enlivening their humdrum lives with thoughts of hidden wisdom handed down from antiquity. They met in the evening because all have businesses to run during the day. It was dark because of the time of year. They try not to attract attention because their beliefs are heretical, even exotic, and they wish to avoid censure and ridicule. No other reasons. When I was silly enough to ask Mr Ransome to describe their beliefs, I had to stem the outpouring after a few minutes, or risk being preached at for several hours. They are undoubtedly earnest, but not dangerous to anything save their own sanity. They are as puzzled by Pryce-Perkins's murder as anyone else.'

'So did they meet for some sort of worship?' Halloran asked.

'Not even that. From what I gathered, Pryce-Perkins invited them to his house to act as an appreciative audience, while he displayed the depth and extent of his learning in matters of the supposed hidden wisdom of the ancients. As the only genuine scholar amongst them — certainly the only one with an expensive university education — he had become their natural leader.'

'An odd activity for an Anglican clergyman surely? To lead a group devoted to pagan and heretical beliefs. What was he doing?'

'That's my problem,' Foxe said. 'I'm certain the clue to the mystery must lie somewhere in Pryce-Perkins's activities and character. Yet so far my picture of the man is still far too vague.

The pensioners seem merely to have regarded him as yet another in a long line of young priests kicking their heels at St. Stephen's until something better came along. The librarian only knew him as a habitué of the library, with an odd interest in books on the restricted-access shelves. Even that chatterbox Oliver Lakenhurst, the bishop's secretary, knew little but superficial gossip — when I could stop him talking about himself and how much the bishop relied upon him in all matters. I'm never going to understand where to look for the killer without knowing a good deal more about the victim.'

'You need to talk to the dean,' Halloran said. 'Nothing moves or breathes in or around the cathedral without our dean knowing about it. He's the true power in the place. The bishop merely comes and goes, between spending long periods at court and occupying his seat in the House of Lords. Ask the dean if he will speak with you. I assure you he'll already know all about your activities at St. Stephen's Hospital.'

'I will,' Foxe said. 'However, none of this is what I came here to tell you. My immediate concern is that house at the head of Mancroft Yard. The one where the young woman's body was found.'

'Are you still meddling with that, Foxe? I thought I'd asked you not to let yourself be sidetracked? That is surely insignificant compared with keeping the mayor and the bishop happy. Besides, wasn't it all some sort of misunderstanding? The girl had merely eloped, not come to any physical harm.'

'Yet there was still a body. A woman died in that house, murdered, even though it wasn't the one it was expected to be. I can't forget that. However, the most important point at the moment is that I've found the house is being used for the purpose of counterfeiting large numbers of silver coins. Someone has set up two coin-stamping machines in the attics. I believe the tale about the place being haunted was invented to keep curious people away.'

'Good God!' Halloran exclaimed. 'Yet another wretched counterfeiter in our midst! It doesn't seem to be long since you found a similar criminal. Is the whole city infested with them? The mayor will be distraught. Not only is that loathsome business a capital offence, it ruins a city's reputation, destroys trust in monetary transactions, and undermines everyone's business. Do you know who is behind this outbreak?'

'I don't know the identities of the ones who are doing the work — save one, that is. Nor am I quite sure yet of who is the actual organiser on a practical basis. I do know that the house is said to be owned by Richard Hatchard, the goldsmith and jeweller. He's been deliberately keeping the place unlet since the last tenant died, and that's almost eighteen months ago. It looks to me as if he must be up to his neck in this business. He has access to precious metals, to forges and to the knowledge of how to produce various alloys. I also believe he's known as a skilled engraver. It's perfect! He has to be the person behind this enterprise. We'll capture all the actual workers, and the supervisor I hope, in a night raid on the house. Someone is bound to talk under interrogation, if only to try to bargain for his life. That will give us the information we need to arrest Hatchard as well — assuming he isn't already in our hands.'

Foxe stopped. Partly because he needed to take a proper breath, but mostly because he could sense the alderman's rising impatience. What was wrong? He had abundant evidence already. All that was required to strike a mighty blow for good government.

'Whoa!' Halloran said. 'Not so fast. I think someone had been trying to mislead you. The man you are thinking of is Robert Hatchard, not Richard. I've never heard Hatchard had as much as a single cousin. But there's a bigger problem in your tale. Robert Hatchard is dead. He died some six months ago of a sudden apoplexy. I believe he was somewhere about sixty years of age, so it may not have been a complete surprise. If probate has been granted, as I would imagine it must have by this time, his widow will now own all his assets, including that house you are talking about.'

'Dead?'

'Undoubtedly. The widow, I'm told, has persuaded a family friend to keep everything going, managing the business on her behalf until she can find a buyer. There's also a younger man working there who happens to be a fairly skilled engraver. I've no doubt she will sell the business and everything else before long. If she hasn't done so already, it's because her husband's death was a great shock coming as it did, so suddenly. She'll have needed to cope with all the formalities and try to keep the place active so she can sell it as a going concern. You'll have to look elsewhere for the man behind the counterfeiting.

Poor Foxe! He was totally deflated, robbed of what he had planned as a moment of triumph. Why hadn't he checked about Hatchard, instead of accepting what he had been told at face value? Now he was even more determined than before to catch everyone inside that house and wring the truth out of them.

For a while after Foxe returned home, the mood of dejection remained. Then he reflected that nothing had been lost. The alderman had readily agreed to arrange for him to have three constables available when the raid on the house should take place, so that all within could be duly arrested. Only his pride had been dented and that might swiftly be repaired.

Soon he began to grin to himself. Halloran had gone to Cromer to restore his sense of well-being through the health-giving properties of sea water. He had spoken with pleasurable recall of the exciting tingling which had spread through his body in the immediate aftermath of each dipping. It was time for Foxe to recall what he had said in response and seek out the same feelings of ecstatic warmth. After dinner, he would summon two linkmen and go to the place Mistress Tabby had recommended. The attending girls there should do for him what the dippers had done for Halloran in the surf. That would soon put his world back to rights!

16

Foxe spent the next day making the arrangements for the descent on the house at Mancroft Yard. He wanted to be completely ready as soon as word reached him that the men working there had resumed their nocturnal activities. He felt sure that whoever was in charge and arranging the supposed exorcisms would want that to be as soon as possible.

His activities during the early afternoon were interrupted by Bart, who had been sent with an urgent request that Foxe should accompany him to a tenement in the area of Oak Street, close to the River Wensum. Many merchants and traders had their premises there, the river providing excellent access for goods moving in and out. On the surface, the place appeared busy and prosperous. However, many of its large buildings shared the timber framing, with wattle or brick infill, characteristic of construction techniques two and three hundred years earlier. It was also an area best avoided at night, since the commercial premises were usually deserted after dark, their owners having long since moved into fine modern mansions, where the air was free from the fumes from dye-works and the streets less fouled with all the signs of busy horse traffic.

Many of the properties along Oak Street had been built with long, narrow gardens to the rear. As the prosperous owners had moved away, these gardens had been filled with sheds and small workshops. Others, like Bedlam Yard to which Bart now led Foxe, had been filled with mean, poorly constructed dwellings and any larger properties left standing converted into a warren of tenements. The yard had acquired its name, people said, from a tavern called *The Bess of Bedlam*, perhaps in commemoration of some ancient church or chapel dedicated to St. Elizabeth, coupled with a reference to the noise and chaos of the area when it had been one of the principal locations for business of all sizes.

The tavern was now long gone, but part of the building it had once occupied remained, along with a narrow entry into the yard behind. Bedlam Yard itself proved to be filthy, deprived of light and air by tall buildings all around, and clearly crowded with some of the poorest families in the City. As Foxe and Bart entered, they found themselves surrounded by dirty, ill-nourished children, some of them nearly naked, who had been playing in what small open area remained. Their mothers sat on doorsteps, smoking short pipes and exchanging gossip. A more unwholesome and slatternly covey of women Foxe thought he had ever seen. His recollection of the perfumed, lovely young ladies of the bordello the night before almost convinced him that these must be females of an entirely different species.

Tabby was sitting outside on a bench, along with a scrawny, undernourished youth whom she introduced as Tom Dancie. Foxe recognised him at once. He was clearly the young man who had been first down the stairs on the night when Kate Sulyard had given her performance as the tortured spirit of the murdered girl.

'Tom lives in the cottage behind us, if you can call it a cottage,' Tabby said. 'He looks after his mother, who has the lung disease. I give her what I can to ease her, but she can never improve while she lives in such foetid, airless conditions as these. I won't ask you to go inside. We'll stay here in what passes for the open air. Pull up that old barrel to sit on. Bart will keep us safe. No one would dare to attack me, but the sight of a well-dressed gentleman like yourself might be too much for them. The coins in your purse would represent untold wealth to these wretched folk and your clothes could also be sold for a good amount.'

Foxe did as he was told, though not without some nervous glances about him at the dark spaces behind several open doors. Who knew who might even now be casting murderous glances in his direction. He tried to settle his nerves as Tabby continued speaking.

'Tom has been suffering terrible nightmares since that night in Mancroft Yard and has been unable to work. He believes he is under a curse, with the result that he is scarcely sane at the moment. I have done what I can to calm him, but he is tortured by guilt. I therefore told him I would call a gentleman who is a powerful force for good in this city. A man who has overcome the forces of evil many times and will know best how to drive the devils from his brain.'

All the while, she looked intently at Foxe, willing him to join in this elaborate charade.

'I also explained that you might be able to find a way to protect him and his mother from the full fury of the law. Tom is only sixteen. Nevertheless, he is certain he will soon be tracked down by the constables and taken off to be hanged. Without him, his mother would surely starve, if the lung disease didn't take her first. She is so wasted already that she couldn't even go on the streets to earn a few pence for a crust of bread.'

Foxe nodded wisely, more to show Tabby that he had received her message and would act on it, than for any other reason.

'Tom,' he said to the boy. 'I believe I can help you, but only if you tell me everything about what has brought this curse upon you. Hold nothing back. I have been searching into the dark vibrations I see in the air around you all the time that Mistress Tabby has been speaking. What I see is a darkened house, with stairs going down to the front hall. It is lit only by the candle you are carrying. Then I see another light, and a ghostly face, and hear the cackling of demons. Then it all goes black.'

Tom's face was now showing nothing but astonishment.

'That's it! That's it!' he cried, shaking all over. 'That was 'er. The girl I killed. 'Er ghost come to take revenge, bringin' the devils o' hell to carry me off to Satan's clutches! But I never meant to do it! I never did! 'Twas only to try to stop her yellin' so loud and wakin' the neighbourhood.

"Go down and see what that noise is, Tom," 'e says to me. So I went an' found her and ... I didn't mean to do it. Honest I didn't, but I had to. So I tells 'im and 'e says 'e'll go an' see. "I did what I said and made all right", he says to me after. "She'll never go running to the constables to get you into trouble. She's gone." Weren't true though, were it? She come back an' he sends me down again, even though I be terrified. Can't you do it I says to 'im? "No, 'e says, I'm needed here. That's your job. Make sure you gets it right this time. I can't always be cleanin' up your messes like afore." That's what 'e said to me.'

'Who said this? When?' Foxe asked quietly. Everything was pouring out in a jumble and it was hard to make head or tail of what Tom was saying. 'Who sent you downstairs?'

'Mr J, weren't it. I didn't want to go! Not after the last time. I tells 'im can't do it. But 'e made me. Said 'e'd beat me cruel if I didn't, and 'ave me an' me mum turned out onto the street. I 'ad to go then, didn't I? An' she puts a curse on me. Calls mea murderer. Brings the devils to drag me down into the pit. I must 'ave fainted, 'cos I woke up lying in the churchyard up against a cross. 'Twas that cross what saved me. But she won't give up. Every night she comes, pointing 'er finger at me and callin' me a murderer. An' all the devils too! For God's sake, Mister, 'elp me! Else I'm doomed to be taken to hell.'

Slowly and painfully, interspersed with many tears and cries of lamentation, Foxe extracted the full story of what had happened that first night in Mancroft Yard.

It had been a normal night at the start. The same as the previous four or five times they had come to that house. They didn't come every night. Mr Holtaway passed the word when they were to assemble, generally from Tuesday to Friday, then a break. This was the second Tuesday.

They would arrive separately, creeping as silently as possible through the arch and round to the back. I had been a fine, moonlit night, though rather warm for the time of year. He'd hoped they could leave early, siince his mother was not at all well. It all depended on the number of coin blanks. At the start of a week, there would be plenty, so they would work steadily until just before dawn. By the time Friday came, they might only have enough left for two hours or less.

- 183 -

Mr J brought all the blanks at the start of each week. He would count them out carefully. So many sixpences, so many shillings and florins, a small number of crowns. Mr J said gold coins were too hard to dispose of, and coppers weren't worth the time and money they took to make. At the end of the week, he would return and count the coins they'd made. The two numbers had to match exactly. No pilfering. Any blanks which had been mis-struck or otherwise damaged had to be handed over at the same time. Between visits, coins and blanks were kept in a small safe in the same attic as the stamping machines.

The three of them, himself, Frank Horne and Sam Colman, were usually in place and ready to start by around a quarter to midnight. Along with Mr Holtaway, of course. He didn't do much. Fancied himself as a kind of supervisor, wandering about and offering unwanted advice. Occasionally, when they were really busy and dawn was getting close, he'd do a bit of fetching and carrying, but nothing else. Frank set the dies into the machine, went around with the oil and made sure they kept working properly. Sam did the heavy work with the handle, stamping out the finished coins, though Frank would take turns to give him a rest. Too little pressure, or a careless placement of the blank, produced a dud, and Mr J complained about the amount of wastage anyway. Much more, he'd said, and our pay would be docked.

Mr J duly arrived just before midnight. His, Tom's, job of scratching and hammering the new coins to make them look used, didn't get under way until they'd made a dozen or more. Until then, he usually just stood and watched as Mr J counted out the blanks for the week and the other two bickered over the number of sixpences – fiddly little things – and the lack of florins and crowns. The bigger coins were easiest to work with, but Mr J told them they were chancy to pass off. The more valuable the coin, the more people checked them over before accepting them.

It was probably because he was loitering about doing nothing, Tom said, that he'd been sent downstairs on his own to see what was making the noises below. He hadn't wanted to go. He didn't like being alone in the dark in that place. Mr Holtaway had told them he'd invented all the stories of ghosts, but you never knew, did you? And in the end he'd been proved right to be afraid.

Mr Holtaway offered him the dark lantern and the others had laughed at him, so he went in the end. As he crept down the stairs, he could hear someone moving about. He could also see a light, as it might be from a dark lantern like the one he was holding. If it had been a burglar, he was ready to dash back upstairs and call for help.

He was moving slowly and carefully to avoid being seen, so it took him several more moments to reach the landing at the top of the final flight of stairs down into the hall. That's when he saw her: a fine young lady, richly dressed, holding up her lantern to get a look at him.

'Had you ever seen her before?' Foxe asked.

'Never! I swear it. She was just there, 'er hair pale and 'er face all white, and wearing that dress the like o' which I ain't never seen afore. 'Twere all covered with things what glittered an' it spread out to either side, far wider than any woman's hips could really be, especially a young woman like 'er.'

'What did you do then?'

'Nothing, sir. Just stood an' stared I did. Dumbstruck I were. To be 'onest, I 'alf thought 'twere a ghost then. But she spoke to me. All angry 'an demandin' she were. I just said, "Who may you be then?" and she snapped back at me. "Never you mind tha', boy. You tell me where Mingay is an' what he's doin' here." That's what she said.'

'What did you tell her, Tom?'

'Well, nothin'. What could I tell 'er? I never 'eard of this Mingay. So I asks 'er again, polite like, 'oo she said she wanted.'

'Did she say any more about Mingay?' Foxe asked.

'Did she 'ell!' Tom replied. 'All she does is yell, "Mingay! Mr Mingay! Are you deaf as well as stupid? I know he's here. Tell him to come out an' face me." Things like that. She were real angry. She were making a lot o' noise right as well. Far too much. We were told to make no noise, or as little as we could. The 'ouse was supposed to be empty, weren't it? With all that row, it wouldn't be many minutes afore the watchman would be round, or a passel o' nosy neighbours. I tried to tell 'er to be quiet, but she wouldn't. No, she started to yell even louder. I 'ad to keep 'er quiet, didn't I? I 'ad to. I never meant to do anythin' else, I swear.'

'So what happened?' Foxe asked gently. This was the critical point. He could not afford to frighten the boy now.

There was silence, then Tom spoke again in a kind of uneasy whisper.

'I put my 'ands around 'er throat, just to stop 'er yellin'. All the time I was sayin' shush, shush, like you does to a baby, but she took no notice. She tried to 'it out at me, but she were only a little mite, so 'er fists felt more like taps than 'ard blows. I must 'ave squeezed 'arder than I intended, 'cos all of a sudden she goes limp an' falls on the ground. I'd killed 'er, though I swear on me mother's life I never meant to.'

The boy stopped. By now he was shaking all over, mixing sobs with his words. Tabby started forward to put her arms about him, but Foxe motioned her back. He still had to find the key point in this narrative.

'What then, Tom? What did you do then?'

'I just stood an' stared at what I'd done. It were terrible, sir. I felt like I could feel the 'angman's noose already about me neck. Then Mr J came down.

'Mr J?'

'The man 'oo organises everythin'. The one in charge. I already told you about 'im. That came down the stairs, that did.'

'What did he say to you?'

'As I recalls, 'e kind of swore under 'is breath, then 'e knelt down and felt the woman's neck. Once 'e stood up again, 'e ordered me to go back upstairs and say nothin' o' what 'ad 'appened to the others. I was just to say there'd bin an intruder and Mr J was dealin' with it. Well, barely five minutes later, 'e comes back and says we're all to go 'ome 'cept Mr Holtaway. So that's what we done.'

'You thought you'd killed the woman?' Foxe said.

'I 'ad, sir! I 'ad! Next day I 'ears everyone talkin' about it. I've been mortal afeared ever since. Will they 'ang me, sir? Really 'ang me? What would me poor mam do?'

'No,' said Foxe gently. 'They won't hang you, I'll see to that. Forget all this nonsense about being cursed as well – '

'But — '

'You were simply frightened by what Mr J said afterwards. I saw the dead woman myself, Tom. I saw the marks on her throat, just as you've told me, but they weren't what caused her death. That was done by someone else, not you. In her excitement and fear at being half-throttled, the woman simply fainted. You've killed nobody. Understand? Nobody. Now, let Bart, Mistress Tabby and I go home. You look after your mother. She's been as frightened as you have, doubtless imagining all kinds of terrible things. Take the medicine Mistress Tabby has given you. That will take the bad dreams away and you'll be able to sleep well again. You're no murderer, Tom. I give you my solemn word on that.'

As Foxe told Tabby after they were on their way home again, part of the story was now quite clear. Mr J, coming downstairs to see what was going on, found Tom standing over the girl. He'd knelt down, checked the veins in her neck, and found she'd just fainted. He then sent Tom upstairs out of the way and killed the woman himself. Why they had yet to discover. After that, he'd moved the body out of sight, gone back upstairs and sent all but Holtaway home, probably via the servant's stairs and the back door. Meanwhile, he'd told Holtaway what to say and do when the constables came. He'd probably also made up that cock-and-bull story about the vagrant on the spot. His whole plan had been to have the body found and the death blamed on the non-existent vagrant as quickly as possible. That way, it would be no more than a three-days' wonder and they could return to work. It had probably been Holtaway who realised the death could also serve to strengthen the ghost story.

All that was needed now was to find this Mr J or Mr Mingay, or preferably both.

'What about Tom?' Tabby asked.

'Look after him and keep him close at home,' Foxe replied. 'He mustn't spoil things by letting on I know he didn't kill anyone. Mr J probably intends to use him as a second scapegoat, if the tale of the vagrant fails. Maybe he'll have to give evidence in court, but I very much hope not. Horne, Colman and Holtaway will try to drag him down with them, but I believe I can frustrate that. Here's what to do. I'll give you five guineas. Change it into shillings and pennies. When I send you the word, give some of it to young Tom's mother and find her somewhere to go out of Norwich. Tell her you'll give her more later, until Tom can get work and keep them. If I haven't given you enough, ask and I'll add to it. Counterfeiting is a capital offence as much as murder, but Tom doesn't deserve to hang or be sent to a penal colony in America. He's suffered enough.'

To Foxe's surprise and embarrassment, Tabby spun around, put one hand either side of his face and kissed him soundly, right there in the street.

'Bless you, Ashmole,' she said, as he struggled to get his breath back. 'You're a good man, for all your strange ways at times. What you need now, is a good woman to go through life at your side. Find one — and do it soon!'

###

Foxe hoped he would have a little more time to plan his seizure of those working in the house in Mancroft Yard. It would be simple enough to rush in with the constables and see them arrested, with all the proof of their activities about them. Simple, but dangerous. The men would be desperate. To be taken alive meant facing an inevitable walk to the scaffold, with no reprieve or chance for mercy. Only young Tom might escape death because of his age. The rest were all grown men and the laws against counterfeiting were unequivocal. It counted as a form of treason. They were the king's coins, stamped with the king's head. Fakes undermined trust in the currency itself, and thus in the kingdom and the vast networks of trade and exchange on which it depended. The very fact that it was still done underlined both how easy it was, at least for a skilled man, and how much profit was to be made. These men might very well have weapons and would fight for their lives. Better to die battling your enemies than be led to death like sheep or oxen.

Foxe had a fair idea how they could all be captured with no blood shed. The drawback was that his plan would involve quite a substantial number of people, each of whom would have to be perfect in their part in the one and only performance. Worse, most of them would be ordinary people, unused to creeping about in the dark and following instructions come what may.

It now became clear that time was not on his side. Last night, the street children told him, Holtaway, Zabek the magician and three other men had assembled near the front of the house at around eleven o'clock at night. Zabek was dressed in fantastic clothes, all covered over with stars and magical signs, and had a tall, pointed hat on his head. The hat was probably stuck over with pieces of glass, because it glittered in what little light there was from the last quarter of the moon.

For a while, the magician had stood before the door with arms outstretched, chanting something in a language none of the children could understand. His chanting was not loud, but its reedy, nasal tone made it seem to echo back from the walls.

During the chanting, the others had simply stood and watched, their backs to the opposite side of the street where the children were hiding. Then Zabek called them to cluster around him and began to talk to them all.

One of the street children, smaller and nimbler than the rest, scuttled across the street, all the while making squeaking noises like one of the many rats which ran about at night. Then he crouched, unseen, behind a barrel someone had left near the front door of the house. Another child followed but made a little more noise as he did so.

'What's that?' the children across the street heard one of the men say sharply. 'D'you think there's someone about?'

'A cat, most likely,' Holtaway replied. 'Thought I 'eard a rat just before. Place is infested with vermin. Attracts cats to hunt 'em.'

For a moment, all the men listened intently, but heard no more. The remaining children, just four of them now, stayed where they were. It would be up to the two behind the barrel to hear whatever they could.

As reported to Foxe next day, those two managed to catch a good deal of what was said. It was far from perfect, but more than enough for Foxe to gather the substance of these men's secretive huddle in the dark.

Zabek, it seemed, was telling the rest of his prolonged and exhausting struggles with the demons within, who were most reluctant to leave what had long been one of their favourite dwellings on earth. Stripped of all the hucksterism and self-congratulation, what it came down to was that the house was now free of malevolent spirits and safe to enter. He had stood at the door but five minutes before and summoned any supernatural creatures to show themselves. He had used his strongest spells. Nothing had happened.

When the magician had finished, one of the men, not Holtaway, had handed him a small leather purse which made a satisfying clinking noise. Zabek had taken it and hurried off down the street, luckily away from where the children crouched behind the barrel. As he went, one of the other men had asked in a joking voice whether the contents of the purse were some of their own. He was sharply told to shut his trap. It didn't do to say things like that on any occasion. You never knew who might be close enough to overhear. After that, the same man who had issued that rebuke told the others that it was time to get back to work. Soon they would move to other, safer premises, but those wouldn't be ready until the following week. For the time being, they would work as normal to use up the supplies of blanks he'd brought them before the girl's body was found. Once they were exhausted, they would spend two nights dismantling everything ready for the move. Five days, six at the most, and they would be set up in the new place. This one had attracted too much attention.

It had been Holtaway who asked if anyone knew what had become of the lad. This had provoked various comments, the gist of which was that he had run mad and was unlikely to return. That was not been enough for the man who seemed to be their leader.

'He'd better be mad indeed,' he'd said in a grim voice. 'I expect to track him down in a day or so. When I do, I'll make very sure he can't go telling wild stories to the authorities to try to save himself. Remember that, all of you. No one peaches on me – or even tries to – and lives to stand in a court of law and give evidence. I haven't come this far to lose it all now. If I go down, I'll make damn sure you all come with me! Now, off home and be here at the usual time tomorrow. I'll take the boy's place until we move.'

After hearing all this, Foxe felt an icy fear for Tom's safety. If he was right, this fellow who had made the threat against him had already killed without mercy, He wouldn't hesitate to do so again, if he thought it necessary. Yet to move Tom away risked tipping off the fellow that someone was onto him. Bart could protect Tom from any assault, but a pistol fired through a window at night, or poison dropped into a cooking pot by an innocent-seeming delivery boy, might elude even Bart's usefulness. The only solution was to seize the gang either that night or the next, before the murderer could carry out his threat.

Foxe decided to set the time for the following day. That was far quicker than was comfortable and trying to assemble everyone for that evening risked disaster.

17

Foxe leaned forward a few inches, so he could peer up and down the street, then pressed himself back into the narrow alley-mouth he had chosen as his hiding place. He needn't have bothered. If he recalled rightly, it was the day of the new moon. That frail sickle of light must still be hidden behind the tall houses round about. The sky was also partly overcast, so even what little light there was from the stars was generally hidden. It was as dark in the street as the fur of a black cat tied up in a bag.

He knew there were several street children crouched along the street to either side of him yet could see none of them. Couldn't hear them either. Safety on the streets at night often depended on staying still and hidden. These children could crouch motionless for hours if necessary, breathing so quietly you might step on them before you realised they were there.

He listened but could hear nothing. Unlike the areas around the taverns and houses of ill-repute, these streets were almost deserted as midnight approached. Earlier he'd heard a drunkard singing some distance away. Once he'd heard the frantic squealing and scuffling of a rat being chased, then caught by a cat. After that, nothing.

He felt a tug on his sleeve and bent his head down to what he guessed might be the level of a child's face.

'Someone comin',' came a whisper out of the dark. 'Two men I think. Frank'll warn us if they turn this way.'

Thank God for young ears honed by the danger of living on the streets, Foxe thought. I still can't hear a thing.

A few moments later, somewhere to Foxe's left, a cat gave two soft miaows.

Another tug on his sleeve. 'Tha's Frank,' came the whisper. 'They're comin' this way.'

Foxe guessed at least another minute passed before he could hear approaching footsteps himself. Two men it was, barely visible in the dense blackness, had not one of them been carrying a small lantern. They came closer, walking steadily but saying nothing, then turned aside to disappear into the entry to Mancroft Yard. Holtaway would doubtless be waiting there to let them into the empty house via the back door.

Would he stay by the door, awaiting the fourth member of the group, the curiously named Mr J, or go upstairs with the other two? To be fully effective, Foxe's plan depended on all four men being inside, and in the attic, when it was set going. All he could do now was wait until that fourth person came.

Foxe had spent all evening fretting over his plans, checking each step again and again. Unfortunately, he was like the manager of an acting group forced to stage the single performance of a complex, action-packed play with a largely amateur cast and no rehearsals. The likelihood of something going wrong was far greater than achieving the desired success.

He ran over the arrangements in his mind for what felt like the thousandth time.

Kate, the two actors who had helped him before, the so-called twins, Richard and Jeremy, Bart and an unspecified number of street children were to congregate outside the theatre. Kate to be made up as the ghost of the murdered girl as before. Nicholas, Charlie, three constables and more street children, including the young burglar to open the door for them, should have assembled in St. Stephen's churchyard. All were to stay hidden and silent until Foxe's message reached them.

Another tug on Foxe's sleeve, this time on his right arm.

'Another one comin'.'

The signal followed more swiftly this time, three soft miaows away to the right. This man must be walking faster, perhaps thinking he would arrive later than he had intended. He too turned swiftly into the entrance to the yard and disappeared.

Foxe scanned the front of the house, looking for some trace of light to let him know what was taking place inside.

There it was! A dull gleam just to the right of the front door, then another in the same pace a floor higher. The other three must have been waiting inside the back door for the last one to arrive. Now they were climbing up to the attic together, presumably sharing the light from a single lantern to minimise any showing outside. Finally, a steadier, stronger light from the attic windows on the left of the house, quickly hidden as the shutters were closed. Foxe guessed they were normally kept shut. Someone, probably Zabek, had left them open and this was not noticed in the blackness of the night until that one, swiftly quenched sign of several candles being lit had shown itself to the world.

Foxe now had to be leave enough time for the men in the attic to settle into their work, before he and his helpers could hope to creep inside without drawing attention too soon. How long would it take for both his groups of helpers to reach their final collecting place outside the front door of the house? Three minutes? Five? They would have to approach slowly and quietly. Foxe had forbidden all lights, save for a single dark lantern for each group. He would rely on the street children to lead the way. Their eyes were by far the keenest, and they knew the city centre's streets and alleys intimately. Say three minutes or so. Neither group had to come far. Allow another two or three minutes for the messengers to reach them, making around five minutes in total.

Foxe decided to wait until he heard the steeple clocks striking the quarter hour. The hour had been struck only moments ago, so that should give at near fifteen minutes for those in the house to settle down and start to relax into normality.

As the quarter chimes began to strike, Foxe bent down and whispered the single word, 'Now!' to his left and right. To his surprise, no one appeared to move, though each gave a single sharp bark like a dog or a fox.

'Them on the ends will go, sir,' the voice to his left whispered. 'Saves runnin' so far in the dark.' Foxe now realised there must have been two lines of street children stretched out either side of him. Those at the far ends would carry his message, as the rest began to cluster around him. He hadn't arranged any of this, but it made perfect sense. The further away from the house the movement started, the less likely it would be noticed within.

It did indeed take five minutes for the first members of his group to begin assembling. They came as silently as possible, each one holding to the coat of the one before them and only the one at the front of the line holding a dark lantern low down to show any obstacles in the way

Once assembled, they sorted themselves out and moved silently to their allotted places. Charlie, the twins and four of the children went through the archway to the back of the house. Their task was to block any escape via the back door. Foxe noticed Richard was carrying a thick plank of wood about four feet long, presumably to wedge under the handle of the back door to prevent it being opened.

Nicholas and two children went back across the road to the alleyway where Foxe had been. He had insisted on coming along, but Foxe was not going to risk him being in the way if anyone inside had a gun. The three constables clustered around the front door, eager to make their arrests. Let them stand in the place of danger. That was what they were paid for. Besides, they had been all for knocking down the front door and rushing inside. It had taken Foxe sometime to convince them to do as he asked and wait outside. He'd allocated Bart to stay with them and make certain they did as he asked. No one dared to make Bart angry. That way you got hurt.

As before, the lad who Charlie had said was a burglar, stepped forward and unlocked the front door. This time it was to be left unlocked. Foxe's plan called for all inside to try to rush to safety that way, only to fall into the waiting hands of the constables. Foxe, Kate, the two actors and no less than six street children slipped inside, all taking up their positions exactly as Foxe had laid down.

The trap was set. It simply remained for Foxe to bring the men headlong down the stairs from the attic.

Foxe crept forward with Kate, the actors and two of the children beside him. He stood for a few moments listening, though his ears seemed full of the noise of his heart pounding in excitement and dread. Once it started, events were likely to follow one another at high speed, leaving no time for second thoughts or change, if they started going wrong. Far above, he could hear muffled thumps and the low murmur of voices. It was time. He squeezed Kate's hand as the signal to begin.

Even though Foxe knew what to expect, the terrible scream the girl gave startled him and made his blood run cold. He had no idea where she could have learned to make such a noise; only that it would wake the dead, let alone attract the attention of four men only two stories above.

As the shriek echoed about the house, the actors once again began their cackling chant of devilish glee. Kate unlatched the dark lantern she was carrying and stepped clear of the foot of the stairs, appearing only as the hideous, rotting face of a corpse lit from below by flickering flames. The actors too stepped back, leaving Foxe and the two children, who now held a thin, black cord between their hands and crouched either side of the lowest step. Kate stayed silent for a moment, just long enough for Foxe to hear angry voices and pounding feet above. Then she began to wail. 'Murder! Murder!' as if her heart would break at the very pity of it. As the footsteps crashed downwards, Foxe also withdrew to the side, standing clear of the path to the front door, but close enough to step forward if needed. In his hand he held the pistol which had been in his pocket all along.

To try to narrate what happened in strict order would result in a narrative as muddled as the events themselves. Far better to take each of the men who were rushing headlong down the stairs in turn and follow their progress as they reached the ground floor.

The first to arrive was John Holtaway, the carpenter and only one who lived in Mancroft Yard. He'd come down the servants' stairs, planning to leave by the back door, the key to which was already in his hand when he descended. Finding the door stuck fast and the keyhole blocked by something, he turned and rushed along the passage towards the front door. As he dashed through the doorway leading to the hall, he encountered two street children holding a thin rope tightly across the opening at ankle height. His speed was such that he fell forward without any attempt to save himself, his head striking the stone floor hard enough to dash out his few remaining front teeth and leave him stunned. In seconds, the children had used more rope to tie his hands and feet, leaving him helpless and confused.

Two of his comrades arrived at the foot of the main stairs together, only to encounter another rope stretched in their path. They too fell headlong, one partly on top of the other, and lay in a heap. Before they could be tied, however, the last man, obviously younger and more agile that the rest, leapt right over both of them, managed to land more or less on his feet, and ran for the front door. When it opened, he let out a cry of triumph, swiftly cut off as his face encountered Bart's massive fist coming towards him. His head snapped back, his feet left the ground and he went over backwards, like a tree felled in the forest, to lie prone and senseless on the ground.

All that remained then was the clearing up. Foxe's plan had worked perfectly, with none of his people even scratched. If the same could not be said for the four counterfeiters, it was of little consequence to men who must soon end their lives via the hangman's noose. Bart picked up the one now lying outside the front door – Foxe assumed he was Mr J – and held him while his legs and feet were bound. Two of the constables checked all the rest were secure, while the third lit a candle from Kate's lantern and went upstairs to see all the equipment for himself. Finally, the oldest constable took a whistle from around his neck and blew two loud blasts to summon the horse and cart waiting out of sight near St. Peter Mancroft church. All four men were thrown roughly into the back of the cart, which trundled off, accompanied by the oldest constable, in the direction of the castle and the county gaol. The other two constables were to stay behind to see that no one tampered with anything in the house. Not only was it evidence of a serious crime, the authorities would wish to be sure it was destroyed as soon as possible, rather than be taken by others to allow them to set up the criminal trade elsewhere.

Foxe dispensed thanks and congratulations on all sides, plus promises of rewards to follow. The street children melted away into the darkness, the actors, the twins and Kate left to make their way back to the theatre, from where they could scatter to their beds. Nicholas, Charlie and Foxe walked back to Foxe's house, swapping excited anecdotes of what each had seen and experienced. Both Nicholas and Charlie were eager for Foxe to explain what had taken place inside the house after Kate had set events in motion.

Foxe was certain he, at least, would be too excited to sleep. Yet once dressed in his nightshirt and lying in his bed, he fell instantly into a state of unconsciousness which lasted until four o'clock of the afternoon the next day. Only then did hunger, and an urgent need for a chamber-pot, jolt him awake. It was going to take several more nights of rest for his body to replenish the reserves of nervous energy he had used on that night at Mancroft Yard. Indeed, for years after, the simple mention of the place would be enough to set his heart racing, and bring back something of the mixed anxiety and elation he had felt during those hours.

###

Over the following days, Foxe was able to work out the answers to the final remaining mysteries surrounding the murder in the haunted house. The process began on the morning of the second day after the raid and seizure of the gang of counterfeiters.

Foxe rose at his normal time, feeling quite refreshed after two lengthy periods of sleep. Nicholas had spent yesterday evening taking dinner with the Hallorans, who were agog to hear all they could about the arrests and his part in them. Since Foxe had not awoken until late that same afternoon, he had declined his invitation, pleading the need to rest some more before resuming his normal activities. To be honest, the thought of spending the evening answering questions filled him with horror. He therefore sent Nicholas in the carriage, while he ate a frugal dinner and retired to his bed almost as soon as it was over.

Now he ate a hearty breakfast and listened to his cousin eulogising the elder Miss Halloran. It was clear that Nicholas was completely smitten. He also seemed to believe that his feelings were reciprocated.

'I have spent the last few days visiting a number of legal practices recommended to me by the alderman,' he told Foxe. 'Two of them have invited me to return to hold further meetings with the existing partners. Subject to positive reports from my current practice – which I have every reason to suspect will be forthcoming – I believe I shall be able to obtain a place in one of these practices, with the promise of a junior partnership within the year. My aunt also tells me she will be very happy to move to Norwich. All that will remain is securing the substantial loan I will require to buy the partnership.'

'Don't worry about that,' Foxe said. 'I will lend you what you need when the time comes. Do you know where you will live?'

'This very day I have arranged to look over various properties.'

'You can always stay here until you find the right one,' Foxe replied. 'You and your aunt.'

'I thank you kindly, cousin Ashmole, but I really must start to stand on my own feet. I promised the partners of my current firm I would not leave before I had completed all my outstanding work. That should give me about a month or more to find somewhere. If I am to make my proposal to Miss Halloran, and secure the approval of her family, I must be able to show myself able to keep a wife with an appropriate level of comfort and security.'

Seeing Nicholas was not to be moved from this position, Foxe let him go about his business with all the headlong enthusiasm of a young man hopelessly in love. To be honest, he almost felt envious. He himself had never suffered from such a violent affection, and was sure he never would. It took someone with a high level of optimism and a trusting nature to feel like that. His own life had conditioned him towards a far more sceptical and realistic outlook on the vagaries of human existence.

Such were the thoughts which exercised his mind as he walked around the Market Place, along Gentleman's Walk, and entered his favourite coffee house.

Unfortunately, he could not escape being asked to relate what had happened two nights before in Mancroft Yard. Capt Brock was waiting for him, eager to follow up on the news which had been occupying the people of Norwich to the exclusion of all else. Foxe took his seat, ordered a large pot of fresh coffee, sighed deeply and did his best to relate all in a logical sequence.

'The man behind the gang,' Brock asked at the end. 'Did you secure his arrest too?'

'I do not know,' Foxe admitted. 'We did seize a young man, perhaps a little older than I am, who seemed to be in charge of proceedings at Mancroft Yard. That, I believe, is the one they called Mr J during the investigation. I also heard mention of a person called Mingay. He may be the overall leader, but I know nothing of him beside his name.'

'Mingay. Mingay,' Brock mused. 'An unusual name and one I feel sure I have heard before. Some time ago, I think, and again more recently. Where was it? Portsmouth? Chatham? Plymouth? No closer to home than those. Yes! I have it. The place was Great Yarmouth, when my ship anchored in Yarmouth Roads to take on supplies. While that was in going on, I went ashore and walked around the centre of the town. I remember there was a small goldsmith and jewellers shop run by a man of that name. I had a fancy to purchase a piece of silver for the wardroom in commemoration of my time as captain. However, when I went inside I very soon decided to look elsewhere. I didn't like the look of the proprietor and the smell of strong spirits on his breath was too great to inspire confidence in anything he might seek to sell me. As I recall, I left quickly.'

'Can you recall anything else?' Foxe asked eagerly. 'Anything more recent?'

'Only that the business fell into bankruptcy about two years back. Anyone could have seen it coming. I believe old Mingay had a son, but the poor fellow would have been left with nothing on his father's death. I've no idea what happened to him. John Mingay, the son was. His father was Henry.'

'Mr J,' Foxe said quietly. ' That's it. I wonder when he came to Norwich? Were there any rumours of criminal activities linked to the shop in Great Yarmouth, Brock? Can you recall?'

'I never heard of any. The gossip around the time that business collapsed was that it had been quite a flourishing concern while Mrs Mingay was alive. When she died suddenly, her husband became morose and withdrawn, took to drink and fell in with a group who gambled for high stakes. His wife, people said, was the real power in that household. With her gone, Mingay threw his money away, neglecting his business and seeming to give up on life. Soon after bankruptcy was declared, he died from a massive apoplexy — doubtless make worse by all the drink. The son simply disappeared.'

That was all Brock could offer, but it was enough to cause Foxe to write a note later that morning to the magistrate in charge of the case, requesting permission to interrogate a prisoner in his jurisdiction by the name of John Mingay. The reply came within the hour, granting permission for Foxe to visit the gaol next day.

Foxe was well known to all the magistrates in the city. Since he had also brought about the capture of that particular person, he could hardly be blocked from talking with him. The legal authorities had little interest in any charge other than counterfeiting. If Foxe wished to see if he could get a confession of murder, let him. They could not hang the man twice and he had already confessed to organising the business of counterfeiting.

Later in the afternoon, Foxe went around distributing rewards and thanks in equal measure. He handed out pennies to the street children, encountering their new leader, Sally Winsom, at the same time. When later he expressed surprise to Charlie that it was another girl, he was told that was usually the case. Having Charlie as leader had been out of the ordinary. They had simply returned to the usual pattern.

'How does this Sally Winsom make a living?' Foxe asked.

'She's a dipper, a pickpocket, like Flo used to be,' came the reply. 'Not nearly as good though.'

There was now a definite bond between Charlie and Flo. Whether it was friendship or something else, Foxe wasn't sure.

At the theatre, Foxe paid the actors and Kate what he had promised them. Richard and Jeremy claimed one extra reward. They had managed to track down Grace Custance's former maid. From her, they had learned the identity of the clothes dealer to whom she had sold the fateful dress. The dealer recalled it well. It was rare for her to be offered a dress of such style and quality. Indeed, she told them, she was reluctant at first to accept it, fearing it would not be at all easy to resell. In the end, she had paid five shillings, more for the prospect of selling the cloth for re-use than in the hope of selling the dress complete.

Imagine her surprise when a young woman, who had been standing by her stall during the transaction, stepped up and offered her six shillings and sixpence for the dress as it was. She had been so surprised she took the money. Few of her customers could afford such a sum and the prospect of an instant profit of one shilling and sixpence outweighed all other considerations. She'd thought she would be forced to keep the dress for weeks, then cut it up and sell the fabric in pieces for next to nothing.

Asked to describe the purchaser, she said she was a young woman with blond hair. Not a servant, in her estimation, though definitely of that class of society. More likely a prostitute in a second-class bordello. Those who worked in the best places of that nature had their clothes made for them. The madams of lesser establishments usually required the girls to sew their own clothes, often giving them money to visit stalls like hers to buy items they could alter or unpick to provide ready-cut elements. Besides, who else would have the occasion to wear such a grand outfit? Certainly not some housewife or the daughter of a tradesman.

Had she been to the stall before? Did she perhaps recall her name?

Yes, she had been on several occasions usually to purchase day-dresses or patterned petticoats. Few people gave their names; there was no need to do to. Yet, now she thought about it, she seemed to recall the young woman had several times come with friends and they had called her Judy, or some name like that.

Foxe was delighted to get the information. Not only did he pay the twins what he had promised them, he added a further shilling – which was what they said they had given the clothes dealer for her information – then another two on top of that. By the time Foxe left the theatre, he was the most popular man in Norwich among those who had helped him in the past days.

Arriving home that afternoon, he found a reply from the dean, the Right Reverend Emlyn Rathbone, D.D., inviting him to call next morning at eleven. There was also a note from Alderman Halloran, expressing his own warmest congratulations, along with those of the mayor and the rest of the corporation of the city. It seems he had asked Nicholas the night before to express these sentiments on his behalf. However, rightly anticipating the young man's mind would be totally taken up with other matters, he had decided to write as well.

The pleasure Foxe felt at receiving such a warm commendation was only slightly lessened by the remark at the end of the note that they were all eagerly awaiting a solution to the matter of the murdered warden of St. Stephen's Hospital. Poor Foxe was entirely bereft of useful ideas on that subject, and only vaguely hopeful that his forthcoming meeting with the dean would improve his prospects of bringing that investigation to a successful conclusion.

18

It occurred to Foxe, first thing next morning, that he had yet to tell Mistress Tabby it was time to make sure Tom Dancie and his mother were moved safely away from Norwich. He sent Alfred round to her house straight away, bearing a small bag of coins to be given to them to pay for their immediate needs. That done, he enjoyed his usual lavish breakfast, and congratulated Nicholas, who had received the offer of a immediate employment, and an eventual junior partnership, from one of the most prestigious legal businesses in the city. All that remained to finalise the deal was for them to receive a suitable character from the lawyers in Diss. Nicholas explained that he intended to write to his aunt that very morning, telling her the good news and announcing that he would return the next day to collect her, so she could help him settle on suitable accommodation. All this, of course, if cousin Ashmole was willing to accept a second visitor for a while.

Foxe was entirely agreeable to this arrangement, so Nicholas departed to write his letter, leaving Foxe to think through the questions he intended to ask the dean. His experience of dealing with grandees of the established church was limited. He knew they were all men of considerable learning, who moved amongst the highest levels of society. It was quite possible the dean would prove to be as prickly and haughty in his manner as any earl or marquis. Foxe was not looking forward to the encounter.

Dr Rathbone, the Dean of Norwich, proved quite unlike the figure Foxe had conjured up in his imagination. When he arrived at the Deanery, Foxe had first been greeted by a soberly-dressed footman and asked to wait for a moment in the hall, while his arrival was announced. He barely had time to admire some fine bronzes standing on tables set either side of the stairway, before the footman returned and told him that the dean would be happy to receive him in the library.

It would have been hard to say whether the style of that room reflected the dean or the other way around. Between neat, well-ordered bookcases of English oak, the walls were plastered in the latest fashion, with plaster swags of flowers and geometrical patterns of oak leaves, set off by the parts in between being painted in a pleasing shade of pale lilac. Mirrors served to reflect ample light into the room, and the paintings that hung there were mostly landscapes in the style of Poussin. Not the dark portraits of grim-faced former deans Foxe had expected. On the mantel and on several half-moon tables about the room, he could see Chinese vases of a quality to make a collector gasp in admiration. Yet all were patterned only in blue and white, thus enhancing the overall look rather than individually clamouring for attention. There was a substantial desk at the far end of the room with globes set in mahogany frames to either side. Probably a terrestrial globe showing the continents and a celestial one mapping the patterns of the stars and their constellations.

Taken as a whole, the effect was both elegant and tasteful, without being ostentatious. Even the fabric used for the two settees which sat either side of the fireplace had clearly been chosen to blend in with the general air of lightness and quiet opulence.

Dr Rathbone himself proved to be a man in his early fifties, with all the signs of a scholar. He was tall, still slim, but somewhat stooping in his posture. Yet there was a firmness in his handshake, and a shape to his jaw, which indicated a man well use to taking charge, and not to be easily diverted from whatever course he had set. Fortunately, there was also a twinkle in his eyes which betokened a keen sense of humour as well.

The dean greeted Foxe warmly in a resonate tenor, with just a hint of his birthplace in it; thanked him on behalf of the cathedral for the excellent work he was doing in ridding the library of a number of highly unsuitable books; and invited him to seat himself on one of the settees to await the arrival of coffee. Foxe was both relieved and delighted by the mention of coffee. He had missed his second pot of coffee with breakfast and his usual trip to the coffee-house on Gentleman's Walk to be at the deanery on time.

As they exchanged the usual polite small-talk and drank what proved to be coffee of outstanding quality, Foxe studied his host.

Dr Rathbone wore no wig, but only a light house-cap on his head. Nor was he dressed in clerical fashion. Instead, he wore a banyan of rich, red damask over a white shirt and dark breeches, with pale silk stockings. Foxe, who had dressed in his best, most formal clothes in anticipation of a different personage, now felt ridiculously over-dressed.

'Perhaps we should turn to the matter which has brought you here,' the dean said. As he relaxed, his voice now containing rather more of a Welsh lilt. I know the bishop has requested your assistance in trying to discover who murdered the late Warden of St. Stephen's Hospital. His death troubled us all greatly. I cannot recall when a crime of that nature last took place in the precincts of this sacred building. Any murder here would have been grave enough. To have a priest killed is doubly shocking.'

'I'm afraid I am somewhat at a loss for how to proceed in that matter, Mr Dean,' Foxe said. 'I began by assuming the most likely place to find the killer was amongst the secretive group who were reported to have visited the warden by night. As you will know, I used the sale of the library's books, together with more from the collection of a Dr Danson, as bait. Dr Danson too was murdered by someone obsessed with trying to buy certain volumes he refused to sell. From what I could understand of the warden's interests, they seemed more or less to coincide with Dr Danson's. I'm pleased to be able to tell you that the sale has raised several hundred pounds for the funds of the cathedral library. It also worked in the other way I intended, finally producing an approach by a man who could tell me of the group the warden was leading. Sadly for my theory about that group including the killer, the members proved to be inoffensive — though misguided — merchants and shopkeepers. What drew them together was a belief in sources of hidden knowledge about the universe and the life within it. The warden was the only genuine scholar amongst them. Most of the time, he seems to have been content to lecture the rest and dazzle them with his learning on esoteric matters.'

The dean sighed. 'I feared as much, Mr Foxe. Henry Pryce-Perkins has been an ongoing problem, both to the bishop and to myself. At Oxford, he proved himself a brilliant scholar. On the other hand, he failed to achieve the academic distinction he deserved through a stubborn refusal to follow accepted teaching. He thought he knew better. In the end, he had to leave without obtaining a degree. I don't need to tell you the scale of the influence and patronage wielded by the Earl of Westleton and his family, I'm sure. Young Henry was taken into the church and duly ordained, rather against several people's better judgement. His outspoken ideas were already clearly bordering on the heretical at that stage. After his ordination, the problem arose about what to do with him. The usual approach to young clerics of his cast of mind was clearly impossible.'

'What approach is that, sir?' Foxe asked. Never before had he been offered such an insight into the workings of the established church.

'I fear I may shock you, Mr Foxe,' the dean replied. 'These matters are rarely talked about openly, especially with lay persons like yourself, but I'm sure I can rely on your discretion.'

'Of course,' Foxe said at once.

'The Church of England, like all large and complex organisations, is more driven by patronage and politics than by the strict application of its rules and procedures. Young clerics whose theological views are too advanced or unusual are generally appointed to distant parishes amongst rural folk. There they can follow their inclinations in obscurity. Even if they preach heresy from the pulpit, we can be fairly certain their congregations will not understand a word. Indeed, in some of these backward parishes, few of the congregation stay awake once the sermon begins. So long as the stipulated services are held, even if by threadbare curates, and people are baptised and buried, little else matters. I didn't add married because church weddings tend to be less usual in such places. Couples choose each other and settle down of their own accord, only appearing in church to have their many children christened – and not even then, in some cases.

'To treat Henry Pryce-Perkins in that way was clearly impossible. His father, the earl, was determined to see his son appointed in time to one of the principal dioceses in the land, preferably York or Canterbury. Yet his son's opinions, usually expressed openly and forcibly, ruled out appointing his son through some suitably wealthy rectory; then relying on him to see himself as too grand for parish duties and appointing curates of more orthodox views to handle those for him. You might be surprised how rarely certain rectors even enter their parish churches, especially if they are pluralists.'

Foxe was enthralled. A thousand questions crowded into his mind. What the dean was now telling him revealed Pryce-Perkins in an entirely new light. No longer the scholar who was no threat to anyone. Here was a dangerous radical in church matters, whose family background demanded appointments and subsequent promotions for which he was manifestly unsuitable.

'Sometimes,' the dean continued, 'these early firebrands rid themselves of their strange notions and settle down into seeking preferment in more conventional ways. Had Pryce-Perkins moderated his opinions — as seemed unlikely even then — he might eventually have been appointed as the bishop of a small, distant diocese. Perhaps St. David's or St. Asaph. I'm afraid my Welsh homeland has too often been the recipient of bishops who are on probation, as you might say. I hope I am not boring you with all this, but it is necessary to understand why Henry Pryce-Perkins was put into the position of warden.'

'Not at all, Mr Dean,' Foxe said and meant it.

'He was made warden for somewhere to put him, while a better, longer-term solution was sought. He could preach heresy to those old men as much as he wished and do little harm. Few would understand him. Several of them are already more or less senile. As long as he carried out the minimal duties of the post, scandal would be avoided.

I'm afraid the bishop even went so far as to hint the fellow was there so he could keep a special, fatherly eye on him. This was to stretch the truth a great deal. The bishop and I did keep a close eye on him, but for quite different reasons. We both knew about the strange people who congregated at his house, but hoped that lording it over them would keep Pryce-Perkins from doing worse on a more public stage. The man's death was a grave crime, rightly to be deplored, but it would be hypocritical of me not to admit it freed us from a most difficult situation. The Earl of Westleton can go on claiming his son was destined to be an archbishop and no one need contradict him.'

'I fear it is I who am now in a difficult situation, Mr Dean,' Foxe said. 'If the warden's strange beliefs had been rendered harmless for the moment, why should anyone kill him?'

The dean considered this for a few moments in silence, then smiled and began on a new subject.

'How much do you know of the character of the Earl of Westleton and his sons, Mr Foxe?'

'Almost nothing. The family treat people like me as beneath their notice.'

'Ah,' the dean said. 'There you have a clue. The earl is cold, arrogant and dismissive of the vast majority of humanity as unworthy of a single thought. His eldest son has now been sent to Ireland to manage the family's extensive estates on that island. Since he shares many of his father's traits of character, I have no doubt he is introducing many improvements, but also greatly increasing the rents charged. At the same time, I believe he will also be doing nothing whatsoever to lessen the native population's hatred of their English landlords.

'The second son is, I understand, a brave and skilful Post-captain in the Royal Navy. He also demands instant obedience and iron discipline in his ships. Any misbehaviour is punished with maximum severity.

'Henry, the youngest son, was cast from the same mould. If I were you, Mr Foxe, I should pay less attention to his heretical views in seeking his killer than to his personality. The old men in that hospital are, as I told you, mostly harmless or senile. But even people of the mildest temper can be driven to violent deeds if the provocation is great enough.'

###

It was perhaps half a mile from the dean's house in the shadow of the cathedral to the gatehouse into Norwich Castle. In every other way, the distance was immeasurable. The mighty cathedral, with its spire reaching up towards heaven, had been built as an expression of mankind's belief in a better, more enlightened form of existence. Inside, the continued round of prayers, and the artistry of the ritual, served to remind those who came of the beauty and decency of which mankind was capable.

The men who had commanded the raising of the vast mound on which the castle keep stood had only a single objective: intimidation. The massivet, grey stone cube which they set on top of their artificial hill made it clear to all that these new Norman overlords were in charge and meant it to remain that way. What was demanded of the Anglo-Saxons, who made up the vast majority of the population, was obedience. They should forget mercy and hope and freedom. Under the feudal system, the lives of ordinary people lay in the hands of their overlords, and everyone's lands, wealth and existence were but the gifts of the king.

The seven centuries since the Normans established their rule had slowly seen this sternly hierarchical system softened and changed, becoming a way of life which still set people in ranks, but was otherwise less oppressive and more open to individual freedom to rise or fall. Some things, however, had not changed. Parliament still passed laws aimed at controlling the populace with a mixture of ferocity and menace. Hundreds of offences, especially against property, carried the death penalty. Those who broke these particular laws, even once, would never do so again. The hangman would see to that.

Perhaps it was entirely fitting that the great castle was now both a prison and a place of execution. Outside the crumbling remains of its gargantuan walls, Norwich took pride in its learning. It praised the elegance of its finest buildings and took delight in the sophistication of the entertainments on offer in its theatres, assembly halls and public gardens. Above all, its educated people valued the politeness and rationality of public conversation. Inside that stone monster on its colossal hill, the rejects of this new society were hidden away in squalor, until such time as the wheels of justice removed their nuisance altogether, either by death or banishment to the remoter parts of Britain's growing empire.

As Foxe toiled up the hill towards the castle entrance, the sense of dread and despair perpetually flowed from its walls began to weigh upon him. Why was he seeking to speak to John Mingay, counterfeiter and, in Foxe's estimation, murderer as well? Foxe's task had ended when the gang were seized three nights ago and handed over to the constables.

The answer lay in Ashmole Foxe's need to satisfy his curiosity on even the smallest issues. That Mingay had delivered the blow which had ended this Judy's life Foxe was certain. What he needed to know now was why? Who exactly was she? What had taken her to that house? Why had Mingay chosen to kill her?

Thus it was that, after finishing his conversation with Dean Rathbone, Foxe made his way to the castle, where he had arranged to have Mingay brought from his cell to answer questions — always assuming he was willing to do so.

When he arrived at the appointed time, a warder led Foxe to the room the governor of the prison used to deal with prisoners, when it proved unavoidable.

'You don't want to go inside the prison itself,' the man to Foxe, 'fine gentleman like you. They're like animals in there, wallowing in their own filth. I wouldn't reckon on you coming out alive, if several of us weren't there all the time to protect you.'

Foxe was therefore taken to a bare, white washroom and given a comfortable chair to sit in, set behind a solid table which appeared to be bolted to the floor. A stone bench, fixed and immovable, was set on the other side of the table for prisoners, too far away for anything other than verbal contact.

Mingay was brought in, already bearing with him the stench of the prison cells and the grime it left on face and hands. Foxe had heard him coming. The chains attached to his wrists and ankles rattled with every step. The warder pressed him down onto the stone bench and attached his chains to hooks set there for the purpose. The governor clearly took no chances of being assaulted by those in his charge.

Physically, John Mingay looked older and smaller since Foxe had last seen him. He still wore the same clothes, but they were now creased and draggled. Yet his fierce spirit was as yet undimmed by the experience of capture and incarceration. Foxe didn't need to press him to talk. It seemed he wanted nothing more than the opportunity to pour out his bitterness at life to who ever would listen.

'Come to gloat, 'ave you?' he said at once. 'Come to crow over me? Or are you one of those religious types who think it their duty to preach to lost souls? You can save your breath in either case. All my life, ill-luck has deprived me of what I was due. I had to watch my drunken sot of a father wreck a good business and take away my inheritance. When I finally helped him out of this world, there were only debts left and the name of Mingay had become a disgrace. I could get no decent work in Yarmouth. I had to trudge miles and miles to escape his shadow, eventually ending up in Bury St. Edmunds.'

'What brought you to Norwich?' Foxe asked softly.

'It was like this. There I was, slaving away for a man with as much mercy in his soul as ravening wolf has, when news reached me that Hatchard, the goldsmith in Norwich, had died. I was also told his widow was trying to keep the business going with the help of some elderly relative. That's when I knew my time had come. I'm a bloody good engraver, anyone will tell you that, so it wasn't hard to worm my way into the business. I could tell the widow was eager to sell. I was eager to buy. I wasn't going to stay at others' beck and call any longer. Not me! By all rights, I should have had my own business in Yarmouth, shouldn't I? Now I wanted my own business in Norwich, as was due to me, and no one was going to get in my way this time.'

'But surely you had no money to buy a business?' Foxe said.

'Of course I hadn't! But I knew how to get it by this time — and get it fast.'

'We both know the answer to that, don't we.'

Mingay sniffed and regarded Foxe with something between anger and contempt.

'Listen, know-all!' he said angrily. 'I knew I could inveigle the Hatchard widow into selling to me at a good price. Silly old cow had no idea what the business would be worth in proper hands! Trouble was, as you pointed out with such attention to what's obvious, I had no money. So I came up with the prefect solution to building up a suitable amount of capital in a short time. Then you came along , damn your eyes! I was almost there and you ruined everything I've worked for with your silly tricks. I'd like to get my hands around your throat and throttle the life out of you for what you've done!'

'Like you throttled the girl called Judy?' Foxe said quietly. Until now he'd more or less allowed Mingay's anger and hatred to spur him into telling his tale. Now it was time to focus on what he really wated to know.

'Judy? You mean Judy Fernley? That dimwitted tart? It wasn't me who throttled her. That was Tom Dancie. He comes rushing up the stairs blubbing his eyes out and saying he never meant to do it. He only wanted to shut her up. Left to him, she would have been back on her feet in minutes, raising the roof and bringing every watchman and constable for miles around. I couldn't have that, could I? So I sent Tom back to work and went down to deal with the silly bitch myself. She was just coming round from her faint, but a few stout blows from an old chair leg put an end to her nonsense for good, didn't it?'

'Why did you call her a tart?'

'Because that's what she was. A tart. A whore. A prostitute. Not a very good one either, if you want to know.'

'Why had she come to that place?' Foxe asked. The reason why Mingay had killed the poor girl was now plain enough. But why had she come to the house and why did he think she was gong to make a noise and attract unwanted attention?

Until that point, Foxe had been so intent on what he wished to know, and so appalled by the atmosphere of the prison, he hadn't even noticed Mingay had two very black eyes and a misshapen nose, doubtless the result of the contact he'd had with Bart's fist. Now there was a thin trail of blood and snot running down from Mingay's one nostril and he tried to raise a hand to wipe it away. The heavy manacle, hooked to the bench, stopped him from doing it, so he sniffed loudly instead and did so several times. Foxe had to stifle his natural urge to take a handkerchief and wipe the man's face. Put his arm within Mingay's reach and there was no knowing what he would do.

'She'd followed me, I expect,' he said through his sniffing. 'Last time I went to the brothel where she worked, the stupid little tart had somehow convinced herself I would take her away from that place and set her up in some cosy nest as my pampered mistress. God knows what gave her such a stupid idea! She was just about acceptable for a night's amusement. Willing to do as she was told and always eager for more. I wasn't going to tie myself to the likes of her. No, sir! Not once I'd got my business. Then I could become a fine gentleman like you and take my pick of proper ladies.'

'She wouldn't take no for an answer?'

"'Course she wouldn't, the hussy. Tried to cling to me and pleaded for me to make her into a lady. As if you could turn a guttersnipe like Judy Fernley into anything other than what she was. Even when I told her plainly I wanted nothing more to do with her, she tried to accost me one day outside the shop. Did that make me mad?! I had to take her into a shed behind the business and knock her about a bit to make her go away. I told her at the time. Even if she was dressed in the sort of expensive clothes real ladies wear, she'd never look like anything but what she was — a girl from the gutter. One who earned her bread by lying on her back with her legs open.'

'But it didn't convince her?'

'I thought it had, but she was like a damned leech. One night she must have followed me to Mancroft Yard. Somehow, she dressed herself up in some fancy clothes and turned up asking for me. Perhaps she thought that if I saw her dressed like a lady I'd change my mind. I don't know. She was stupid enough.'

'So you killed her.' Foxe said.

'Had to, didn't I? She knew where I went and she hadn't got the sense to stay away. I couldn't risk losing everything for the sake of some sixpenny whore. How was I to know you'd come poking your nose in where it wasn't wanted? After we sent the others home, Holtaway and I dreamed up the perfect solution in the story of the unknown vagrant. I must have left the front door open that night or she couldn't have got inside. Since she had, we had to invent someone who would also get inside, kill her there and conveniently disappear. If that failed, we could blame Tom Dancie. He thought he'd killed her anyway. But that left the chance of him confessing why he had been in the house in the first place. Our story was better. It looked as if it was going to work too. Coroner's jury gave the usual verdict, the magistrate wasn't interested enough to make more than a token investigation, and another unknown person was tipped into a pauper's grave. Even when some potty gent tried to claim she was his daughter, it did nothing save muddle things even more. But you – you ruined everything with your poking and prying. I hope you rot in hell! Chaplain says that's where I'm headed, so I'll get the devil to have a nice pot of boiling oil ready for you when you arrive! Damn and blast you!'

'You didn't care if poor Tom Dancie was hanged for a crime you committed?'

'Why should I be? Miserable little runt isn't worth a fart in a forest.'

Foxe had got what he wanted, so it was high time to get out of that loathsome place. He called loudly for the warder, who appeared almost at once and tried to take Mingay back to his cell.

Once he was freed from the wall-shackles, Mingay fought like a maniac to get at Foxe, howling curses and obscenities in his direction and trying again and again to spit in his face. Only when the warder cuffed his prisoner soundly about his head did the stunned man suffer himself to be dragged away.

When the doors had been unlocked and Foxe was released back into the open, he gulped in huge lungfuls of clean air and hurried to his home as fast as he could. There he stripped to the skin and washed himself down all over, telling Alfred to take everything he had been wearing away and either burn or sell it. He never wanted to see it again, so foul was the memory of that afternoon and that confrontation with Mingay. Even when he was pressed later by Nicholas and Mrs Crombie, Foxe would never say exactly what had taken place in the bare room with the unrepentant murderer. All he would tell them was that a poor girl, Judy Ferney, had met her end as the result of her misguided belief in her own ability to persuade Mingay to help her better herself; and that, if any man deserved to be hung, it was John Mingay.

19

Foxe could be relentless in pursuing a particular mystery, but once it was solved, he liked to set it aside and move on as quickly as possible. That felt especially true of the murder in Mancroft Yard. The ugliness of the emotions involved, from greed to hatred and selfishness, had left a very bad taste in his mouth. He wanted nothing more to do with any of it.

He also felt impatient to be rid of the question of who had killed Rev. Henry Pryce-Perkins. The fact of that man too being a less than pleasant character was no reason why he should not have as much right to an untroubled existence as the next man. Nevertheless, Foxe found it hard to feel more than an impersonal curiosity about who ended Pryce-Perkins's life and why. It wasn't helped by the suspicion that the fellow's family viewed his murder as more of an affront to their status than the loss of a loved and cherished member of the family.

Still, Foxe was determined to use all his perseverance and skills to reach an answer in this annoying case too. He therefore rose early the next morning, put on suitable clothes for what looked as if it might prove a damp day, and ate a rather less ample breakfast than he usually did. When he left the house, he turned in the opposite direction to his usual walk, headed along the upper side of the great market, passed the theatre and Assembly House and entered through the gate of the Chapel Field gardens, newly rearranged and elaborated for the pleasure of the people of Norwich.

Once inside, Foxe paid his entrance fee of one shilling to an attendant whose eyes were still bleary with sleep. Then he strode forward at a good pace down the main avenue, where other attendants were only just beginning to open up the various booths and the pavilions where visitors could purchase refreshments. His route took him on past the bandstand. It was still silent and shuttered at this early hour, though later a group of musicians would gather there to provide medlies of popular airs to serenade both strollers and those who occupied the seats provided for the popular pastime of watching the world go by.

Despite the thin drizzle which had stated to fall, the flower beds still offered the colourful displays for which they were famous. Mostly, the only sound he heard was that of his own feet on the path, for the birds had ended their spring chorus and sat, damp and dejected, to watch him pass. During the day, these gardens were quiet. Only as the evening came and turned into night would the efforts of the various orchestras and brass bands hired by the garden's proprietors fill the air.

Most people went to the gardens to see and be seen. To stroll the long pathways greeting friends and acquaintances as they passed. To pass muttered comments to one another on the unsuitability of some lady's costume, or the brazen effrontery of some lady and gentleman enjoying the air together, when it was well known that each was married to someone else.

Foxe had not come for any of those reasons. He wished only to walk to clear his head of the taint of the visit to Norwich Castle and in the hope that brisk movement in the open air would stimulate his mind.

The few people who greeted him as he passed, head down and attentive only to his own thoughts, received the vaguest of acknowledgement. His mind was elsewhere; his eyes blind to the harmonious arrangement of flowers and trees amongst which he walked. Even the cold drizzle could not distract him from his purpose.

Foxe began again at the beginning. He started by reviewing everything he had discovered – or failed to discover – about the circumstances surrounding the surprising murder of Henry Pryce-Perkins. The people amongst whom he moved, few as they were. The subjects which seemed to have occupied his mind. In particular, he found himself searching again and again for some series of provocations, as suggested by the dean, which might have culminated in one final outrage great enough to provoke the taking of a life. Foxe was convinced that such a pattern must exist, if only he could find it. This was no carefully calculated killing, planned in advance, in pursuit of revenge or personal gain. He was sure of that. To pick up a rough flint in the dark and use it to strike a man down argued for a sudden outburst of fury, rather than the eventual result of a process of cold logic.

Foxe next reviewed all the possible candidates for the role of killer, not omitting that favourite character of lazy magistrates, the unknown vagrant. There had been no theft involved. Nor would any footpad have expected to find rich pickings on the body of a dead clergyman. Footpads and their like rarely killed anyway. They threatened their victims, usually with a knife, and forced them to hand over their valuables. One or two might knock a victim down to rifle his pockets, but the last thing the average footpad wanted was to take the risk of being hanged for murder. Leaving dead bodies around was too likely to draw the immediate attention of the constables and end in them being captured and brought before a magistrate.

Those who had found Pryce-Perkins's body had also made no mention of a struggle. There were no signs that Pryce-Perkins had been attacked or tried to defend himself. The position of the blows to his head rather suggested he had been approached from behind. He had probably been unaware of any threat until the first blow was struck. His killer had knocked him down, then struck him two or three times more while he lay on the ground. After that, he simply dropped the flint he had used beside the body and walked away. It must have been over in less than a minute.

So who could have wished Pryce-Perkins dead? Who could he have wronged so greatly? Until only a few months before, he had been at Oxford. Nor, after he had been appointed Warden of St. Stephen's Hospital, had anyone mentioned growing anger or discontent amongst its inmates. So far as he had been able to learn, Pryce-Perkins had carried out his minimal duties fully, but sought little or no personal involvement with any of the pensioners. His only contacts appeared to be with the men who made up the supposed Lodge of Hermes Trismegistus —

and with the cathedral librarian, of course. The latter could be excluded right away, unless Pryce-Perkins had failed to return so many volumes to their correct places on the shelves that the librarian had been driven to distraction and killed him to save himself the trouble of re-shelving so many books. That thought brought a smile to Foxe's face, but was nothing to be taken seriously.

His process of elimination had left two groups of people. The lodge members and the pensioners themselves. He had already dismissed the notion of some earnest acolyte of hidden wisdom being driven to murder by Pryce-Perkins's unwillingness to recognise anyone else's contribution to the study of the writings from the wise men of the past. Pryce-Perkins had been their openly acknowledged leader. The one true scholar amongst them and the only one with both access to the relevant books in the cathedral, plus a working knowledge of the ancient languages in which nearly all of them were written. Rather than being lacklustre in his devotion to their cause, the man had been the driving force behind everything they did. Nor was it likely that any of them were rivals for the role of leader, ready to strike Pryce-Perkins down to clear their path to that position.

If they were set aside, that left only the pensioners. According to the dean, who was in a position to know, several of these old men were either on the border of senility or had already crossed over. Many were frail or crippled with arthritis, suffered from poor sight or other diseases of old age. Pryce-Perkins was young and in the best of health. What on earth could have persuaded one of these feeble old men to commit the ultimate sin of murder towards a man who was, on past experience, unlikely to hold the post of warden for many more months.

All that left was the anonymous vagrant and Gunton's suggestion that one of his senile colleagues killed Pryce-Perkins in a fit of insane rage, then promptly forgot he had done it. In either case, Foxe might as well give up right away and accept his failure.

By this time Foxe was feeling the effects of vigorous exercise on top of a meagre breakfast. He therefore returned to the main avenue and sought out one of the newly-opened restaurants, where he consumed two glasses of good ale along with two large, but sadly mediocre meat pies.

That food and drink managed to put new heart in him. He was not yet ready to give up. He still had one idea lurking in his mind. What it needed now was a visit to Mistress Tabby to see if she could answer a question that was bothering him.

Foxe decided he had already walked more than far enough that morning. It would be easy to hire a chair to take him to Tabby's from where he was; far less easy to find one in the vicinity of her house to bring him back home. He therefore decided to return home and order his carriage to be made ready and waiting in half an hour. He had Alfred bring him another coat. The one he was wearing was now wet through, thanks to the steady drizzle which had fallen all the time he had been walking in the gardens. That just left him time to go into his shop and tell Mrs Crombie the last details of the death in Mancroft Yard. When his carriage came round, he directed the groom to take him to Mistress Tabby's house and to wait outside until he was ready to return.

Foxe found Tabby in her kitchen for a change, not in her garden. Even she didn't much like being outside in the rain. Now she was busy taking the bunches of herbs, which had been hung up to dry twelve months before, and crumbling them between her palms. That done, she picked out the coarse stems and put the remaining powder into large earthenware jars. This was her supply of dried ingredients to last her until she should be able to pick fresh herbs again the following year.

She acknowledged Foxe's arrival with a nod and a smile, waving her arm to indicate that he should seat himself on the other side of the room until she had finished her task. The smell of herbs filled the air; bitter, pungent, yet also somehow refreshing and calming. As he sat and watched Tabby at work, Foxe felt a kind of lethargy creep over him; a powerful sense of physical relaxation and mental distraction. His mind filled with fleeting memories of watching his mother at work in her kitchen, when he was little more than a toddler. Of the sense of comfort and warmth she always seemed to bring with her. Most of all of the knowledge he had then that she had the strength needed to protect him from the world's blows. He hadn't thought of his mother in years. She died when he was only twelve. Now, in a strange way, he felt her presence once again and found himself torn between joy and sadness at what he had lost.

How long he sat there, Foxe had no idea. Only that — slowly, slowly — the stresses and problems of recent days began to leave him, so that he felt cleansed, yet helpless as a kitten.

When she had completed the last bunch of herbs, Tabby dusted off her hands, came around the large kitchen table at which she had been working, and stood looking down at Foxe.

'You need a good rest, Ashmole,' she said sternly. 'You think you can go on and on, running your mind at full speed and losing sleep over these mysteries you set yourself to solve. From the look of you, you've reached the end of your reserves of energy. It's a simple choice, Ash. Either you think about your own needs a little and slow down, or wait until your body and mind force you to stop by wrecking your health.'

She went over to the other side of the room and opened one of the cupboards. From it she took a large bottle, its stopper sealed with wax. From another cupboard, she took a small wineglass of the type often used for port or madeira wine. Breaking the seal on the bottle, she filled the glass with some of the greenish, viscous liquid it contained.

'Drink this,' she commanded. 'No arguments. Drink it. I should warn you it tastes foul.'

Foul tasting the liquid most certainly was. It somehow combined a sickly sweetness with an underlying taste of rotten fruit, along with bitterness enough to set the teeth on edge. At the same time, it warmed as it went down like the very best brandy.

'My god!' Foxe gulped. 'Whatever does this evil brew contain!'

'Never mind that, Ash,' Tabby replied in her best lecturing style. 'Take the rest of this bottle with you and drink a glass of it every night before you retire to bed. You can follow it with a brandy to take the taste away. It'll put some heart back into you. If you stop rushing about so much and allow proper time to rest, you'll be back to your old self in no time.'

Foxe accepted the bottle reluctantly. It was never a good idea to ignore Tabby's advice. For one thing, she seemed to have an uncanny understanding of whatever you were doing and when you were doing it. If you ignored her, it simply brought down worse strictures on your head, together with endless lectures on your foolishness and lack of gratitude. He would simply remember to have a glass of best French cognac to hand to take the taste away.

'Now,' Tabby said, smiling again. 'Before you ask your questions, tell me whether you have found the final pieces in the puzzle over that poor young woman's death in Mancroft Yard.'

'Tabby dear,' Foxe protested. 'Please, for heaven's sake, give me something to take away the taste of this witch's brew! Do you use slugs and rotten apples to make it?'

'Naturally,' Tabby replied, 'along with essence of fisherman's stockings and a liberal helping of pig dung. Don't be such a baby! Here, I'll fetch you a pot of ale. Drink it and stop whining. It's making you feel better, isn't it?'

Reluctant as he was to admit it, Foxe could definitely feel a returning of his strength and a clearing of his head. He gulped his ale and told Tabby all that he had discovered about John Mingay's lust for wealth, and his sense of being entitled to what his father had pissed away in drunkenness. When he reached the part about Judy Ferney's misguided belief that he would take her away from the bordello and set her up as a respectable lady, Tabby had tears in her eyes.

'Poor child,' she said. 'So many of those girls cling to the belief that they can find a way out of prostitution. Usually by persuading some customer to set them up as his mistress. It does sometimes happen, of course. Take your Mrs Danson. Mostly, however, the only things the wretched young women have to look forward to are poverty and disease. The moment they start to lose their looks, the madams throw them into the street to survive as best they can.'

'Judy Ferney had the ill luck to settle on a man with no emotions beyond ambition and revenge on his father. From his words, I wouldn't be surprised if he had helped Mingay senior on his way out of this world. Sadly for him, it was already too late to save anything from the business.'

'This world is a wretched place,' Tabby said. 'Anyway, that business is over now and young Mingay will soon get the punishment he so richly deserves. Time to forget about it and move on. I must just say, however, that you exceeded even your usual level of cunning this time. Still living up to your name, obviously. Have you found the killer of Henry Pryce-Perkins yet?'

'That's what I came to speak with you about,' Foxe replied. 'I wondered it you'd ever had any dealings with St. Stephen's Hospital and its pensioners.'

'I have indeed,' Tabby said, 'and there's a long tale to that. I'm not usually approached by anything or anyone connected with the church. The idea of a Cunning Woman is too reminiscent of witchcraft. But one of those old men, Ben Allsop his name is, suffers badly from rheumatism. He was coming to me for salves to lessen his pain even before he became too infirm to live on his own and was given a place at St. Stephens. I'd simply continued to treat him. The successive wardens had accepted me for what I am – a simple herbalist. Until that prize fool Henry Pryce-Perkins came along, that is.'

Far from banning her from the place, she explained, Pryce-Perkins had shown an obsessive interest in what he termed "her craft", demanding to be told exactly what she did and what recipies and handed-down approaches she followed.

'He was a complete nuisance,' Tabby said. 'Either he tried to turn me into a witch — or the priestess of some imaginary secret cult, handed down from our pagan ancestors. Time and again I told him I used only two things in my work: my knowledge of herbs and plain common sense. He wouldn't believe me.'

'Did you keep going to see old Ben?' Foxe asked.

'I did, but only until he gradually became too senile to even be aware of who I was. The other thing which kept me away in the end was the arrival of that man Gunton. He's an even bigger fool that Pryce-Perkins knew how to be. Gunton fills his hours with bible-reading. He also cherishes the foolish belief that every word of that book is the literal truth. He used to be a churchwarden, you know — and, I'm sure, a thorn in the side of every parson who came to his parish church. Gunton knew the bible inside out and would lecture them on all their supposed mistakes in not following what it said. You could never tell him anything. Soon, he started claiming to be deputy warden of the hospital and ordering the others about, as well as boring them with bible reading. Even worse, he preached them impromptu sermons about the terrible torment awaiting them, if they didn't repent and follow his perverted version of Christian beliefs. I swear several of them have started to lapse into senility simply to escape. What with Gunton *and* Pryce-Perkins, I couldn't stomach going to St. Stephen's any more. Old Ben isn't long for this world anyway. Sleeps most of the time, as people do when death is approaching. It's as if nature is gradually easing them on their way into oblivion — or the next world, depending on your belief.'

'Thank you, Tabby,' Foxe said. 'You've helped me see my way to a conclusion of this whole sorry business.'

'You know who the killer was?'

'I think so now. I cannot be entirely certain yet, but I hope to be very soon. Whether I shall ever be able to prove it, I have no idea. Probably not. But at least I will be sure in my own mind and will know what to say to the bishop.

'Will the case not come to court then?'

'Oh no, that would be quite impossible. Unless, naturally, the guilty person insists on confessing publicly and is willing to go on repeating his confession. If he had any wit, he'd know all he has to do is deny everything and he will be safe from the law. Even if it went to court, he'd most likely be declared unfit to plead through insanity. It doesn't matter though. I doubt he will ever commit another murder. He only did so this time because the circumstances must have driven him to it.'

'You're being very mysterious,' Tabby complained. 'Can't you say outright who it was?'

'Not until I am certain. Give me twenty-four hours and I will be able to tell you everything — if you haven't worked it out yourself before then. Now I must go. I need to spend some time running through all the details in my mind and working out precisely what to do next.'

'Very well, Ash dear. You'll give my best regards to Nicholas, won't you? He hadn't visited me much recently.'

'Too busy visiting certain other people,' Foxe said with a grin. 'He's gone back to Diss today anyway. I shall have my house to myself again this evening.'

'Gone back? Why? I thought he was to stay for some weeks.'

'Sorry, Tabby,' Foxe said, 'I forgot to tell you. He's arranged himself a position in a law firm in Norwich, with the promise of a junior partnership within a year, subject to good performance. He's gone back to Diss to explain all the details to his aunt, my cousin Harriet. They will both return to stay at my house while they look for somewhere suitable to live. I strongly suspect young Nicholas also has his eye on gaining a wife in a couple of years.'

'A wife? Heavens, Ashmole,' Tabby exclaimed. 'What else have you conveniently forgotten to tell me?'

'I thought people said you had second sight,' Foxe replied, smiling. 'I shouldn't need to tell you anything.'

'I can see I need to box your ears for you,' Tabby snapped back, though she was laughing at the same time. 'Impertinent young puppy! Be careful I don't turn you into a toad.'

'A fox, surely? Goodbye Tabby. I'll let you know what happens.'

'Remember to take the medicine I gave you,' Tabby called after him. 'You may be sure I'll know it you don't. I wish I'd put an extra dose of snail slime into the bottle!'

Foxe's good humour lasted until he was back in his own house. It promised to be a far nicer and drier evening, and the city was looking its best as he travelled along in his carriage. The market traders were starting to pack up for the day, many of them selling off perishable items cheaply to some of the city's poorer inhabitants. They'd have to ignore any bruising or sense of taint in what they bought in return for a large reduction in price. Most of the better sort of people were already at home and eagerly awaiting dinner; though a few of the harder-working professionals were still to be seen making their way homewards, mostly on foot, but a few in chairs. Later in the evening, the city would be thronged with well-dressed men and women heading for the theatres or assembly rooms; or to one of a score of other places where entertainment would be offered. The streets would then be densely packed with carriages and sedan chairs, and the linkmen would be making ready their supply of torches to guide people back home at the end of the evening. Norwich was often as busy, many claimed, as London itself, just with everything crammed together into a much smaller area.

That night, however, Foxe had other things on his mind than seeking amusement, either of a cultural nature or of a more earthy kind in his favourite bordello. He had to plot.

20

Tabby's medicine, duly swallowed that night and as foul as ever, must have been powerful stuff. Foxe awoke next morning refreshed and as prepared as he ever would be for the struggle which would lie ahead. It was quite clear now that it would be useless to resort to an open accusation of murder. As he had told Tabby the afternoon before, he hadn't a shred of evidence. A simple denial would see his whole case fall to the ground. Nor did he think an attempt to extort a confession out of the killer would be effective. How would it appear if Foxe was discovered to have tried to bully one of those old men into admitting a crime? Everyone's sympathy would be on the side of person he knew to be the killer. A few tears and exclamations of weakness on his part would be enough to convince the world Foxe had failed to discover who really killed Rev Hon. Henry Pryce-Perkins and was trying to extort a confession to cover up his own failure. Still worse, he was attempting to fix the blame on a harmless old pensioner. An appeal to the man's conscience would also likely prove fruitless. He almost certainly believed he had done nothing wrong.

This was a time for cunning, not force. A time to outwit his opponent into giving away the truth he would otherwise have continued to conceal. A time to smile and look silly, while all the time piling provocation upon provocation until the killer once again was brought close to that boiling point of furious anger with which the crime had been committed. There was some danger involved, of course. The man was certainly insane. Provoking him in that way might well induce some act of violence against Foxe himself.

That was a risk he was now prepared to take to get at the truth. Pryce-Perkins had been taken by surprise, at night, when he was struck down. It was daylight now and Foxe, younger by many years than his potential attacker, would be very much on his guard. The only real problem was that, if he succeeded, the killer would have to be left on his own while Foxe went to get help. To take someone else to secure the madman was impossible without alerting him in advance. Foxe's only hope was that he might be able to alert some of the other pensioners to hold the killer, or lock him in a suitable room.

All these thoughts and many more went through Foxe's mind as his carriage once again made its way to Tombland, then passed through one of the great stone gates of the Close. At almost the last moment before they arrived at St. Stephen's Hospital, Foxe remembered his coachman, Henry Burkiss, was with him. Hurriedly, he warned Burkiss to be ready at a moment's notice to rush into wherever Foxe might be, if he heard shouting and his master calling for help.

'Can you find some straps or something else suitable for securing a prisoner?' Foxe asked him. 'Something strong?'

'I got two spare suspension straps in the box at the back o' the carriage, master,' the groom said. 'They're powerful strong and they has buckles too. The front straps on the carriage is starting to look real worn. 'Tis all these potholes and uneven roads. If you don't keep a close eye on 'em, they be apt to break all o' a sudden and throw the passenger out into the roadway. I could get them.'

'Do that,' Foxe replied. 'but quietly now. There may be someone inside already watching us. Make it look as if you're just spending the time waiting for me checking over the carriage . Can you do that?'

'I can, right enough. I'll just get those straps out and pretend I be checkin' 'em for size. Then I'll keep 'em in me 'ands an' all, should they be needed.'

'Splendid!' Foxe said, trying to look as if he'd been doing nothing more unusual than giving his groom some routine instructions. 'I think I'll be in that cottage there. The one just to the left of the warden's house at the end. Make sure to stay alert in case I have to go anywhere else. Look, there's one of the pensioners coming out now to see what's going on. With any luck, he'll come over to exchange a few words with you when he sees you fiddling about. These poor old fellows get very few visitors. Encourage him to stay and chat, if you can. He might prove useful.'

Foxe banged on Gunton's door hoping the man was inside and not in the communal dining room or the chapel. His luck was in, though when the self-appointed deputy warden opened the door, it was plain he was not at all happy to see Foxe standing there. He hovered indecisively, as if torn between opening the door wide and slamming it shut in his visitor's face. Foxe solved his quandary by barging past him into the little living area, trying — not altogether successfully — to combine being ingratiating and menacing at the same time.

'There a few matters on which I need your opinion, Gunton,' he said firmly. 'About Pryce-Perkins and his time here as warden. Sit down, man! You're making the place look untidy.'

All this while continuing to stand himself, thus towering over the elderly pensioner. It was vital to keep the man off-balance.

'It must have been a great privilege to have such a man as Rev. Pryce-Perkins as your warden.' Foxe continued. 'After all, he wasn't the typical young clergyman who's given this job.'

'It were no privilege —' Gunton began, screwing his features up in disgust, but Foxe cut him off.

'Exactly. A great privilege. Especially since he was, I believe, at the forefront of the latest thinking on matters of religion.'

'If that's what you calls it —.' It was no use. Foxe talked over him relentlessly.

'No more supernatural mumbo-jumbo,' he continued. 'No more nonsense about angels and visions and miracles. Just the plain teaching of a great thinker and moral philosopher, free from silly notions like being the Son of God and that kind of thing.'

Gunton was growing red in the face now, as Foxe deliberately trampled over what he obviously held most dear. Whether Pryce-Perkins had ever espoused those particular ideas hardly mattered. He might very well have done. They were widely shared by certain philosophers who saw an attempt to overthrow superstition and long-accepted ideas in religious matters as a kind of enlightenment through the power of reason. Men like Diderot and Rousseau in France, and Locke and that American fellow, Franklin, in the English-speaking world. All that mattered was to jolt Gunton so hard he would forget caution and reveal his true feelings — the ones which had led him to commit murder.

'I expect your warden explained everything to you all in his sermons, didn't he?'

Gunton could be held no longer. 'Explain? Explain? 'Twas nothing but rank blasphemy and heresy!' the old man cried. 'I told 'un, many times. You just forget such wicked notions and read what it says in the Good Book. That's all the learning anyone needs to know the will of the Lord and the savin' grace o' his Son. Right there it is, an' in plain English for all to read. That's my learnin', I told 'im. I studies those holy words every night without fail.'

'But weren't you a carpenter, Gunton?' Foxe said. 'Your warden was a member of the nobility and a man who had studied at the university.'

'Dun't it say that God will humble the proud in the imagination of their 'earts and bring down the mighty from their seats. Dun't it say that in the Good Book, plain to see?'

While he was speaking, Gunton had stepped over to a table at the side of the room and taken up a medium-sized Bible in his hands. Now he waved it in Foxe's face as he must once have waved it at Pryce-Perkins.

'Do you know what 'e said to me?' he rasped. 'D'you know what that arrogant young pup said to me? "Complete nonsense!" 'e said. "A good half of that so-called holy book of yours is made up of Jewish myths and other fantastic tales. Even the supposed writers of the New Testament couldn't agree on the same story. They weren't explaining what they had seen and heard. They were collecting stories and rumours and stitching them together over decades to support their twisted religion. Have you read the manuscripts in the original Greek and Hebrew? I have! You can see where parts have been cobbled together and the earlier words altered to make them fit. Don't you dare try to lecture me, you ignorant little fool! I have more knowledge of the bible and its various versions in my little finger, than you have in the whole of your body." That's what he said to me. Rank blasphemy an' all it were!'

Foxe was beginning to feel nervous that he might already have provoked Gunton too far. He'd assumed the man was a fanatic, who might have been tipped over the edge on a single occasion. Now it looked as if he was, indeed, truly insane. Spittle was flying from the corners of his mouth and his eyes blazed with pent-up fury. Foxe tried to step back, but Gunton was on his feet now and kept coming towards him.

'I knew what was behind the warden's scorn for the true faith. I knew! It was Satan hi'self. I see'd 'is picture in one o' those accursed books as the warden had on his desk. The Devil 'isself, complete with 'is 'orns an' 'is tail and 'ooves. Like a girt great goat, 'e were. All surrounded with signs and strange letters. I knew what was goin' on there, right enough, 'Twas witchcraft, that's what it were! The warden and those other wicked men 'e'd gathered about him was conjurin' up the Devil an' the spawn 'o Hell. Pollutin' our cathedral an' all.'

'What books were these?' Foxe asked, though he knew very well what Gunton must have seen was an open grimoire. A book of magical spells and incantations used by those who believed they could call up spirits and ancient gods and bend them to their will. One had been amongst the first set of books he had sold for the library.

'Evil books!' Gunton was shouting now. 'Wicked, evil books! Full o' witchcraft and the temptions o' the Evil One. The warden had fallen into the pit in his pride in all 'is fake learnin'. Worse still, 'e'd led others astray. Now 'e was set on bringin' us into the realm of Satan with 'im. 'Witches! Devil worshippers! All 'on 'em, 'im an' those others! Well, I wasn't 'aving that.'

'How did you manage to look at the warden's books?' Foxe asked mildly, hoping now to bring Gunton back from the brink of final and irreversible insanity. 'Did you go into his house when he was out?'

'Course I did!' Gunton yelled. 'Mr 'Igh an' Mighty Pryce-Perkins thought it were beneath 'im to sweep 'is own floors or make 'is own bed. Made us to it. That's when I saw those wicked books. Right there, they was. Lyin' open on 'is desk. That were the final straw. I knows what God says in the Book of Leviticus: "Thou shalt not suffer a witch to live." That's the word of the Lord, that is, an' I 'eard it speakin' to me. I prayed and The Lord strengthened my arm and put the weapon in my 'and, so as I could strike down the blasphemer and the devil worshipper. "Send 'im to 'is master," The Lord said to me. "Send him to Hell!"

It was too late. With a final howl of rage and fury, Gunton flung himself at Foxe with the bible forgotten and both hands reaching for Foxe's throat.

Foxe was undoubtedly the stronger man, as well as being more than thirty years younger, but Gunton possessed the element of surprise and the strength which comes with blind frenzy. The two of them crashed to the floor, with Gunton on top, so that Foxe had the wind knocked out of him during the vital few seconds when he might have prised Gunton's hands from around his throat. Now he found himself fighting for breath while a madman, foaming at the mouth, steadily choked the life out of him, all the while yelling fragments of nonsense interspersed with calls on God to help him strike down the evil-doer. The best Foxe could do was kick the chair and try to make as much of a fight of it as he could. While Gunton raved at his god to destroy the stain of witchcraft and heresy, Foxe hoped against hope that his coachman had stayed alert and would soon, very soon, come to rescue him.

After what felt like half-an-hour, but could have only been a couple of minutes, the door burst open and Henry entered. He wasted no time in dragging Gunton off his master. Even then, it took the coachman and three of the other pensioners to subdue Gunton, and secure his arms and legs with the leather straps from Foxe's carriage. All the time they did so, Foxe sat where he had fallen, gulping in precious lungsful of air and trying to lessen the pain in his throat. Finally, with Gunton, still raving incoherently, laid on his bed and trussed up like a turkey at Christmas, Foxe was able to croak to Henry to run and fetch help.

It came in the form of a verger, closely followed by a sexton. Moments later an elderly clergyman arrived, still clad in his surplice and bands. This proved to be the temporary appointee as warden of St. Stephen's until a new priest could be found. As he told Foxe later, he had been in the middle of conducting the Morning Service in one of the cathedral's chapels when he noticed all the shouting, closely followed by Foxe's coachman bursting in yelling for help. Now, standing over the unlikely sight of one of his pensioners tightly secured and howling gibberish at the top of his voice, the temporary warden showed admirable calm and common sense.

First he told the sexton and verger to fetch something to act as a stretcher, then sent the other pensioners back to their rooms. The moment the two cathedral servants came back, he directed them to take the madman and lock him in the woodstore behind the warden's house.

'It's dark there,' he said, 'and he'll be quite safe until I've spoken to the dean. He's the formal source of judicial authority in the close. It will be up to him what happens next.'

Finally, once quiet had been restored the warden listened carefully while Foxe explained all that had taken place.

'I never met Pryce-Perkins myself,' the warden said at the end, 'but it was common knowledge he was in the process of losing his faith. How sad that he didn't have the good sense to keep his doubts to himself. As for these so-called studies in supposed ancient wisdom, I call them plain nonsense. Couldn't the man see they contained at least as much superstition and error as he claimed was true of Christianity. You took a great risk, Mr Foxe, in doing what you did. Still, I suppose you're correct when you say it was the only way to get at the truth. Doubtless Gunton's condition would have grown worse. A man who commits one murder finds it easier to commit another. Anyone who failed to match up to Gunton's warped conception of Biblical truth must have been at risk — even me.'

'I imagine what began simply as religious zeal somehow degenerated into fanaticism,' Foxe said. 'Maybe all those hours reading his bible were too much for him in the end.'

'Parts of the Old Testament are very strong meat for an uneducated mind,' the warden replied, shaking his head sadly. 'That's why the church stands firm in the view that its guidance and teaching are necessary to reach a true understanding. Well, I must hurry to inform the dean of all that has taken place and seek his ruling on what is to be done next. You, I am sure, will be only too happy to return home and put the sad results of this day behind you. I can't imagine how distressed the dean will be to discover we have been sheltering the murderer of poor Pryce-Perkins; nor how he will go about breaking the news to the bishop. There are times, sir, when to be nothing but a lowly priest not far from retirement seems a blessed state.'

###

Foxe was not at all surprised to receive a note from the dean next morning asking him to call as soon as possible.

Once again, they sat in his elegant library, drinking a good deal of the excellent coffee the cook had prepared. Foxe found the dean already knew something of what had taken place at St. Stephen's Hospital. All he wanted from Foxe was confirmation of the details.

'It is a very sad affair, Mr Foxe,' he said at the end. 'As you can imagine, I have charged the temporary warden with looking into all the prior circumstances. I already knew something of the reasons for Gunton being given a place in the hospital. It was at the request of the priest of his parish. Gunton had been a loyal churchgoer for most of his life, even serving as a church-warden for many years. When his wife died the loss seemed to hit him badly. He neglected his business and spent nearly all his time shut up alone in their rooms above the shop. From being a neat and well-presented fellow, he fell into slovenly ways, rarely washing or changing his clothes. He also lost a great deal of flesh about his body through forgetting to eat.'

'Did the servants not take care of him?' Foxe asked. 'He must surely have employed a maid and a cook.'

'That was, in hindsight, the very first sign that his mind was failing. The servants all left, telling those outside that he had become irritable and prone to fits of anger. The cook said he had thrown a dish of potatoes in her face because she corrected him when he said they were turnips. The maid couldn't stand the way he began to follow her about asking her if she was taking care to avoid the snares of lust. After a little while, it became obvious he could no longer fend for himself.'

'He had no children?'

'None,' the dean replied. 'According to his vicar, he had few if any relatives. Those he had must have lived in far distant places, for none of them had even attended his wife's funeral. Under the circumstances, the most likely outcome for him was the workhouse. That seemed an inappropriate end for a loyal servant of the church, so he was found a place in St. Stephen's. It was hoped that the quiet regularity of the life there, and company of the other pensioners, might restore him to a sense of balance.'

'It was a merciful decision,' Foxe said, shaking his head sadly. 'It's a shame it didn't produce the desired effect.'

'On the contrary, looked at from the outside it appeared to be successful. He smartened himself up, ate regular meals again, and even tried to play a role in organising the others.'

'As deputy warden.'

'Exactly. I thought it a harmless eccentricity. What I hadn't reckoned with was being kept in ignorance of his continued descent into madness. While the previous man was warden, all seemed well enough. The change came with Henry Pryce-Perkins. He was far from the ideal person to be appointed as warden. We all knew that. It was purely a stop-gap. A respectable place to send a turbulent and schismatic young priest while a long-term solution was found to avoid his family's embarrassment. It was clear he felt the post to be beneath him, but the bishop hoped he had soothed the man's ruffled feelings by explaining no suitable appointment for a man of his undoubted abilities was available. The post carries few duties, Mr Foxe, save for supervising the daily prayers and keeping an eye on the old men's welfare. They say the devil makes work for idle hands, don't they. That proved true in this case. Bored and uninterested in any kind of pastoral care, Pryce-Perkins tuned to ever more heretical studies and gathered misguided disciples around him.'

'Had he not been interested in such matters at Oxford?' Foxe asked. 'The librarian suggested as much to me.'

'Yes and no, Mr Foxe. He had been studying the earliest days of the church. A time before Christian teaching had managed to overcome the many wild and semi-pagan ideas which attached themselves to groups of disciples operating without any proper oversight. It is a legitimate field of study and carries no suggestion that those interested in it are in any way unorthodox. I have no notion what persuaded Pryce-Perkins to go further and begin to cast doubt on the faith itself. Perhaps it was discovering those unfortunate volumes in the cathedral library, which you are now helping us to dispose of. What puzzles me, though, is how Gunton came to understand what Pryce-Perkins was doing.'

'I can explain that, Mr Dean. When I decided how best to approach Gunton, my aim was only to provoke him in some way by praising the late warden. I reasoned that if he had hated the man enough to strike him down, hearing him lauded as a treasure to the hospital would force him to disclose what had driven him to kill. Since I had no idea in what particular ways Gunton and Pryce-Perkins had clashed, I picked on something I thought might do the trick. I had been told Gunton was somewhat extreme, believing the Bible to be the Word of God, every word of it. I therefore borrowed what I knew of the ideas of the deists, and other so-called enlightened thinkers, to belittle its importance.'

'And it worked?'

'Only too well. Gunton swiftly became enraged. It was soon clear Pryce-Perkins must have poured aristocratic and scholastic scorn on the man's beliefs, especially his faith in biblical infallibility. I could almost hear the Oxford-educated son of the Earl of Westleton sneering at the attempts of a Norwich shopkeeper to debate with him on matters of theology. By the time I realised what a powder-keg I was playing with, it was too late,'

'There was the other element in this tragedy, Mr Foxe. Without knowing it, we had put together an arrogant and uncaring priest with heretical ideas with a lonely old man who had found some purpose in life through reading his bible over and over again. The more bloodthirsty passages of the Old Testament, studied without guidance, seem to have exercised a fatal influence over his failing mind. The Church of England, Mr Foxe, prides itself on avoiding all dangerous extremes in matters of theology. We reject the Papist's descent into idolatry, just as we deny the grim doctrines of Calvin. We are equally wary of the emotional enthusiasms of John Wesley and his followers. If we cling to our tradition, it is because it has stood the test of centuries. Thanks to Price-Perkin's neglect of his pastoral duties, no one in authority knew that Gunton's obsessive, unguided reading was turning him into a fanatic. His fellow pensioners stayed silent, probably because they did not know to whom to convey their concerns. Yesterday, I gather, they were all eager to share tales of Gunton's ultra-puritanical views and his violent outbursts if he felt crossed in any way. They simply tried to avoid him and let him have his way whenever they could.'

'I also blame myself for failing to speak to anyone other than Gunton at the start,' Foxe said. 'Or rather, for allowing him to be present when I questioned the pensioners as a group. All swore they could contribute nothing to my enquires. It never occurred to me they might be frightened to speak out in his presence. At the time, he seemed entirely rational. He even suggested one of the other pensioners as a candidate for killing the warden in a fit of madness, then forgetting he'd done it.'

'That would be poor Old Ben,' the dean said with a smile. 'The others call him that to differentiate him from Gunton, whose name is also Benjamin. Old Ben is quite harmless. His senility is now almost complete, so that he neither knows who he is or what he is doing in that place. He can barely shuffle about either. A less convincing murderer it is hard to imagine. You mustn't blame yourself in any way. Many of us had far more obvious reasons to suspect what was going on, yet all of us missed it. I am relieved you did not come to any greater harm than you did.'

'I would have done, had it not occurred to me at the last minute that a man who has killed once will not hold back from violence on subsequent occasions. How is Gunton now? Has he recovered his reason even a little?'

'He is sane only in short bursts, I gather,' the dean replied. 'For an hour or so he will appear quite rational, then he will recall recent events and be transformed into a complete madman. For example, in one period of insanity he told those taking care of him that his home had been invaded by a red fox, which had tried to tempt him into evil. When he threatened it with the bible, the beast emitted a blast of brimstone, before becoming the snake from the garden of Eden and wrapping him in its coils. He has also claimed that he barely escaped being dragged down to Hell by Satan and his demons. Then he demands that he should be released, saying he is the Lord's appointed destroyer of witchcraft and devilry. If anyone questions such fantasies he at once flies into a rage and tries to attack them as he did you.'

'What will happen to him? It's clear he could never face a judge in court.'

'The obvious course would be to consign him to Bedlam, but I cannot bring myself to act with such cruelty. I am still reviewing what might be best for all concerned, but I am inclined to try to find a place for him in a private madhouse. I'm sure the church can meet the cost under the circumstances. Somehow, he will be quietly put away. The Pryce-Perkins family will be told that it was finally discovered Henry had fallen foul of a wandering madman. Scandal will be avoided and the whole matter laid to rest. My earnest advice to you, young sir, is to leave it all behind you. Gunton's future is not your problem. Take some rest and some healthy exercise. I gather sea-bathing is becoming popular to restore health after periods of over-exertion. Or you could go riding. In my youth, I was a fine rider and spent many an afternoon in headlong pursuit of a fox.'

The notion of the grave and respectable Dean of Norwich hallooing after foxes nearly caused Foxe to burst out laughing. Fortunately, he managed to cover it with a cough.

'Whatever you do,' the dean continued, 'know that you have my deepest gratitude for bringing this matter to a conclusion. I am sure the bishop will also join me in those sentiments. Now I must bid you farewell and prepare to meet with the cathedral organist. The fellow does nothing but complain about the state of the organ, and ask for yet more money for repairs and renovations. To hear him talk, he can barely persuade it to play at all. Yet, next Sunday, I have no doubt I will hear it thunder forth in its usual fashion.'

###

Foxe neither went riding nor entrusted himself to the freezing waters of the German Ocean. In their place, he went next day to visit Mrs Danson. In all the fuss of the past week, he had quite forgotten to take her the money he had made by selling the first batch of her husband's books.

She professed herself astonished by the sum Foxe brought her, and lavished praise on him for his skill in obtaining such good prices. For his part, Foxe disclaimed any particular skill beyond finding eager buyers for an unusual range of volumes, then reminding each one that others were waiting, should they balk at the price asked. Of course, he wouldn't have been Foxe had he not basked in the warmth of her approval and considered himself no end of a fine fellow as a result. It occurred to him again that Mrs Danson, freed from the oppression of her husband, was a remarkably fine-looking woman and a pleasure to talk to. Since she still had more books she wished to sell, there would be other times when he visited her house with the proceeds. Perhaps he might invite her to walk with him in Quantrell's Pleasure Gardens or accompany him to a performance at the theatre? She would look good on his arm, as well as providing delightful company. He cared not a whit for what others might say about her dubious start in life. Wasn't he the man who had once gone to the Mayor's Ball with two partners: one an actress and the other the madam of an expensive bordello? Still worse in the eyes of the censorious, weren't they sisters as well, both known to be sharing his bed at different times?

Even so, Foxe told himself sternly, he was determined to avoid any emotional entanglements for the foreseeable future. No messages had come either from Dublin or Italy. The last thing he wanted now was risk more heartache. He would enjoy Mrs Danson's company, but that was all. It was time to preserve merely polite behaviour towards the ladies of Norwich and avoid all deeper involvement.

A fine intention, no doubt. The question he failed to ask himself was whether the ladies of Norwich would stay content with such as decision. He was still young, notably rich and well regarded at the most important levels of local society. More than one mother with unmarried daughters regarded him as an ideal candidate for matrimony, now that his wilder days seemed to be behind him.

Life otherwise began to return to normal after what had proved such an unpleasant interlude. Foxe found he could not take pleasure in his success, despite receiving letters of congratulation from the mayor, the bishop and the deputy lieutenant for the county. Two innocent, if misguided, people had been murdered. Four guilty men had ended their days abruptly at the hands of the public executioner. One other was now destined to spend the rest of his life locked away in a private madhouse. None of it was any cause for celebration.

Nicholas returned with his aunt and they busied themselves finding a suitable place to live in the city, while making arrangements for their goods to be transported from Diss. Foxe owned a number of fine properties, but all were let on leases with several years still to run. The best he could do was put Nicholas in touch with his own attorney: an honest and dependable man who would make sure he was not cheated. Charlie would start his book-binding training soon. His obvious pleasure in this arrangement was further increased by the gift of his own set of tools, each set in its proper place in a roll of fine leather.

All in all, as the summer moved on and the city wrapped itself in its usual adornment of flower gardens and shady walks, Foxe's life would have seemed to most outsiders to be almost idyllic. He, however, was beginning to find it to find it dull. He knew it was high time for another investigation.

Printed in Poland
by Amazon Fulfillment
Poland Sp. z o.o., Wrocław